Field of Bones

Maddie Castle

Book 6

L.T. Ryan

with

C.R. Gray

For information contact:

contact@ltryan.com

https://LTRyan.com

https://www.instagram.com/ltryanauthor/

https://www.facebook.com/LTRyanAuthor

Chapter 1

I HAD NEVER BEEN AFRAID OF A SPINNING BLUE CIRCLE.

Now, I couldn't imagine something more terrifying.

The heat of the laptop radiated onto my thighs. By my feet atop the cheap Berber carpet, Tempest panted hard. It was almost as loud as Bentley's heavy breathing at my ear. Grace was quieter, but her big head was obstructing my view of the screen. All I could make out was that spinning blue circle and the word, *Loading*.

The librarian behind the desk in the corner had shot my German Shepherd a few dirty looks, but the place was calm otherwise. In the children's section, I heard a mother and her child. A young man sat at the computers half a dozen yards ahead of me.

Considering my history in law enforcement, I'd always kept a careful eye on my surroundings. Now, I was somehow more cautious than usual.

The flash drive loading on the screen before me—I hoped—had come from Daisy Miller. She'd been missing for almost a year, and this was the first concrete lead I'd had since.

Within the last week, Daisy had been in this very library. Along with a sweatshirt that she left in the drop ceiling of the library restroom, concealing the tiny flash drive.

The drive was valuable. She'd wanted me to find it. But she didn't want anyone else's eyes to see it.

I didn't know why, and I wouldn't. Not until the damn thing loaded.

My first thought had been to go out to the car and plug it into my laptop out there. But Grace and Bentley had insisted we do it here, inside the library. My laptop needed as much battery as possible, and there was no place to charge it in the car. They also wanted a good view of what we were about to see.

That only added to my fear.

None of us knew what was on this flash drive. But we believed Daisy had been kidnapped and held captive all this time. That meant some disturbing images or information could appear in the next few seconds. I didn't want Bentley and Grace to see those. That saying, about how some things can't be unseen, was nothing but facts. If I could take a sponge and scrub half my memories away, I would.

Daisy was their family though. I wasn't a cop—only a PI. It wasn't my call. All I could do was sit and wait and—

It loaded.

Stomach in knots, I opened the zip file.

We all leaned in closer, our breathing hitched.

Open First_forBentley

ForGrace

ForMaddie

Thank God. Not only was it from her, but she knew that I knew. That there were some things the family didn't need to see.

"Do you want to read it in private?" I asked Bentley, turning to meet his gaze.

A hard swallow bobbed the Adam's apple in his throat, covered in thick dark hair. He shook his head. "Go ahead."

I did so.

A two page Microsoft Word file filled the screen.

Dear Bentley,

I'm so sorry. Probably seems like a grim way to start this out, but every day since it happened, those are the three words I wish I could say most to you.

I'm sorry for all the bullshit I put you through. I'm sorry I took your kindness for granted. I'm sorry I expected so much from you. I'm sorry I didn't understand what it was like to stand in your shoes. To love a kid you want so badly to help, but to be forced between two brick walls.

Now, I get it. I look back on those court hearings when you were fighting for custody, and all those times I showed up at your door, and every fight we had about every shitty boyfriend and bad decision I made, and I get it. Back then, I resented you for not doing enough. Now, I know you did everything humanly possible. Way more than you were obligated to. It wasn't your job to look after me, but you did so to the best of your ability, and I'm the one who screwed it up. I'm the reason I am where I am right now.

I guess I get it now because you weren't obligated to do so much for me, and you did anyway. The thing is, I'm obligated to move mountains for someone now, and I, too, am stuck between two big ass brick walls.

Not literally, but I'll go into more detail there with Maddie.

If you haven't figured it out yet, congratulations, Uncle Bentley. You have a beautiful little niece. She looks like Bella. Before I had her, I always thought people were crazy when they said that about babies. Babies look like weird little aliens. They don't start to look like people for a long while. But this little one does. She looks so much like my big sister. So that's why I named her Bella.

I'm going to go into more detail soon, and I hope the information I give you is enough to find me and bring me home. But if it's not, and something happens to me along the way, please make sure my baby has the life you wanted to give me. If you find her, and you can bring her home, I'd love that. Just to clarify–in case this letter one day ends up in a court document, Bentley Roycroft is the only person I trust wholeheartedly to raise my daughter if I cannot.

I don't want you to feel obligated, though. You weren't obligated to take care of me, and you did. I'm not in any place to ask you for more favors.

The last thing is that I love you. I'm not angry about any of the fights, or any of the boundaries you tried to set, or any of the mistakes you may have made. I don't think you made any, honestly. But now that I'm a parent, I get it. Every breath we take, we question.

I don't want you to do that, though. I want you to know that, in my eyes, you did everything right. You gave me every chance that no one else would. You loved me when no one else did. You cared for me financially, physically, and emotionally when the rest of the world abandoned me.

You may not have been my dad, but I always wished you were. I love you, I'm grateful for you, and I don't want you to question that for a second.

With love,

Daisy

PS congrats on the new relationship thing. I can't safely log into my social medias, but I was able to do some digging, and you guys are really cute together. She is out of your league though, so don't screw it up. You're not gonna land someone that hot again :P

. . .

Bentley chuckled at that, and I smiled. But that was only one page of the document. I scrolled to the second.

Grace's document is just a letter. Share that with her whenever you can. The other document, share only the details you have to with my family.

The file for you, Maddie, is my story. Every gory detail of my captivity. Yes, captivity. I use that word specifically because I'm sure you need it to get the authorities involved. You'll need them. Lie low though, because I don't know what he'll do to me and Bella once he realizes you're onto him.

The evidence you need to get the FBI on this, aside from my written statement?

Bring a dog and a shovel.

"Are those coordinates?" Grace asked, voice shaky.

If I had to guess? Yes. The numbers following that letter were coordinates.

I copied and pasted them into Google Maps. A twenty-two minute drive from here.

Shutting the laptop, I stood. Bentley said something I didn't catch. I was too busy looking at my phone, dialing the number for Ashley Harper. She answered on the third ring.

"Hello—"

"I need dogs and a search team at the address I'm about to send you." Propping the phone between my shoulder and ear, I shoved my laptop into my bag. "It's Daisy. She got us coordinates. I'm heading there now."

Chapter 2

"That's not happening," Bentley said, trailing behind me out of the library. "You're not doing this alone."

The car door was heavy under my grasp. No matter how fast I wanted to charge out of here, it wasn't my first time dealing with civilians in a situation like this. I took in and gradually released a deep, calming breath. Spinning to meet his gaze, I did my best to soften my expression.

Cool wind fluttered the curly brown locks around his face. Tucking one behind his ear did nothing to release the tension in his taut jaw. "A few cops are meeting me there. I won't be alone, Bentley."

"He doesn't actually care about you being alone," Grace said, shoving past her father. She was a few inches shorter than me yet stood taller than us both. "We want to know everything as soon as you do."

Daisy told us to bring a shovel and a dog. That told me this was Deluca's dumping ground. By nightfall, we'd be uncovering bodies beneath the soil.

"You don't want to see this. *Neither* of you want to see this." I dropped my laptop bag into the passenger seat and shut the door. "Just call an Uber and get a ride to the hotel. I'll be there as soon as I can."

"It's not her." Bentley's voice cracked. "I know what you're going to find. I know it's not going to be pretty. But it's not Daisy. I just want to be with you as you learn whatever you learn, Maddie."

I frowned. "I'll call you as soon as I know more—"

"You need someone to drive while you read anyway," Grace insisted. "She left you her entire story, and there are going to be clues in there. You can't wait around to read it. We have a twenty-minute drive. You can read on the way, and when we get there, we'll stay in the car. We won't move a muscle. We won't see whatever it is you're afraid of us seeing."

The kid made a good point. "Guys—"

"We won't get in the way," Bentley said. "Just like I didn't get in the way with Eric. I let you handle it. But you let me be there, Maddie. Until the very end, until you had to take the reins, you let me be there. Please. *Please* just let us be there now."

Another deep breath.

If I were in their shoes, I would be asking the exact same thing. Of course, I'd been a cop, so I knew how to handle these situations a bit better. But the fact remained. I wasn't heartless.

"If the cops want you out, you gotta go," I said, looking sternly between them. "We aren't back home. I don't have pull here. I sure as shit don't have jurisdiction. That means I need to be on my best behavior if I don't want to get kicked off this case, and so do you guys."

"Deal." Bentley held his hand out for the keys.

I handed them over. "In the driver's seat."

He jogged to the left side of the car.

Grace started for the backseat.

"You get shotgun." I leaned against the rear door. "I'm sitting in the back with Tempy."

"But you can't get comfy back there."

True. Grace also couldn't read my laptop screen from the front seat. If she sat in the back, she would read every word over my shoulder. Daisy made it clear she didn't want her to. At the very least, this girl deserved privacy.

"I'll make do."

* * *

I PAID NO MIND TO THE SWAYING OF THE VEHICLE, THE FARMLAND WE were driving through, nor Grace and Bentley arguing over which map application would get us there quicker. Vaguely, I knew it was occurring, but my focus was on the word document in my lap.

THE KIDNAPPING

There are turning points in everyone's life. One precise moment that categorizes every other moment since and prior. The before, and the after.

That night, when I ran away with Mr. Deluca, was one of those moments. Even heading into it, I knew so.

The day before, I had never been so excited. It was like when I was a kid, and I knew that Bella and Bentley were taking me to an amusement park on Saturday. I was all but pulling pages off the calendar in preparation for that evening.

It was all planned out. It had been planned out for exactly one month.

I'd only known him a handful of them, but I believed he was my knight in shining armor. Yes, our love was young, but that only meant it would last longer. That it was pure. He loved me. He loved me, and he lifted me from a life of catastrophe.

There wasn't a better word for who I was then. An addict. A sex worker. A teenager. A soon to be mother.

I was a tornado, and he was a mountain. I tore through all I touched, and he stood tall. I shattered everything I encountered, and he was unbreakable.

He settled my violent wind to a gentle breeze.

That should've been the first sign. If there was anything he was good at, it was settling my violence into submission.

I should've run at that realization.

In the months leading up to this, he'd talked about his home in central PA. He was only in Columbus on business. Paired with everything Bentley had said about Pennsylvania, it sounded like a utopia. When Deluca told me to pack a bag, that he was taking me to his personal oasis, it sounded like the last page of a fairytale. Happily ever after.

Obviously, he was full of shit.

Because of the situation with Kevin, the fact that he was still chasing me even though I'd paid my debts and had no desire to be with him, Deluca suggested we go quietly. Once we arrived, we'd let Bentley know. It was best, though, if we got out in the late evening. It was an eight-hour drive. We'd get halfway there before midnight, we'd stay at a hotel, have a nice breakfast in the morning, then arrive at our new home before dinnertime.

I'd yet to tell Deluca about my pregnancy. My plan was to do so when we got to his oasis.

You'll notice I call it that a lot. That's what he refers to his home as. His oasis.

That drive, though, I remember as clearly as my face in a mirror.

He had told me to get some sleep, but I didn't. I lay awake in the passenger seat of his black Range Rover, eyes turned out the window, watching the countryside float by. When we crossed the West Virginia state border, I took a mental snapshot. It was the quarter way mark. It wouldn't be long, and my happily ever after would begin.

The Pennsylvania State border made me smile. That big blue sign that read "Pursue your happiness," seemed a little silly, but more welcoming than I had ever felt. I was used to being undesired, unwanted.

But there was that blue sign, and the man I loved had his hand on my knee, obeying each traffic light and stop sign, protecting me in the simplest of ways. Soft jazz music vibrated the speakers. I never listened to jazz, not before Deluca, but that night, it was my personal anthem. Sage and musk filled my nose, radiating from his chest. Cool wind drifted in from the cracked window. A hint of cigarette smoke complemented the rest.

It was the only thing I hated about that night. It was the only thing I hated about him. *He smoked full flavor cigarettes, just like my mom. When I found out I was pregnant, I'd quit smoking, but he still did. I hated that smell, not because I was envious, not because I wanted to smoke myself, but because it reminded me of home. Of the life I wanted desperately to forget.*

Now, that smell is the only thing I like about him.

It was about 4 AM when we stopped for the night. The halfway mark.

I wish I could tell you the name of the town. I don't remember it.

I do remember that it was a tiny hotel. Certainly not upper-class. It was the first building I had seen for miles, aside from a few barns. Maybe a dozen miles back, there'd been a diner, but one of the windows was boarded up, so it had probably been closed for a while.

There wasn't a name on the hotel sign. Or maybe there was, but I can't remember. I do know it was one of those retro light-up ones. Maybe the bulbs were burned out. In red letters, it said '$99 a Night.' Those are the only words I can remember clearly. Deluca went inside to get the room, and I stayed in the car, staring at the pool in the center of the hotel plaza. It was a large u-shape, with the pool in the center. Behind it was a glass door with a sign that said, 'Breakfast Ends at 10.'

While I waited, a little fantasy played out in my mind. The two of us having breakfast at 7, playing in the pool together until 10:30, and getting back on the road by 11.

I don't know if any of this is going to help you, and I'm sorry if a lot of it feels like filler. I'm just trying to give you as many details as I can recall.

Deluca was in there for a while. Now, I wonder if it was because he had a rapport built with the manager or owner of the hotel. When he came back out, when he led me to our room, he just seemed too comfortable. Like he'd been here before. Like this was a routine. Like this very place was the oasis he spoke of so fondly.

I even said so as we climbed the cement stairs on the other side of the pool to the second floor. "It's the only place for miles, and it's about halfway home," Deluca had said. "I've stopped here a lot over the years."

Hopefully that'll help in your investigation.

He held the door open for me, and I wasn't shocked by what I saw inside. I was a sex worker, after all. I was familiar with hotels like this.

Thin red carpet with yellow diamonds in a checkered pattern from wall to wall. Peeling, floral wallpaper from the eighties. A white backdrop, with red and yellow flowers. It matched the carpet too well. Too exact. The bedspread was no different. It was almost the exact same pattern as the walls.

There was a dresser at the foot of the bed with an old box TV on top of it. The whole place reeked of cleaning agents, mothballs, a touch of pot, and something I couldn't quite place.

Now, I imagine it was a mixture of bodily fluids.

As he always did, Deluca told me to go clean up. He always wanted me clean. Freshly showered, freshly shaved. Makeup never mattered, but cleanliness did. He didn't want to touch me if he thought I was dirty.

As always, I did as he told me.

I showered, I shaved—even though I had shaved just before we left. I blow dried my hair, I moisturized any chafing skin, and I stepped into the nightgown he'd laid out for me.

Just a simple white, baby doll nightgown. It didn't cover much, and that was the point.

I'd gotten used to it in my line of work. Certain customers liked certain things. Deluca liked white and dainty. I thought it was because of his borderline obsession with cleanliness. I wonder, now, if it is because of the color white's association with purity. Like I was some pet project. The prodigal daughter. He wanted to rebuild me, only to destroy me.

That was what came next.

I don't want to talk about the details. A summary will have to do, and I hope it's enough to help you wrap your mind around this sick bastard's psyche.

Consent had always been important to Deluca, until that night. He was rough, and aggressive, and I wasn't prepared for it. I accepted it, because I didn't know what else to do. He's at least three times my size, five times as strong, and it was useless to fight. So I didn't.

I tried to justify it at first. Gaslight myself, I guess.

'He's excited. That's all. He didn't hear me tell him to slow down. He didn't mean to hurt me. He would never hurt me on purpose. This is just exciting for him, like it is for me. Today's the first day of our life together. It's fine. I'll be fine. I was fine every other time this happened, and those guys didn't love me. Not like Deluca does.'

Then he closed his fingers around my throat. A gentle grasp wasn't unusual for us, but this was not gentle. It started with one hand, then progressed to two. I was on the bed, and my lip was already bleeding from where he bit me. Not just a trickle of blood, but so much that my mouth was full of iron. And I still tried to convince myself that it wasn't happening.

But then, both of those hands closed around my throat, and I realized. I saw that look in his eyes. The same look I'd seen in the eyes of boys at the foster homes. The same look I'd seen in the eyes of my johns. The same look I'd seen in Kevin's eyes.

Obscure hatred. Hatred I could never understand.

The kind of hate I had never seen in a woman's eyes. Only a man's. A man who claimed he loved women, who desired women, and yet, hated me—all of us, more than likely—for reasons I could never fathom.

Was it that their intense desire brought them shame? Was it the power we held over them when we batted our eyelashes? Did it make them feel small? Did they have to hurt us to prove that we were smaller?

Maybe a psychologist could answer that for me one day.

When I saw that look, though, I knew. I knew I had to do whatever I could, or I would never walk out of that room.

I pissed myself.

That was enough for him to release my throat.

Everything was black around the edges, but I rolled sideways. I don't know if I moved quickly or if he moved slowly, but I made it to my feet, then to the door, only for him to slam me against it. Just before his hands closed around my throat again, I said, "I'm pregnant."

He stopped.

The heat and the calluses on his palm reminded me that I was not yet safe, but he stopped. He stood there, entirely frozen, staring at me, and even if it was only for those few minutes, that hate vanished. I almost convinced myself that the last hour had been a dream.

Eventually, still holding me against that metal door, he said, "You can prove that?"

I opened my mouth to speak, but he squeezed my throat. I nodded instead.

"How?" he asked.

With a shaky hand, I pointed to my purse.

Before he went for it, he grabbed my wrist and pulled me to a metal pole in the corner of the room. It was warm to the touch, so I had to imagine it was for either heat or a water pipe.

His suitcase was right there, between the metal pole in the corner of the room and the dresser. After forcing me to sit, he fished through it. He came out with cuffs. Which didn't come as a surprise. Deluca was into that sorta thing.

He cuffed me around the pole, then went for my purse. Rather than dig through it, he dumped it onto the bed. Probably onto my piss, now that I think about it.

There, he found the ultrasound. My name was on it, as was the clinic I'd had it done.

Rubbing his hand over his jaw, his breaths picked up.

And again, I knew. I knew what I had to do.

"This–this doesn't change anything," I said, somehow managing to stop my quivering lip. "I love you. I love you, and I know you love me. We're gonna have the most beautiful baby, and we're going to have the most beautiful life, and—"

"Shut up!" There it was again. That look in his eyes. "Shut your damn mouth, Rory."

That wasn't my name. I still wonder why he said it.

Maybe you can figure it out.

But I did as he said. I shut up.

I stayed quiet even as he fished in the suitcase again, only to come out with a syringe. The only words I uttered as he stabbed it into my arm was, "I love you. I love you so much."

Because if I had learned anything over the years, it was that there was no use in fighting hate. He hated women, he hated me, and I couldn't change that while playing defense. I could only do so if I played the submissive damsel.

Chapter 3

The exact coordinates were two miles deep into the woods from the nearest road.

With the blistering summer heat, I loaded my backpack with all the bottles of water I could find in the car. No one knew the password for my laptop, so I made sure to shut it down before I got out. Bentley wouldn't read Daisy's journal because he knew he didn't want to find what was inside. But Grace? It wouldn't have been easy for her to practice restraint.

Stepping out onto the muddy grass, I snapped my fingers. Tempest jumped out behind me. The terrain ahead wouldn't be too difficult to maneuver. The hill I had to climb was a gradual upward slope. May have seemed like a small thing, but in Pennsylvania, it could've been a ninety-degree mountain cliff.

Although the soil was damp, that wasn't such a bad thing. It gave me more traction. Dry dirt on an upward angle will crumble out beneath you. Mud would slide, but it would do so slowly. Hopefully long enough that my foot would catch on a tree root. With all the rich foliage, I had branches and leaves to grab hold of along the way up as well.

The driver's door swung open.

A sigh forced my shoulders downward. "Bentley, you have to—"

"I know, I know. Stay put." He raised his hands in surrender. "And I will. But I gotta know."

"You gotta know what?"

"Why your face was all screwed up like that." Glancing into the car at

Grace, he lowered his voice. "While you were reading. I know it was bad. And you don't have to go into the details, but please tell me why. Was she suffering? Does he beat her regularly or something?"

There was something unique about Daisy's writing. She didn't drop you down into a scene. It's not that her words made you visualize every moment, every image she saw. No, it was deeper than that.

She dropped me into her mind. She didn't have to explain every picture on the wall and the texture of the bed linens to make me understand her.

Did I have enough to help her? No. Not yet.

I only had enough to understand her, enough to empathize.

"It was the night she ran away with him," I said. "She gave me some valuable details, and she explained what happened, and—"

"*What* did happen, Maddie?"

I shook my head. "If she wanted you to know, she would've addressed it to you."

"She doesn't want to hurt me, but I can handle it. My head is a thousand different places. I keep imagining every awful possibility, and..." Tears bubbled in his eyes. He blinked them away. "It can't be worse than what I'm imagining."

Maybe that was true. Maybe it wasn't. One way or the other, I was not going to recount Daisy's rape to him.

"All you need to know for now is that she did find a way to survive, Bentley. She's smart, and she's surviving. Okay?"

A hard swallow. Ever so slightly, he squared his shoulders. That gave him solace. Knowing that she didn't lie down and die gave him solace.

"When the cops show, point them in the right direction." I nodded up the hill. "Shouldn't take me more than an hour to get there, but once they do, I could be up there for hours. If I am, go to the hotel. I'll be there soon as I can."

* * *

I HAD ONLY MADE IT TO THE TOP OF THE HILL WHEN A STATE POLICE car showed beside mine. My knee wasn't impressed with the hike thus far, so I figured it was a great time to take a break. The officer, Harold Grant, was a few years younger than me, a lot spryer, and climbed to the top in half the time it took me to get here.

Luckily, he had a canine as well. His name was Bob. Bob the dog. I made a few jokes about it, which he joined in on. Apparently, his girlfriend had named him.

Although we were following the dropped pin on my phone, we felt a bit aimless. There were some deer trails, but much of this hike was pulling branches and bushes aside for one another. Bob and Tempest didn't mind, but Grant and I weren't huge fans.

Cresting the top of yet another hill, a creek came into view. At least ten feet wide, a few deep, and as brown as the mud at the bottom of our shoes.

"Ah, shit," Grant said under his breath.

I found a big enough rock on my left, sat, and began untying my tennis shoes. "Come on, wasn't this what you were fantasizing about at the Academy?"

Snorting, Grant leaned against a tree to do the same. "Yes, ma'am."

"I'm not that old." I yanked off my socks and tucked them into my pocket. "I don't need a 'ma'am'."

"After everything you've done, yes, ma'am. You deserve a 'ma'am'." Grant stumbled and caught himself on a low-hanging branch. Raking some blonde waves from his face, his eyes met mine. "I hope you know that's the only reason we're out here. My sergeant only signed off on me coming because the tip came from you."

"Huh." I stood up with my tennis shoes in hand. "Didn't know if anyone knew me out here."

"Country Killer never made it out this far, but we were worried he would." Grant tied the laces from both of his shoes together and hung them over his shoulder. "The first time, and the second. We weren't surprised to see your name in both headlines."

"Wish I wouldn't have been." Mud smooshed up around my toes, and I fought a gag. Tempy and Bob were already waiting at the water with wagging tails. He was a pretty boy, with a black blanket back, traditional blonde mask, but light, amber eyes. "Guessing you brought him because he's trained in human remains."

Another, "Yes, ma'am."

"Good thing. Tempy's expertise is narcotics." Fastening my backpack, ignoring the twigs that poked the soles of my feet, I started for the creek. "I get why you guys don't think you have a case out here, but this witness wouldn't lie."

"Who is the witness, if you don't mind my asking?"

"Don't mind one bit." I spared him a glance, using a tree branch to keep myself steady as I stepped into the water. "Just glad there's one friendly face on the force. I'm gonna need that if I want to find her."

Brows furrowed over his blue eyes, he cocked his head to the side. "Your witness is missing?"

"She is," I said, trudging into the knee-high muddy water. I commanded Tempest to do the same, and I explained. For the next fifteen minutes, maybe twenty, I explained everything I knew so far.

When I wrapped it up, detailing what I had just read from the flash drive, Grant muttered some profanities. "And no one else cared to open up an investigation?"

"Harper did. You'll meet her soon."

Bright summer sun blasted into my eyes as we came into a clearing. Wildflowers stretched across it in all directions. Trees framed the edges. Except for in one spot. There, carved into the otherwise dense forest, was a dirt path covered in tire marks. Not a quad trail, but an access road carved by someone with a big ass truck. I used my hand as a visor. Tempest and Bob were a hundred yards ahead, chasing one another in a big circle.

"But Harper had no jurisdiction. Nothing happened in Pittsburgh. Nothing that we know of, not enough to open a case. For months, we've just been following breadcrumbs. The flash drive was the first solid lead we had. And if it..."

Bob wasn't playing anymore. He was lying down.

Tempest crouched out next to him, paws outstretched in front of her, butt wagging in the air, but he just looked at Grant and panted.

"Is he signaling?" I asked.

Grant swallowed hard. He gave a short nod. "Yes, ma'am, I believe he is."

Faster than me, Grant picked up speed across the field. I kept limping, cursing at my knee the whole way. This field had to have been the size of a baseball field, maybe a high school football field. Bob was at the far end of it, close to the tree line. The field sloped ever so slightly at that edge.

It took me getting halfway across the field to realize that Bob lay in a patch of mud.

Wildflowers stretched in all other directions. But there, in a roughly six by four patch, there were no flowers. Only soil and clay.

A fresh grave.

I stopped.

I stood still and gazed around in a slow, careful circle.

The clearing only had one small access road. I knew this would be his burial ground, but I didn't expect a cemetery.

Reaching the patch of soil, Grant grasped hold of his walkie-talkie. His voice trembled when he said, "We've got something. We need forensics."

"And a tractor," I called. "I have the feeling we're gonna be digging a lot of holes today."

Chapter 4

Grant and Bob the dog followed that access trail. It was our only hope of getting all the authorities up here. I sat with Tempest in the grass at that shallow, unmarked grave.

At first, that was all I did. I sat, and I stared at the muddy four by six patch of dirt.

There were flowers everywhere else in this field, and I thought about picking some to lay atop it, a well wish for the body left behind. But that would interfere with the scene. The cops, the FBI who I imagined would soon arrive, needed to see this field exactly as Grant and I had found it.

So I only sat, and stared, and mourned for the woman we were about to find beneath the soil. I mourned for her family, for the life she'd lost too soon.

And then I got back to work.

Because that was all that made sense to me. I could either wallow in my feelings, or I could fight to make things right. I could absorb all of the words Daisy had given me because those words were knowledge. Knowledge was power.

That'd been why the Nazis banned books. No matter how silly they may have seemed, words and ideas stretched out across a page packed the same power as the bullets in my gun.

Not because knowledge and ideas were dangerous, but because they endangered the oppressor.

So I read on, using the PDF of the document I'd sent to my phone at the library.

. . .

The Trip

The last thing I remember was everything going black moments after Deluca stabbed me with that syringe. I don't know how he got me into the car undetected, but that was where I woke up.

We had driven to that hotel in a Range Rover. I woke up in a trunk. My hands and feet were bound, but I was flexible, so I managed to untie the rope around my ankles.

Range Rovers don't have trunks, so not sure how he changed vehicles, but he did. Maybe the first one was stolen, and maybe the second was too.

One way or the other, the dim glow from the trunk's seal told me it was daylight. The same jazz music he had played on our way to the hotel now vibrated through the speakers to my right, so loud no one would hear me scream. I had written mystery novels, and watched plenty of them on television, so I knew what to do next.

I kicked, and I kicked, and I kicked. I wish I could say I was lucky when I kicked out a taillight, which gave me a chance to stretch my bound hands through the opening.

I wasn't lucky.

He turned down the music, pulled over, and stopped the car.

When I heard him walking around the car, each footstep crackling the gravel beneath, I mentally prepared myself. I told myself that my feet were free. If I could get out of the trunk, I could run.

I just needed a way to disable him. When he got to me, I would head butt him in the balls. I would scream. I would flail and flop like a fish out of water.

I did none of that.

He opened the trunk, and I found myself paralyzed again. He was so big. 6'4", muscular arms, muscular chest. Things I'd once found so appealing were now my greatest nightmare.

There I was, curled in a ball in a trunk, no weapon, hands bound together.

I realized then that I had no other options.

People always say that, "Women are just as strong as men." I was one of them.

It's a lie we tell ourselves. Physically, my beauty was the only power someone my size had over someone of his stature. No matter what, I couldn't have gotten out of that trunk. Especially not when I saw the gun in his hand.

My only power was my quivering voice and my big blue eyes. "I—I didn't know where I was. I'm sorry. I'm so sorry. I didn't mean to—"

"Shut up."

That's all he said as he positioned the gun in one hand, aimed it at me, and stabbed me with a syringe with the other.

Everything went black again.

Next time I woke, it was to raindrops on my face.

Everything ached. Guess that had to be expected after rolling around like unpacked groceries in a trunk all day. All day, to clarify, because raindrops plopped onto my face, and when I opened my eyes, cloud-blurred stars stared back at me.

So did the bottom of Deluca's chin.

Coyotes howled in the distance. There was a small light shining somewhere on my left, just enough to illuminate his face, but I didn't have the strength to roll my head in that direction.

He was carrying me. And for a moment, a brief moment, I wanted to believe that everything I recalled was a nightmare. That this was the dream. The man I loved was carrying me, his bride, through the threshold into our new life.

Then I felt that rope around my wrists again.

That realization, then it all went black again.

The next time I woke, sheets with a number of threads I could hardly count to cradled me. A glass ceiling stared down at me. Beyond it was a blue sky.

At least, part of the ceiling was glass. Just enough to provide a gorgeous view of the night sky while lying in the California king bed. Deluca always had a thing for stars and birds, so I wasn't surprised. A bit grateful, in fact, because when I tried to roll over, only to find leather cuffs cementing me to the bed, I consoled myself with the realization that if I died here, at least it'd be below a pretty view.

I didn't let panic get to me, though. Every piece of this room, I committed to memory. Four walls surrounded me. On the right was an open door to a walk-in closet. It was as big as my bedroom growing up. Beside it was another door. Beyond it, I could make out the marble floor, granite sink, and glass doors of the shower. Even the edge of a clawfoot tub.

To my right were a series of windows that stretched from floor to ceiling, ending in an A-line peak. My answer was out those windows. This was his home, and he'd brought me here, because all that lay behind that glass was wild. Trees that stretched on endlessly. Rolling mountains. In that very moment, coming to terms with the fact that I was tied to a bed, I watched a bear and her cubs venture through the grass before the trees.

No one would hear me scream here.

"Ma'am!"

I jumped.

My phone fell to the soil.

I followed the sound of his voice, finding Grant at the entrance of that access road again.

With Bob at his side, he gestured down the access road. "My sergeant's asking for you."

Chapter 5

The sergeant in question was named Javier Torres. He introduced himself with a firm shake and concerned brown eyes. He had to have been approaching fifty but was still a good-looking man. A five o'clock shadow covered his strong jaw, complemented by warm, sepia skin. He stood a head taller than me with big shoulders and a round belly beneath his Kevlar vest. Torres, like Grant, asked for the long story rather than the short one.

From start to finish, I told him everything I knew so far. It hadn't seemed like I knew much until now. Daisy's background, the apathy I'd received from the Columbus PD, my personal connection to the case, finishing up with the flash drive. In the time it took to rehash it all, a dozen cruisers and twice as many officers filtered into the field.

Shaded by the heavy tree coverage, we stood on the outskirts of it. Torres stood, at least. I had found a nice enough rock and sat on it halfway through. Torres, leaning against a tree a few feet away, puffed on a cigarette. "You got that on you?"

"The flash drive?" I asked. He nodded, and I said, "It's in my car. Didn't want to risk carting it through the woods."

"I'm gonna need it, you know."

"Yeah, of course."

"And the boyfriend, the one who started all this." He nodded to the right. "Is that the guy sitting in the pink Subaru at the bottom of the hill?"

Feeling my cheeks heat, I cleared my throat. "Yes, sir. It's my car."

"My daughter would love all those butterflies." A friendly smile. "Good call."

"They've grown on me, but it wasn't my first choice. One of my clients owns a car dealership. Pretty much gifted it to me. The butterflies were just part of the package."

Torres chuckled. "No, no. I meant the family. Leaving them down there. That was a good call."

"Oh. Right." Trailing my hand down my thigh, I gripped just above my knee for more stability. It wasn't screaming in pain yet, but it was getting there. "Thank you, sir. Even for letting me sit in this far."

"We're happy to have you." Another deep drag off his cigarette, gazing past me at an officer trekking up the hill.

She, like me and Grant, had a dog at her side. Hers was a Bassett hound with big, adorable floppy ears.

"We know the role you played with that bastard out west," Torres said. "The sacrifices you made. Thank you for your service."

Hearing people say that used to piss me off. Yeah, I was grateful for the good I had done. But I was pissed my body didn't work like it used to, that I lost my job, my chance at a position in the FBI, my dog, even my best friend and fiancé.

Now, it only made me uncomfortable. Taking compliments had never been my strong suit.

Doubted I'd ever be happy with my bum knee, and I'd always curse the sky for losing Bear and Ox, but I loved my job. I loved my boyfriend. All the way around, I loved my life.

Letting go of that anger made approaching this much easier.

"I appreciate that, sir." Snapping for Tempest to join me at my side, I took a few steps inward and lowered my voice. "I know this is your case now. I'm not a cop, but even if I was, I wouldn't have any jurisdiction here. But there really isn't a conflict of interest. I've never met Daisy. I want to find her, obviously, but I would never jeopardize the case by leaking information to the family or anything like that. I just—well, I'm really passionate about this, and I don't want—"

"You could."

I cocked my head to the side. "I'm sorry, sir. I don't understand."

"You got plenty of experience." He took one more drag off his cigarette and flicked the butt to the ground. Squishing it with his combat boot, he lowered his voice as well. "When Grant told me who you were, first thing I did was call down to Pittsburgh. Jones had nothing but good things to say about you. We already know what the media thinks."

Maybe I should've started putting two and two together by now, but I still stared at him in confusion.

"Look, it's a small town." He hooked his thumbs beneath his vest. "I had a grand total of five detectives. Three of them retired. I've filled the seats, and they quit, and I got two new guys in there, but they're all fresh out of the academy. I still got one to fill. It's yours if you want it."

Brows raised, I snorted. Probably not the best thing to do in that situation, but it just seemed far-fetched. "I couldn't pass my physical exam, sir. That's why I'm a PI now."

He shrugged. "Minor issue."

I open my mouth, but no words came out. I didn't know how to respond to that. It was the last thing I expected Torres—or any sergeant, for that matter—to say to me.

"Torres!" someone called behind me. "You're gonna want to check this out."

"Think about it, Castle. No reason to decide right now." Walking past me, he gestured for me to join. I did. Albeit, a few feet behind. "Either way, I want you on this case."

"Well, thank you, sir. I appreciate that."

"As long as you promise to think about it."

Respectfully, I had more important things to think about right now. Like the orange flags perched every few feet apart across the field. Those weren't unusual. We used them at every scene to mark evidence.

But I'd walked this field, and I'd only seen flowers. No footprints. No debris. No garbage or anything of the like.

A young man stood beside one of those flags. His white cheeks were an unusual shade of green. He opened his mouth, but probably only caught a few flies. No words came out.

"What do you got, Mathers?" Torres asked.

"I, um—" He cut himself off with a hard swallow. "These flags. They're marking all the places the dogs laid down at."

Explained why his face was green. Mine likely was too.

"How many are we at?" Torres asked.

"Thirteen, sir," Mathers said.

We were at the corner of the field, closest to the access road. Those flags only extended a few yards.

The field was at least five hundred yards in each direction.

A shaking breath left Torres's nostrils. Gazing out over the field, surely coming to the same conclusion I just had, he hooked his thumbs through the straps of his vest. "I'll call to see when they're getting here with the tractor. No use in digging with shovels."

"That's a good idea, sir," Mathers said, voice quiet.

"The BAU," I said, still staring out over the field. "You might wanna call them in on this too."

Chapter 6

I KNEW IT WAS BAD. EVERYONE KNEW WHAT WE WERE ABOUT TO FIND would be bad.

No one expected it to be *this* bad.

Time moved in slow motion as the dogs laid down at a new grave, then another, and another. I stood there watching with a knot in my throat and a dozen more in my stomach. This wasn't my first rodeo with a serial killer. Maybe I should have been used to this by now.

But then I saw a dog lay down for the nineteenth time, and this field was pretty damn big.

"Where you at in that book?" Torres asked, standing a few feet to my left.

"Maybe ten percent in?"

"How much reading do you think you can get done before they dig all these up?"

A valid point. What good was I doing? Standing here, watching with my thumb up my ass, was helping no one.

Loosening my tight shoulders, I eased out a calming breath. "Right. I'm going to have a seat. Let me know if you need me."

A short nod in response.

Wildflowers smashed under our feet as Tempy and I walked back to the rock just inside the foliage. In the ninety-degree sun, I doubted she appreciated my zombie stare into the open field considering her black fur. Still, I must've looked a bit green, because with every step, her eyes stayed on me. She nearly walked into a tree herself.

Once we reached the big rock I had declared my comfy seat, I popped open my water bottle and Tempy's collapsible water bowl, then poured her some. I scratched her head as she lapped away. "It's okay, baby. Everything's okay."

She plopped onto her bottom and panted up at me with relaxed ears. No matter what was going on behind her in that field, that face could always bring a smile to mine.

I found my phone in my pocket, swiped it open, only to be greeted by fifteen new texts. Three from Bentley, seven from Grace, two from Harper, and three from Alex.

I didn't know what to say to Bentley or Grace yet. Harper was first on the list.

I'm on my way.

Don't leave the site. We can ride to the hotel together.

I texted back, *Sounds good.*

Alex said, *What the hell is going on?*

Lancaster has never asked for help.

But I heard you were there, so fill me in.

I responded with, *Sorry, busy at the moment. Harper can fill you in.*

As busy as I was, Bentley and Grace were still sitting at the bottom of that hill. It was time I clued them in. Before I'd even opened their text, there was already a knot in my throat.

Bentley texted, *Find anything yet?*

Sorry, not trying to bug you, but we saw a bunch of cops heading up. Did you find anything?

Okay, I'm starting to get worried. You're okay, aren't you?

That last text was sent only four minutes ago.

Before I responded to it, I had to see what Grace said.

Maddie.

What's up?

Have you found anything?

Okay, I know you found something. We just saw all those cops.

What did you find?

Not Daisy, right?

Wait, that sounds like I don't want you to find her, and I do, but ideally not at the burial ground.

You know what I mean.

Another deep breath. Too much to text, and yet so few words. Still, I found myself dialing Bentley's number and holding the phone to my ear. He answered on the second ring. "You're okay, right?"

"Yeah. Yeah, I'm fine." Hopefully my voice didn't give me away. "We've found something. A couple things, actually."

Silence for a few heartbeats. "Bodies?"

Pinching my eyes shut, I did my best to keep my voice even. "Yeah. But there's nothing to suggest any of them are Daisy. Alex is coming. So's Harper. I guess Lancaster requested Pittsburgh's help since Harper is already familiar with the case. They'll have more answers for us after they all have a look."

"Alex?" Anxiety tinged the edge of his voice. "Alex isn't familiar with the case, is she? Why did they want her?"

He already knew the answer to that. He just wanted confirmation.

"The coroner needs some help."

Silence. "Some? Or a lot?"

"Look, we're not sure about anything just yet." I swallowed hard. "I'm gonna ride back to the hotel with Harper. You and Grace should head there. Get something to eat, take a shower, just relax, okay? I'll let you know when we have some concrete information."

"So, a lot."

I wished I had good news to give him. I wished I could explain why—in the most twisted, shameful way—all these bodies were a good thing. I wanted to tell him that somewhere along the way, in one or all of these graves, were more clues. I wished there was a light in this very dark tunnel.

There was. Rationally, I knew there was. It was just very hard to see at the moment.

"I'll see you later, okay?" I asked, doing my best to keep my voice soft.

"Yeah, okay." He cleared his throat, likely to even out his voice as well. He, like most of us here, was on the verge of tears. Who wouldn't be in this situation? Didn't mean that Grace had to see him like that. "Okay. Keep me posted. And stay safe."

"Always."

"Love you."

"Love you too."

As the call ended, I returned the phone to my hoodie pocket and took a moment. I wanted to come to terms with what I was about to read before I read it.

I took a deep breath, inhaling the scent of wildflowers, hearing the birds chirping in the treetops. Tempest still smiled up at me and I scratched around her ears.

After another deep breath, I was ready to know more of Daisy's story.

So I swiped open the file, and I continued reading.

More terrifying than the big window and the bear on the other side was the glowing red light in the corner. Where the wall of windows met the ceiling, there was a black lens with a red light below it. A security camera.

He was watching me.

I was tethered to the most luxurious, expensive bed I'd ever seen, in the fanciest bedroom I could imagine, with a swollen lip, aching limbs, wearing only that white nightgown my captor loved so much, while he watched me through that camera.

There was no use in trying to fight. The cuffs I wore were for hardcore bondage. I knew, because we'd used them for that. No matter how hard I fought, I wasn't escaping them. If I screamed, that bear might hear me, but no one else would.

He spared me. He kept me alive. I had to be grateful for that.

Not to say that I became one of those lunatics. Deluca would never convince me that he was a good man. After this, the knife of betrayal was buried deep in the center of my chest, all the blood I had left for him had spilled.

But he didn't have to know that.

Sex work is acting. Unappreciated, undervalued acting. I'd been doing it for years. There was a part Deluca wanted me to play, so I would. I would do whatever it took to survive. So I did.

I didn't call out for him, but it wasn't long before he came in. I didn't even hear him at first. The birds outside the window, I heard clear as day, but not his footsteps. No squeal of hinges from the door. Not even the slight bump of it falling open.

It was his voice that alerted me.

"How long?" he asked.

I sputtered, "H-how long for what?"

"How long have you known?" His tone was so cold. It had never even been cool before.

If there was one thing I could say with absolute certainty about Mr. Deluca, it was that he had charisma like no other. Well-articulated, always, and witty. But never cold.

"How long have you been pregnant, and how long have you known that you're pregnant?"

"I—I'm about five weeks," I said. "I found out last week."

He crossed his arms and leaned against the dresser parallel to the bed, facing me. "That's quite early."

I stayed quiet.

"How do you know it's mine?"

That took me aback. In hindsight, it shouldn't have. Now, I know what he saw me as. Then again, I was still adjusting to the fact that he wasn't the man I thought I loved. "Because you're the only one I've been with—"

"Don't give me that shit." He squared his shoulders, eyes wide, but brows furrowed. "You're a whore. It's your job. How am I supposed to believe a word that comes out of your mouth?"

My eyes stung with tears. I still don't know if it was out of grief, or fear, or if I was already playing the part he wanted me to. One way or the other, I was glad, because as soon as he saw those tears, that hate in his eyes softened.

"We had a plan," I said. "The moment you told me you loved me, that you wanted a life with me, I gave it up. I was still dancing, but I never went home with anyone. Only you. That was in—what? May? You're the only person I've been with since."

Just the slightest bit, his shoulders softened. "We're gonna do some tests to confirm that."

Even if I weren't tied to his bed, even if I weren't convinced he would kill me, I would've agreed to that. Given the context, it was a fair request. So my tone was genuine when I said, "Of course."

"When was the last time you got high?"

"July eighth," I said. "You know this. You know that's my clean date."

He reached into the pocket of his jacket, pulled something out, and set it on the dresser. A small clear cup with a blue lid. "Is your piss gonna prove that?"

God, how sick I was of no one believing me when I talked about my clean date. But there was a part to play. "Yes, sir."

At that word, his jaw relaxed. Apparently, I deserved an Oscar.

I also saw it as my opportunity to get a jab in. "I mean, aside from whatever you gave me last night. That might show up on the test."

There it was. The slightest pinch of his forehead, widening his eyes. Not much, and it didn't last for long, but it was there. Remorse. "It was benzos. They won't hurt the baby."

And screw the mother, I guess.

"Good," I murmured. "Good, I don't want anything to happen to our baby."

"As long as you're telling the truth, neither will I." His tone was flat. Emotionless.

Still, I wanted to cling to the hope of the chivalry of those words. I wanted to believe that I, and this child, mattered to him. It'd save us both if we did.

In the same breath, it was the first time in my life that chivalry sounded dirty. I'd always loved when men opened doors for me, even when Kevin had insisted it was his duty to protect me.

That's how they got me.

Chivalry was oppression wrapped in a pretty package. I'd started to see it with Kevin, but it wasn't until this moment that the dots connected. He protected me, partially because he saw me as a weak little woman incapable of protecting herself, but more so, he saw me as his property. He protected me in the same way a middle-aged man protected his luxury sports car.

I was not a person to him. I was a commodity, an object.

Fact is, I was *a weak little woman incapable of protecting herself. But only because I fell for the fantasy of a knight in shining armor.*

If I hadn't fallen for the chivalry, all the empty promises, if society hadn't conditioned me to think my best shot in life was a man who'd take care of me, I would've never wound up tied to this bed.

"If you need something, call for me," Deluca said. "'Till then, get some rest."

"CASTLE," A FAMILIAR VOICE CALLED, DRAGGING MY ATTENTION FROM the story on my screen.

Her brown ponytail flapped in the wind as she climbed up the hill. Alex's brown eyes leveled on mine. She wore the same navy windbreaker I'd seen her in a thousand times with *CORONER* stamped on the back in yellow letters. Over her shoulder hung a duffle bag with the same inscription.

I closed my phone and stood. Tempest did the same.

"You ready for the longest day of your life?" I asked her.

She grunted, shaking her head. "What's the count at now?"

That was a good question.

Chapter 7

"Nineteen, last I heard," I said. "You guys made it here quick. No traffic?"

Alex grimaced. Behind her, tiptoeing over rocks and mud, Harper said something under her breath.

"She drives like a maniac." Alex nodded Harper's way and crouched to greet Tempest. "I saw my life flash before my eyes a hundred times."

"She's dramatic." Harper scratched Tempest's head as well. "What have you got so far?"

"Enough for the FBI to form a profile, I think," I said. "Not enough to find Daisy, or Deluca. I'm only a few chapters into her story, though. There's a lot more in there. I've been highlighting key details, but I don't know if it's going to be enough."

"What kind of details?" Alex asked.

Torres called from the far side of the field, at least a few hundred yards away. "You gonna make introductions, Castle?"

The temperature had dropped with the descent of the sun. A slight glow still shined behind the trees, turning the sky glorious shades of pink and orange. It almost looked like it was on fire. Given the tractor was just finishing up its first dig, with over a dozen more to go, that fire in the sky felt more literal than metaphorical.

"Let's walk and talk," I said, gesturing for them to follow me. They did, Alex on my right with Tempest between us, and Harper on my left. "Deluca's got money. A lot of it. We already knew that, but it might help us narrow people down around here. I do believe this is his home. He was going to kill

Daisy—or at least begin his torture on her—on their way here. No point in looking for missing girls in this area. All these bodies are going to be from elsewhere."

"What did he tell Daisy he did for a living?" Harper asked. "Have you gotten that far in the book?"

"So far, he never has. Given his schedule, the fact that he could travel all the way to Columbus and stay there for weeks or months on end, he's either gotta work remotely, or not at all."

"Trust fund baby?" Alex said.

"That's what I'm leaning toward, but I can't say for sure yet," I said. "He also spared Daisy because she was pregnant. Right after she told him so, he called her Rory."

"That info might be able to help us," Harper said.

"I'm ninety-nine percent sure he's a narcissist, but I don't know if he's a sociopath." Which was a hard thing to say as I looked at the few dozen markers on the ground, pointing out each place a dog had lain down to signal a body. "The night he kidnapped her, right after she told him that she was pregnant, he drugged her. She woke up the next day in his bed, tied to it, and he asked when the last time she got high was. She said before she was pregnant, aside from whatever he gave her the night before. And he felt bad about that."

"Not about her, but the baby," Harper said, almost as a question. I nodded, and she continued. "Because he hates women, but he wants a family."

"Maybe." I shrugged. "Maybe Rory was an ex, and she lost their baby? I don't know."

"Anything else we should know right now?" Harper asked.

We were halfway across the field by then, and I had many notes to share with her. I wasn't sure which were most important at this moment. "He's got a thing about cleanliness. I don't know how much of that overlaps into his everyday life, but he associates it sexually. He doesn't prioritize makeup or aesthetics in the girls, but he does want them freshly bathed and wearing white lingerie. Very dainty, very girly."

"Ugh," Alex said. "Like, *little* girls?"

"Daisy was barely legal when they started seeing each other, if that tells us anything," Harper said. "Shit, what's the sex of the kid?"

Chills stretched up my spine. My stomach ached, and I swallowed the bile that burned up my esophagus. "Girl. Her name is Bella."

Harper blew out a slow, deep breath. Alex said nothing. Neither did I.

What was there to say?

The one thing that gave me solace was what I'd learned while working with the FBI on the Country Killer case. Predators like this tended to stay in a certain age range. We wouldn't know until we dug up all these bodies, but Deluca preferred his victims developed. Young, barely adults, but nothing at this point suggested that he was interested in babies. Bella wasn't even a year old yet. She wasn't the object of his fantasies.

Not yet.

I hoped the bastard was dead before she aged into his fascination.

Only a few dozen yards from the tractor, now no longer in use, Torres came into view with a handful of other officers I'd yet to meet. One wore a blue vest with white letters on the back that read, *CORONER*. He was an older man, white, balding, with thick round glasses. He introduced himself as Billy Robinson. After a handshake, I introduced Harper and Alex to him and Torres.

"We're glad Pittsburgh could spare you," Torres said, shaking Harper's hand. "Thanks for making it here so fast."

"We just hope we can help," Harper said.

"I could use some down here." Robinson kneeled beside the grave and gestured for Alex to join him. Harper and I followed. As Harper kneeled, I lowered myself to my butt for a better view inside. The tractor behind me revved up, then began backing away from the grave.

Only the victim's hand was exposed. Unlike most murder victims, this one was close to six feet down. That told us our murderer wasn't hand digging. He, like we just had, used some type of heavy equipment to dig this hole.

Because she was buried so deep, Robinson held a stick with a small brush attached to the end. It was practically a sterile broom. Sterile, because any evidence we found here would need to be preserved for the trial. There wasn't enough room in the hole to climb down and carefully sweep the debris from her face, and there were plenty more graves to uncover here.

Carefully, he swept the brush back and forth. Slowly, her arm became visible, and then her face.

It was her.

I tried to retain my composure, but seeing the girl from the missing person photos like this—six feet under, pale skin now leathery, muddy, and her pretty black hair covered in dust and dirt, with that thick black bruise around her neck—I had to look away.

"Late teens or early twenties, I'm guessing," Alex said. "What do you think? Maybe a month down here?"

"Or less," Robinson said. He continued dusting the debris from her chest, exposing a white nightgown. Both hands were folded above her ribs, just like any funeral director would've done. "Fingers seem to be intact, so if she's in any systems, we should be able to get a match."

"You will," I said. "Jane Martin. Twenty-one years old, disappeared a little more than a month and a half ago out of Baltimore. Also a sex worker. Several arrests for solicitation and possession."

Robinson looked up at me with his head cocked to the side. "She your missing girl?"

"No," I murmured, doing my best not to visualize Daisy laid out in this grave. "No, but my missing girl wrote about her. I was hoping I misinterpreted something but doesn't look like it."

"You're sure it's her?" Torres asked.

"Guess I won't be until you run those fingerprints," I said, gesturing to the body. "But the small nose, the high cheekbones, the dark hair. If she isn't Jane, she looks a lot like her."

"He's got a type," Torres said.

"He does. Sex workers or exotic dancers with dark hair, light eyes, and light skin, who have drug problems." Eyes inside the grave again, I squinted at her fingers. Though folded on her chest, something looked off beneath them. "Is she holding something?"

"Could be. Hard to tell from up here." Alex squinted at the figure. "Do you mind if I climb down, Robinson? I think I can squeeze in that gap by her face."

Robinson was on the heavier side. No chance he was climbing in there, but his quick nod told me he appreciated Alex's effort.

"Can someone give me a hand?" Alex asked, looking between the officers.

A few stepped up, offering their palms as she carefully scaled her way into the dirt. Watching each movement, she kept her feet away from Jane's body. Still, her foot landed on Jane's hair, and I grimaced.

I'd worked cases like this before. I wasn't sure why this one was bothering me so much. Maybe because I was so close to it. Maybe because I wasn't sure if Bentley could recover from losing Daisy twice, and I knew this investigation would put her in more danger than she'd ever been.

Alex murmured something in Spanish. I was far from bilingual, but it roughly translated to, "*I'm sorry, sweet girl.*"

Gripping a tree root inside the grave to keep her steady, Alex bent for Jane's hand with gloved fingers. As she peeled them apart, a series of cracks sounded.

Chills swept over my skin.

Gently, Alex straightened holding a figurine. She grabbed one of the brushes from the mat beside the grave and cleared the debris. It was roughly the size of a computer mouse, so from here, I couldn't make it out.

"What is it?" Torres asked.

Alex held it upright for us to get a better view. With the dimming sun, I still couldn't make out all the details. The only thing I could tell was that it was black. "A ceramic of a bird, I think? Maybe a crow, or—"

"A raven," I said. "It's a raven."

Chapter 8

What did the birds mean? Why were they significant to Deluca?

He used them as some type of identifier. Daisy, he considered a hummingbird. Jane was a raven. The hummingbird was because of Daisy's tattoo. The raven was because of the city Jane was from.

Their significance was still lost on me.

I explained the relevance of the birds to Torres, Alex, Robinson, and Harper. Harper already knew what I did, but she didn't understand their importance to Deluca either.

"Once you get further into that book," Harper said, "maybe we'll have a better idea."

"Probably." Using Tempest's vest for support, I struggled onto my feet. "She's very detailed. Scene by scene, she's breaking down exactly what happened. Soon, we should have something valuable."

"She gave us something pretty damn valuable already." Torres looked around the field, nibbling his lower lip. "We're gonna find more new graves. I don't doubt that. But the problem is, we're in a race now."

That we were.

"What do you mean?" Robinson asked.

"This isn't a dumping ground," Torres said, gesturing to Jane. "Look at her. He laid her out like it was her funeral. With dignity, maybe even respect. It's hard to imagine, given what he did to her, but this is sacred ground. No doubt in my mind, he comes back here. Maybe daily, maybe weekly, but if he hasn't figured it out already, he's going to soon."

"He thought he was safe," I said. "That's why he hunts in other cities. Here, at his home, he thinks he's safe. Now, seeing us tear up his cemetery?"

"He knows he's not," Harper said. "He knows we're looking for the killer."

Torres shook his head. "Hopefully he hasn't figured out Daisy's the reason why."

Another shiver raced through me.

"We've got plenty to do here," Alex said, looking up at me from her perch in the grave. "Aside from reading that book, you don't have anything else you can be chasing right now? No other leads?"

I opened my mouth to say that I had nothing, but then I remembered. "There is something. The bag."

"The bag?" Harper asked.

"The shopping bag Daisy put the jacket and flash drive into," I said. "It was from a convenient store, I think. Nature's Basket or something?"

"Nature's Pantry," Torres said. "It's a little farmer's market a town over. I'm pretty sure they close at eleven. I can send some guys over to ask around unless you'd like to go."

"We'd like to," Harper said before I had the chance. "How long does it take to get there from here?"

"Depends on how long it takes to get to your car, but probably forty-five minutes to an hour."

"Next on our list then." I snapped for Tempest to stand, and she did. "You want me to drop that flash drive at the station?"

"Call me when you're finished at the shop, and we'll go from there," he said. "I'm probably going to be here all night waiting for the feds to get in, but you got my number, Castle."

"What was their ETA last time you talked?" Harper asked.

"Six hours, two hours ago. No update since," Torres said. "Want me to fill you in when I've got one?"

"Yes, sir," Harper said. "Thanks so much again."

"No, thank you." Torres gazed down at Jane in the grave for a few heartbeats. "For finding this guy. Hard to believe it's one of our own in this town, but glad we know about it now."

I was just glad to finally work with a cop who believed me.

* * *

My car would've handled the uneven gravel and dirt that lined the access path up this mountain. Covered in butterflies and flowers or not, Subarus were great for off roading. Harper's luxury vehicle was not. Luckily, she had a way with words. With the right bat of her eyelashes, one of the young deputies was more than willing to drive us to her car at the bottom of the hill. Tempy and I sat in the back of his pickup while Harper loaded into the front.

Along the way, I debated if there were any avenues we had yet to go down. So far, no. Legally, we had explored or were currently exploring every lead we had.

Legally.

But I knew someone who worked outside the legal system.

As soon as we settled into Harper's car, I clicked around on her dashboard. "This car has Wi-Fi, doesn't it?"

She shooed my hand away and took over. "You need to login so you can email me those files?"

"And make a call." I squinted at the factory Wi-Fi password on the dashboard and typed it in on my phone. "Service is shit out here."

"You're not kidding," she said under her breath. "Email me that file before you make your call. I can have my phone read the journal aloud to us while we drive. You caught me up on what you read so far, right?"

I agreed and did so. As Harper complained that it was taking too long for the email to come through, I dialed a number that I was sure I'd be dialing a hell of a lot more in the future.

Dylan, my newly found half brother, answered with a groan. "I go to bed by ten PM every single night, Maddie. Do you know what time it is?"

I read the clock on the dashboard. "Nine-forty-two. So just in time, right?"

"The next eighteen minutes, I would like to spend following my usual routine."

"Which is?"

"Watching ASMR videos of people scrubbing rugs."

Harper gave me a look, apparently listening to my conversation. Couldn't blame her though. She was still refreshing her email, and it was hard not to hear somebody through the phone these days.

"Would I be able to pay you for the inconvenience?" I asked.

"It can't wait 'til morning?"

"Maybe it can. But maybe you could help me find a missing girl and her infant daughter sooner rather than later."

He grunted. "Go on."

"I don't have an exact vicinity yet, but would you be able to get me a list of people within, say, a fifty-mile radius who make damn good money?"

"Yes, I can, but I would need something a bit more descriptive. Like an exact number. I believe our ideas of good money are different."

I rolled my eyes, but didn't have time to argue semantics. "What do you think, Harper?"

"Mid to high six figures or more," Harper said. "Either works remotely or comes from money."

"Also owns his home. It's on multiple acres, so it won't be in a housing development or anything like that," I said. "He might be Italian, if that helps?"

"I can formulate the list, but if we're talking about a fifty-mile radius, you're still looking at at least a few hundred people."

A valid point. "But if they're on that list, and we get a lead elsewhere, it might be enough to at least go check it out."

"Alright," he said with a sigh. "Anything else?"

"Yeah, one other thing. I'm looking for a hotel off a highway that comes from Columbus, Ohio, to Lancaster, Pennsylvania. It won't be a chain. The building is U-shaped with a pool in the center, two floors, all accessible outdoors. Not the kind of hotel that you walk into the main entrance."

He made a noise that was hard to decipher. "That's all you have?"

"It'll be somewhere halfway between the two cities," I said. "The sign either doesn't have the name on it, or it was one of those retro light-up ones. I know for certain that the red lettering will say '$99 a night.' About ten to twenty miles back on the highway, there's a diner, but one of the windows was boarded up, so it could be abandoned or under construction."

"That's more to work with."

"Also a good chance that the business is involved in something nefarious," I said. "Might have suspicious tax records, an owner who's been in jail a few times—something like that."

"Much more to work with," Dylan said. "You do realize that this will take me all night, correct?"

I knew where this conversation was headed, and I was already prepared for it. "Damn it, Dylan, just send me the invoice. I don't care how much it costs. I'm trying to find—"

"A missing girl and her infant child, yes. I know." There was an edge to his voice now. "There's no reason to cuss at me. I am trying to help."

"You're right. I'm sorry." I rubbed my eyes and down the bridge of my nose. "The stakes have just gotten higher. I can't get into the details, but it's not just Daisy. The guy we're after, he's done a lot of horrible things, and—"

"And that is why I'm no longer interested in your money for this particular case," Dylan said. "In the future, when you're working a case where you're being paid, I would also like to be compensated. With this particular one, though, I will lend my help freely."

My stiff shoulders relaxed. Warmth filled my chest. "Thank you."

"Thank you as well. I read the missing person's report after you had me look into the library. The girl deserved more than the police gave her, and I'm glad you stepped up."

"I'm sure she'll say the same thing about you when we find her."

Chapter 9

The Visit

Shortly after Deluca came in to question me, he returned with breakfast. Waffles—which tasted a bit freezer burned—yogurt, and a precut apple. "It's important that you eat well," he said.

Initially, he cut each piece of waffle and fed it to me. I was already thinking ahead. Even if I was stuck here, I couldn't lay in a bed twenty-four hours a day, seven days a week. There was no use in running. Where would I go—to lunch with the bear in the front yard?

No, I needed him to realize that I would stay calm, that I wouldn't hurt myself or the baby if he released me.

So I gagged on the waffle. I held my breath and pretended it was stuck in my throat.

Brown eyes wide, he shook my shoulders. I kept holding my breath, mouth wide open, pretending to struggle for air.

I must've been turning blue by then, because he hurried to the leather straps and released my hands. Yanking me up with one hand, he slapped my back with the other. I spit the waffle onto his leg. It was the only thing within spitting distance.

He cussed under his breath about it, and I apologized. Internally, I smiled.

After that, he took the fork and instructed me to continue eating. I used the spoon to cut the waffles, slowly ate the yogurt, and then the apple. He watched each and every bite. I didn't speak.

When I was finished, I said, "It was very good. Thank you."

He said nothing. Only grabbed the breakfast tray and set it on the dresser, keeping his eyes on me.

It wasn't necessary. I wouldn't say that, but there was no reason to watch my every move. He may have believed I was stupid, but I'd spent most of my life on the streets. I knew what being royally screwed looked like.

There was no way out. Not yet. I wasn't going to jam the spoon into his eye socket and make a run for it. The man was a mountain. I had no chance at disabling him long enough to find a pair of car keys and vanish into the forest.

Fact was, given all the nature we were surrounded by, I was safer in here than I was out there.

But I wasn't done yet.

As he started across the room, eyes on those leather cuffs, I said, "Can I use the restroom?"

"You can hold it." He reached for my hand, and I didn't stop him.

"I really have to go." I stretched out for his wrist as well, sliding my fingers down until they overlapped his. My touch was gentle, sweet. Rather than a tight jaw and narrowed eyes, his expression matched mine. Only difference was his was authentic and mine was a show. "I'm sorry. I know I'm being a pain, but I don't want to make a mess. I just—I really *have to go. Can't you come with me? I just need to pee—I promise."*

He looked at me for a few heartbeats, like he was searching for the lie. There wasn't one to find. I really did have to pee.

Deluca straightened. "You'll take that drug test while you're up."

I nodded in agreement. Together, we stood, and we walked to the bathroom off the bedroom. I'd already gotten a good look at it, but I'd never seen a toilet like this. It was in its own little closet. The tub, the shower, and the sink were all out in the open when you first walked into the room, but the toilet was tucked in the corner behind a door.

"Wow," I said, chuckling, "that's smart. Keeps all the nasty stuff out of the rest of the bathroom, right?"

"Yes." He held my hand until we stood there in the doorway, then gestured for me to go inside. I did. As I sat to do my business, he fished around in the pocket of his sweatpants for that little cup with the blue lid. Passing it to me, he said, "Toilets create an aerosol when you flush them. It spreads the germs from inside all over the room. Most public restrooms have E. coli on every surface."

"Ewww." Doing my business into the cup, I gestured to the rest of the bathroom where he stood. "Wouldn't want my E. coli on all this, huh?"

He said nothing, just held out his hand for me to return the cup. I did.

As he set it on the bathroom counter, I said, "I've never been in a bathroom this nice. I always dreamed of taking a bath in one of those though. The porcelain, clawfoot ones?"

Still, he said nothing.

"Maybe I could try that sometime," I said. "I am a little dusty from the car."

"Depends on what the doctor says." Deluca gestured for me to stand and follow him. I did. "Wash your hands."

Again, I did. You'll find that a lot as you continue reading. He told me to do something, and I did it.

I've done things that I never imagined I'd be capable of. Awful things, because if I didn't, I was afraid I'd lose my life.

No matter how miserable I would soon become, I've never truly desired death. I've only desired an end to the suffering.

But, after that, how could I not have hope? He was taking me to a doctor. I'd be able to tell them that this lunatic was holding me hostage. They'd call 911, and they'd arrest him, and this nightmare would end.

Maybe that was the worst part. The hope.

I washed my hands as he told me to, I returned to lying in the bed as he told me to, and I stared at the birds flying overhead until I dozed off.

The sun was still up when the door opened again. This time, Deluca wasn't alone.

A woman in scrubs walked in behind him. The pants were pink, and the top was covered in puppies.

I never got her name. She would later deliver my daughter, and I still don't know her name.

She was somewhere between late middle-aged and retirement. Typically, women in that age range display a sort of motherly demeanor. She did not.

None of her features were particularly attractive or unattractive. Her big, round blue eyes were colder than a blizzard. She was on the heavier side, but her face was oval-shaped with sharp angles. High cheekbones, a strong jaw. Not the kind of person you'd stop to look at, but not the kind of person you'd imagine working with a serial killer.

"How far along are you?" was the first question she asked.

Like I had told Deluca, I said, "Five weeks."

"Have you been taking prenatals?" She sat on the bed beside me and snatched my arm from my side. Pressing her thumb over my wrist, she looked at her watch. "If so, for how long?"

"Only a week or two."

My gaze followed a sound from the hallway. The same door the doctor had come from. It was almost like a vacuum being pushed over hardwoods. Then a small computer came into view. It wasn't until Deluca rolled it to the bedside that I realized it was an ultrasound machine. A small one, but an ultrasound all the same.

The doctor said nothing as she fished around in a basket below the monitor. She straightened back up with a portable blood pressure monitor. Yanking my arm again, she fastened the cuff around my bicep.

I lay there in silence, watching the birds through the skylight again.

My stomach was in my throat, my chest ached, and my eyes burned.

There went the hope.

That minute or two as she took my blood pressure had me more nauseated than the last forty-eight hours.

Deluca, I could wrap my head around. At least in some capacity. All my life, I heard about horrible men. The past few years, I'd met more than I could count. It wasn't the first time a man seemed good, seemed kind, and I'd fallen for it. That was common enough when the men who were paying for your body viewed it as an object. After all, that's what it was. That's what I was. Something to be bought and sold.

The worst part was the doctor.

Maybe because she was so cold and sterile, maybe because she didn't care that I was young enough to be her granddaughter yet lay chained to a bed by her friend.

Maybe because, as all girls are taught, I believed I could trust women. My mother, no matter how screwed up she may have been, would've never done this. Only monsters did this. Only men did this.

It was the betrayal, come to think of it. Girl code. Growing up, even men had taught me to fear men. Bentley had told me if I ever needed help, run to a woman. Men weren't to be trusted, but we protect each other from them. We take care of each other before we take care of a man.

This was the first time in my life I realized that wasn't true for all women. It was the first time I realized that women could be just as horrible. No, she wasn't the one who tied me to this bed. No, she wasn't the one who'd raped me the night before. No, she wasn't the one who beat me and held me against my will.

But she did exactly as my captor asked her to.

At one point while she was conducting my ultrasound, her phone rang in her pocket. She had a phone in her god damned pocket, and she did nothing. This man, this monster, tried to kill me last night, and she did nothing.

She may not have been the cause of this, but she was no better than him. She was, at the very least, part of it.

Even if you do not begin the violence, if you perpetuate it, how are you any different?

Once she finished the ultrasound, she told Deluca he could put my cuffs back on. As he did, she said, "She's telling the truth. I'd estimate her between five and six weeks."

"And everything looks okay?" he asked.

"As long as she's not having any pain or bleeding, yes, I'd assume everything is fine. But this early on, there's not much to see on an ultrasound." She shut down the machine, pulled off her gloves, and found another pair in her pocket. "I'd like to do some blood work. We can check her levels and continue to do so weekly, as well as test the DNA of the child."

"You can do that while she's still pregnant?" Deluca asked.

"Yes. It also tells us the sex." She dug around in the basket where she'd gotten the blood pressure machine again. "Assuming that keeping it is your plan."

"It is," Deluca said.

"Then I will collect the sample and have a basic analysis done by the end of the night. It'll take a week or two for the DNA to come back. It will also cost a pretty penny to keep this anonymous. The basic analysis is simple enough, but the DNA test is more complicated."

"Money is no object," Deluca said, sitting on the other side of the bed beside me. "Just make sure she's healthy."

He took my hand—my shackled hand—and twined his fingers between mine. As if this was something out of a romantic comedy. As if we were a couple who had strived for a child for a decade and were finally blessed by the good Lord.

I wanted so desperately to yank my fingers from his. I wanted to cry. I wanted to scream and shout and punch and stab.

But I couldn't. I couldn't do any of that.

So I held his hand tighter. I gave him what he wanted, because if I didn't, I knew what would happen.

Chapter 10

We'd pulled into the parking lot a few minutes before the chapter ended. We hadn't looked at each other once since.

As we listened, I highlighted all the key details. The file was still open in front of me when I pressed the pause button on the dash.

Beyond the windshield sat a cabin. It was roughly the same size as my trailer, just different dimensions and aesthetics. My siding was rusted, while this place was logs from the gravel below to the peak. There was a small front porch with a few rocking chairs. On the green door hung an *Open* sign. Though hard to see in the dark, a sign on the roof read *Nature's Pantry*.

"Uh." Harper cleared her throat. "I'm gonna need a minute."

Yeah, I could've used one, too. But every moment I took consoling myself was a moment wasted, a moment further from saving Daisy.

"Take your time," I told her. As I stood from the car, even as I grabbed Tempest from the backseat, I didn't look Harper's way. Sometimes, a case made us emotional. Rarely did talking about it help. Not until we got justice for the wronged.

Even then talking about it didn't help much.

With Tempest at my side, I eyed my surroundings. We'd driven through a small town on our way here—mostly middle class homes with a tiny square in the center—and then a lot of trees. This place was no different. Trees to my left, and to my right, and a not so busy highway behind me. Straight ahead, tucked in the corner of the porch, a security camera blinked red.

Could be valuable.

A bell rang overhead as I pulled the door open. And a quick glance around had me rolling my eyes.

I'd expected it to be a market, but it was a health food store decked out with shelves upon shelves of supplements and weight loss drinks. A beige sign with green letters above one of them read, *Organic, All-Natural Energy Source.* I could almost guarantee that if I flipped those bottles around and read the label, there'd be some type of amphetamine inside. But that was the cosmic joke around all these health foods and supplements. Of course caffeine was organic. It came from a plant. Regardless of whether pesticides were used, every plant was organic. The whole organic industry was a scam.

Which wasn't at all the point, but it gave me a better understanding of Deluca. According to Daisy, he was a very fit man. That, tied in with the store, showed me a bit more of who he was.

God, I hope he didn't insist on Daisy feeding the baby an organic, vegan diet too.

"We don't really let dogs in here, miss." A guy, somewhere in his mid-twenties, spoke sheepishly behind the counter. His name tag read *Todd*. "I'm real sorry. You can tie 'em up outside though."

"Sorry, wherever I go, she goes." I gestured to her service vest and walked to the counter. "I'm a private investigator working with the local sheriff's office."

Eyes widening, he swallowed hard. Now that I was closer, I understood why. The smell of skunk permeated the air around him. "Is—is there anything I can help you with?"

"I'm really hoping so." I passed him my phone with the picture of Daisy. "Have you seen her in here before?"

He squinted and zoomed in. "Maybe. Does she got a baby?"

"She does." My heart skipped. "She would've been with a man. Late forties to mid-fifties?"

Nodding slowly, he looked at the image a moment longer. Then he passed my phone back. "Yeah, I remember her. Why? Is she in trouble?"

"That's what we're trying to figure out." I tucked the phone back into my pocket. "When was the last time you saw her?"

"Eh, a week ago, I want to say?" He shrugged. "Probably won't see 'em again for another month or two."

"Why do you say that?"

"They don't stop in all the time or nothing. Most folks don't, you know. We've got the best produce selection for a hundred miles, but it's still too far for most. That's how things are out here. It's half an hour drive just for me to get home, and that's close. Everything is just so far apart. If you're going to take a trip anywhere, it's probably going to be to Walmart."

Supposed that made sense. It was common enough in a rural setting. Even if I still didn't see the produce section he was talking about.

"Right," I murmured. "You don't happen to remember what they got when they were in here, do you?"

"Not off the top my head, but just the usual grocery stuff."

This place didn't specialize in usual grocery stuff. It specialized in 'health foods.' "Not supplements or anything like that?"

"Some protein shakes, maybe," he said. "But there is something weird about them."

"Yeah?" Did the guy act like a serial killer in front of everyone he met?

"Yeah, it's weird." He nodded outside. "The guy always sits up front, and the girl sits in the back. The windows are tinted real dark, so I've never seen inside or anything, but just struck me as odd, you know?"

Not really. It was pretty common for new mothers to sit in the backseat with their baby. They could often soothe them better than the simple sway of the car.

If I had to guess why it was relevant here, and why this cashier got a weird feeling from it, it was because Daisy wasn't only sitting in the back. She was likely blindfolded. She probably gave him certain looks, hoping that he would pick up on it, that he would notice something was wrong and call the cops.

Todd here didn't seem like the brightest bulb, however.

"Did you find anything else about them odd?" I asked.

"Well, most folks around here drive pickup trucks. Stuff that can handle the snow. But that guy she's always with, he drives a Mercedes, I think."

That could help us narrow things down. "Has he ever mentioned where he lives?"

"Just that it's a drive to get here, but everybody says that."

Still, not a dead end. "You said it was last week that they stopped in here, correct?"

"Yes, ma'am."

"I noticed the camera out front. Looks like it's in working order. Think you could get me a copy of it?"

Biting his lip, he shrugged again. "I'm just a worker. But I can give the owner a call."

"Great. Call them."

* * *

WITHIN AN HOUR, HARPER AND I WERE LOOKING THROUGH THE TAPES with Todd. He couldn't remember which day she was here, so he was flipping through each clip individually. That's why it had taken an hour for him to find it.

It wasn't a dead end. But it wasn't much either.

Like most security cameras, the quality was grainy at best. Deluca was smart and parked the car facing the security cameras. Since license plates in Pennsylvania were on the rear of the car, all we got was the make and model. Which, of course, would help Dylan narrow down his large pool of suspects, but it was still a very large pool to pick through.

We did get our first image of the bastard. Not much notable there either. He was exactly as Daisy described him. Somewhere north of six feet tall, with a big, bulky build. He had a typical fade—long hair on the top, short on the sides. In these images, he wore large aviators that obscured most of his face.

Exactly what we expected. A handsome, early middle-aged white guy. Tall and muscular.

Once we had a suspect, sure, we could use this image as evidence. Was it enough to find him? We weren't sure yet.

It was almost 11 PM, and I needed to sleep. Tempest needed to eat. That meant we needed to go back to the hotel, where I would have to talk to Bentley. If not for Tempy, I would've asked Harper to go back to the dig site.

As we were pulling out of the parking lot of Nature's Pantry, Harper's phone rang. Over the speakers, a familiar voice sounded. "This is Detective Ashley Harper, correct?"

"Yes, sir, it is," she said. "Who may I ask is calling?"

"Special Agent Mason Phillips," he said. "I'm assuming you are with Miss Castle?"

"Yes, sir, she is," I said. "Fate's bringing the old crew back together, huh?"

He chuckled. "Seems like you're the fate in question."

"Hey, I just go where the cases take me," I said. Harper gave me a funny look, and I mouthed, "FBI."

"You're lucky, you know," Phillips said. "If one of these bodies they just dug up wasn't dead before you were in high school, I might be accusing you of taking part."

I snorted. Yeah, I'd worked more serial killer cases than most. Not because I asked for them. Simply because they fell into my lap.

"Regardless, I'm excited to meet you all," Harper said. "I'm guessing you landed?"

"We have, and if Miss Castle is still driving that pink Subaru, I'm assuming that we are staying at the same hotel," he said. "If the two of you would like to come down and discuss your findings with our team, we can do so in the hotel lobby."

"Give us an hour, and we'll be there," I said.

For now, back to reading.

Chapter 11

Taste of Freedom

As I lay there in bed, waiting for my next meal or bathroom break, I knew. I knew I had to pretend I was grateful for this.

Although, 'pretend' wasn't a fair word. Half of me was disgusted with myself for it, but I was *grateful.*

How pathetic is that? I was grateful for the mercy of a killer. Even now, I'm grateful that my story didn't end the way the lives of so many women who'd loved Mr. Deluca had ended.

Of course, at that time, I didn't know just how awful he was. But I knew he'd done this before. That kidnapping was orchestrated. It was not his first time. He was an expert. It would take time before I understood his intricacies, but as I lay there in bed, I had no doubts. He'd done this, and worse, more times than I could count, I imagined.

In that moment, when I acknowledged the sickening part of myself that was grateful, I remembered that it had nothing to do with me.

He didn't spare me because he saw something in me. He didn't spare me because I was special. He spared the fetus inside me.

That baby girl. She's who I was, and am, grateful for.

When I first learned I was pregnant, I started picking out baby names and envisioning how I would decorate the nursery. I fantasized about what kind of dog I would get in a few years. I pictured her first day of kindergarten, and then middle school, then high school. College after. Every time I look at my baby girl, that's still what I envision.

A blurry silhouette of black with a square hat. "Isabella Roycroft," being called over the speakers. Cheering for her in the back of the auditorium, watching her head whip toward me. I wouldn't be able to make out her face, because you could never see the people walking across the stage at graduations.

I didn't get to do that. I didn't get to graduate high school.

And if I do die, I want to make known that those previous sentences were not typos. I didn't get to *graduate. Because I was doomed from the start. My mom was a junkie, my dad was a deadbeat, and I was an orphan before I was a teenager. Yeah, I took the drugs, but they weren't what I wanted. I wanted a family. I wanted normalcy.*

Every time I was beaten by a foster parent, or abused by a foster sibling, I was reminded that I would never have it. Every time they made me move schools, which kept me from maintaining grades at all, let alone good ones. Every time I ran from the abuse the system put on me, the evil little voice whispered in my ear that I would never get what I wanted.

If I were a man, a serial killer, they'd write books about how my mother was to blame because she didn't hug me enough, or she was promiscuous. But when a foster kid winds up a dropout with a drug problem, it's their fault that they didn't work hard enough.

These thoughts ran circles through my mind as I lay in that bed.

One thing I knew for damn sure, though? I would do everything for my daughter that my mother didn't do for me. Bella saved my life, and I would make certain that she had one worth living.

Day one, no escape ideas came to me. Day one, I had to survive.

So, when he came into the room with dinner, I went back to playing the part.

Squinting at the plate, I sniffed the air. "Spaghetti?"

"Pizza."

"Is it homemade?" I asked, eyes following him as he walked around the bed. "You did promise me you were going to make me homemade pizza one day."

His head jerked my way. I almost flinched. But there wasn't anger in his eyes. There was confusion.

Why was I being nice? Why was I speaking as though we still had a future?

It was like he was conflicted. Like he didn't want to watch what we had burn, but he didn't know how to put out the flames. He certainly didn't expect me to do so.

Yet, I had. Or was, at least, trying to.

"One day." Deluca set the plate on the nightstand and began untying my restraints. "Frozen is gonna have to do for now."

"Never minded frozen either." Smiling, I straightened up in the bed. "Thank you."

He gave me that look again. Confused, conflicted.

As I took a bite, and then another, he continued giving me that look. I kept my shoulders loose, my gaze relaxed, and the faintest hint of a smile across my lips. When the staring went on for too long, I let that smile widen.

Covering my mouth between chews, I said, "What?"

He said nothing, only squinted a bit. "You amuse me, little bird."

"Yeah?" I swallowed my bite of pizza. "Why is that?"

"You know why."

I arched a brow.

"You're not stupid, and neither am I," he said. "This isn't a game, Daisy."

It was. No matter how serious he claimed it to be, this was a game, and I was a damn good player. "I know."

"Then you understand where you are," he said. "You understand what's happening."

"I understand that I'm not leaving this room unless you allow it." Wiping crumbs from the corner of my lip, I shrugged my shoulder. "I understand that you've been hurt, and you don't trust easily. I thought you and I had built enough of that up, but I see I was wrong. And that's okay."

He squinted. "What's okay, exactly?"

"This." I gestured around. "This is the comfiest bed I've ever laid in. That window?" I pointed overhead. "I'm sure the view of it at night is amazing. And the sheets—don't get me started on the sheets."

Still, he gave me that look. Confused, conflicted.

"You're right. I get it now. This is an oasis, and I'm lucky to be here." Smile stretching higher, I shrugged again. "I mean, it's not exactly what I had in mind, but it's still a dream come true. It's what you promised me. Right now, you're not sure how to feel about everything I told you, or if I'm like those other girls who hurt you before, and I get it. You need time. And once you've had it, I'll be right here waiting."

Every word of that made my stomach spin and my chest tighten. But it was what he needed to believe. He needed to believe that I was still in love with him, that I would be a perfect prisoner. That would buy me my safety. Even if I hated it, it was my only choice.

Deluca said nothing.

I continued eating.

When I finished, I asked for a glass of water. Rather than tying me back up and leaving the room to grab one, he unlatched the leather buckles around my ankles and extended a hand. I took it.

He led me down a narrow hallway that opened into a large living room, kitchen, and dining space. It was an open concept. The intricate woodwork of the baseboards and coffered ceilings told me the place was old, but it had been extravagantly renovated. Thick white oak floors were smooth beneath my feet. They always stuck out, because they were the one thing that didn't fit in. The rest of the wood looked old and redone, but those floors were new.

Except for the new, white marble countertops, the old cabinetry in the kitchen was likely original to the home. I can't say for certain, but judging by the turret in the upstairs bedroom that now belongs to me and my daughter, I have to assume it's an old Victorian. This may help you narrow something down.

In the center of the room, separating the living space from the kitchen, was an island. The butcher block on top looked old, but that artificially weathered kind of old. Above it hung copper pots and pans. All the appliances were new, as were the big white sectionals in the living room, but the kitchen table had to have been half a century old. Like everything else, it was refinished, but there was no denying the character in the wood.

While everything in the master suite was new and modern, the common areas here were full of that. Character. All the stools around the kitchen island matched in a hodgepodge sort of way. One was wooden with a brown leather seat. Another had teal legs and a mocha colored suede seat. The last had those same wooden legs with a beige seat. Above the windows overlooking the field and forest was a unique stained glass portrait. A hummingbird flying over a meadow of wildflowers.

"That's why you liked my tattoo, huh?" I asked, gesturing to it. "Looks just like that hummingbird."

"It did remind me of it, yes." He gestured for me to sit at the island. I did. He kept his eyes on me as he reached into a cabinet above the sink. "My mother had that installed when I was a boy."

"So you grew up here?"

"I did." His eyes were like beams, following every move I made. When I propped my elbows on the counter and hunched over it, appearing comfortable, he hurried into the fridge and spun back around with a jug of milk. "It'll be a lovely place for our child to grow up too."

In spite of the knot in my throat, I smiled. "It will."

It wouldn't. The day my daughter turned two weeks old, he shattered that hummingbird window, raining glass on me and the baby who lay on the couch beneath it. But that's a story I'll get to later.

We sat in silence as I drank the milk. Periodically, I complimented this feature of the home, or that, or the interesting color choices, but mostly, I was silent. When I finished it, I thanked him.

He took the glass, set it in the sink, then leaned over the island. A deep breath heightened his shoulders, then gradually released. "Would you like some fresh air?"

"I would love some."

Deluca had me follow him into the living room, where he instructed me to sit on the sofa. I did. He kept me in sight as he opened the closet beside the front door. A moment or two later, he returned with a pair of men's sandals.

Size eleven, if you need to know that.

They fit me like clown shoes, but I wasn't complaining.

He led me out the front door down a set of intricately laid brick paver stairs. At the bottom of them, he wrapped an arm around my shoulders. He squeezed tight.

And I looked around.

Just as I had seen out the window, there was nothing to *see. A field, trees, and a blue sky.*

Still, I pretended to be bewildered.

"Wow, look at the bark on that one."

"The feathers on that bird are so pretty!"

"Isn't it so beautiful the way moss grows up a tree?"

He responded calmly, sometimes sweetly, to each remark I made. He was so normal, so typical, that fleeting thoughts kept passing.

Is this a dream?

Is he really trying to hurt me?

Maybe I'm remembering it wrong.

It wasn't, he was, and I wasn't.

But he seemed so good when frozen in a still frame like this. If you saw him walking down the street, you'd never suspect this. In fact, you might hope that he'd smile at you and ask for your number.

He was perfect, and that was probably why he'd gotten away with it for so long.

That reminder came when we circled back to the front of the old, white Victorian. We sat on the steps, his arm still around my shoulders, and watched the birds for a while.

Eventually, he said, "Now do you see why I made the frozen pizza?"

I cocked my head to the side.

"I own this mountain." His eyes scanned the field and trees before us. "I own hundreds of acres. There is one small access road. I pick up my mail at a PO Box. Delivery services don't, and can't, come here."

"Oh. Yeah, that makes sense." It made sense that Pizza Hut didn't deliver here, at least. Wasn't a hundred percent sure what that had to do with anything though.

Gripping my shoulder tighter, he met my gaze. "My keys are always kept locked away. You will not make it out of here alive should you try to escape, Daisy. If I don't find you, the wilderness will get you."

Chapter 12

Emily Gayton, Nora Martin, and Mason Phillips. The same three FBI agents who had worked on the Country Killer case.

Since we already knew one another, the greeting was mostly introducing Harper. It was an awkward conversation to have in a hotel lobby. Especially mid-summer at a Holiday Inn. A handful of people were already in the lobby, scrolling on their laptops or fishing around at the vending machines.

Gayton suggested we sit in the courtyard for some privacy. No one protested.

Despite the darkness, summer was in full swing. Mosquitoes swarmed us, likely attracted to the streetlights overhead. The wrought-iron bench was less comfortable than the rock I'd sat on in the field earlier.

But as we delved into the case, Harper and I explaining everything we'd learned from Daisy's journal, the conversation carried me away from the pain in my knee and the literal pain in my ass.

"What I still can't wrap my head around is the nurse," Harper said. "Why would anyone help him? Let alone a woman?"

"As feminist as I consider myself to be," Gayton said, shaking her head, "don't be fooled. Women can be—and often are—just as bad as the men who perpetuate violence against us."

"Especially mothers," Phillips said. "They'll do just about anything to protect their children. Even cover up murders. Daisy doesn't say that they looked similar, but from the way you describe the interaction, I have to assume that's the case here. Whoever that woman is, she sees him as her child. And he could do no wrong, even if he kept a young woman in chains."

"I agree." Martin took a sip of her coffee. "With both of you, as well as Harper. It's unlikely to me that any woman off the street would align herself with him. Considering the age of both parties, I'm not sure I'd guarantee that this woman is his mother, but there's some similar dynamic at play. Maybe a sister, or cousin, but even a friend is unlikely."

Probably. But I didn't give a shit.

Regardless of what cop shows touted, putting so much emphasis on a monster's psyche didn't save lives. It practically romanticized the bastards.

Just like I thought with the Country Killer. I didn't care if his mommy was mean to him. I didn't care if he experienced some trauma as a kid. We all did. Everyone was screwed up. Seeking out why a horrible person did horrible things might be beneficial for psychologists trying to help them heal or for the victims themselves.

But no one could convince me that deconstructing a villain's mind was more important than the facts at hand. We had a good bit of those.

"The nurse's relevance to this case stops at that," I said. "She has some degree of healthcare experience—whether an RN, LPN, CNA, or even something less educated—and she's connected to Deluca. Yeah, probably because they're related. But we have actual evidence that I think we should be looking at before we spend too much time on whoever the hell that bitch is."

All eyes turned to me. Harper's were wide. Martin studied me as carefully as she would've studied the nurse. Phillips squinted me over. And Gayton gave a short nod.

"Alright," Gayton said. "What evidence do you have?"

"For starters, the hotel Deluca stopped at the night he kidnapped Daisy." Leaning in, I propped my elbows on my knees. "I think we have good reason to believe the owner has some kind of deal with him."

"That's possible," Gayton agreed. "But thinking so doesn't give us a warrant, Castle."

"We also don't know what hotel it is," Phillips said, lifting his shoulders in a shrug.

"I'm working on that," I said. "But there's more than that. The more bodies we dig up, the more evidence we're gonna find. What's the count at right now?"

"Thirty-six." Martin rubbed a hand over her mouth. "But the dogs have laid down a lot. Right now, we're guesstimating anywhere between fifty to a hundred."

Shivers stretched over my arms. I rubbed them away. "He drives a

Mercedes. He gave a DNA sample for testing on Bella. Not to mention the house itself. There can't be that many homes on this much land. Which is another thing. Have we done a check on the field? Do we know who owns that land?"

"State Park," Phillips said. "Property of no one. We checked for cameras as well, and we couldn't find any."

Biting my lip, I gave a nod. "So there's a chance he doesn't know we're onto him yet."

"That's what we're hoping for, yes," Martin said, ending her sentence with a sharp inhale. "The fact is, to have gone this long without getting caught, he's got to be highly intelligent."

"But he's got too much free time to have a high-profile career," Harper said. "Maybe went to college, but even so, he's not using his degree."

"I said highly intelligent." Martin shook her head. "Not highly educated."

"The two aren't mutually exclusive." Gayton set her coffee on the wrought iron patio table between us. "But, as Castle made clear, we have more concrete evidence to look at. We'll take a good look at anyone and everyone within a hundred miles who lives in an old Victorian."

"An old Victorian on a shit ton of land," I said. "We need more on the library too. Everyone who was there that day at the same time as Daisy. I want to interview every one of them."

"We will," Gayton said. "But, as established, warrants take time. I'm sure the judge will sign off on it by morning. Regardless, we don't want to go knocking on people's doors at this hour."

"Especially not around here," Phillips said, wiggling his brows. "People love the Second Amendment around here, don't they?"

"Yours truly included." I gestured to the gun on my hip. "Won't be a bad thing to start knocking on doors first thing in the morning, though."

"I'd also like to question witnesses in Maryland." Martin took a sip of her coffee. "All those library patrons could be helpful as well."

"Sure, but that's quite a distance," I said. "We're close on this. If we leave, by the time we get back, he'll know we're onto him. Clearly, he takes Daisy with him when he travels. If they leave, the trail's gone. We'll never find them."

"That reminds me, actually," Gayton said, tilting her head to the side. "How did Daisy get you the coordinates?"

"No idea yet," I said. "We're only halfway through her journal."

"Has she mentioned anything explicit about the home yet?" Martin asked. "Does he bring his victims here, torture them, and then kill them? Or does he kill them on the road and then bring them here?"

"She described Jane in the poem she posted online." Harper relaxed in her seat. "Can't be sure yet, but I think she met her personally."

"Comes back to high intelligence," Gayton murmured, crossing her arms and leaning back in her seat. "Both girls, he took from neighboring states. Crossing state lines is clever."

"Useless to look at any local disappearances." Phillips nibbled his lower lip. "He knows better than to shit where he sleeps."

"All his victims are between late teens and mid-twenties, dark hair, light skin, blue eyes, petite build," I said. "And they're all drug-addicted sex workers, which is why nobody cared to look for them until now.

"But, again, I don't see what the point would be in looking at those cases when we have bodies to look at. He didn't remove their teeth or cut off their hands. Most of them likely have records. Those who haven't decayed already should show up in the fingerprint database. Same goes for dental records of missing people. We have two specific leads. The witnesses at the library and the hotel. I guarantee you, one of those is going to lead to a breakthrough."

Again, Harper gave me that look. The one that said, *Shut the hell up. Don't you realize who you're talking to?*

Of course I did. But they were invited in. They had no jurisdiction here. The local police did. And they were on my side.

"I'm sorry, Castle," Gayton said, brow furrowing. "Do you have something you want to talk about before we go on here?"

I had plenty of opinions about all this. Opinions about them. Opinions about the justice system as a whole. Opinions about the lack of attention Daisy's case received.

But I didn't want to talk about it. I wanted to save an innocent young girl and get justice for the ones we were too late to help. "No. I just want to solve this case. And—"

"And you've got something on your mind," Gayton said, not unkindly. "We're all on the same team here. We'll be less effective if there's tension between us. So if you've got something you want to say, say it."

"I don't think either of us has time to argue semantics—"

"We've already established that we can't go knocking on doors at this hour. We're waiting on a warrant to get the names from the library. And we have analysts working on finding that motel, but that is still going to take time, so I disagree. We all have time."

No matter how harsh the words were on paper, they didn't sound that way coming from her mouth. They sounded direct. Blunt. She wanted to address the elephant so we could work around it.

"Alright, you know what, yeah," I said, throwing my hands in the air. "I'm pissed that I'm the first person who's given a damn about these girls. That me and a preteen girl found a pattern that you guys didn't. My tax dollars pay you guys, yet *I'm* the one who uncovered this murder—all these murders, with the help of someone you all gave up on searching for years ago. The cops in Columbus didn't care when Bentley reported Daisy missing. The cops in Baltimore probably gave up on Jane the same way. I'm pissed this guy has killed somewhere between fifty to a hundred women, and nobody cares because they were poor addicts who relied on sex to make money. I'm pissed the world is the way it is, but I'm even more pissed that when you called me, Phillips, you made a joke about how you'd accuse me of being involved in these murders if you didn't know better.

"Because this isn't a joke. None of this is a damn joke. Somewhere between half a million and a million people are reported missing every year in America, and sure, somewhere around ninety percent of them are found, but we also find about five thousand unidentified bodies every year. I don't think Eric Oakley or Deluca are the only guys you have a hard time finding. That's your whole job as a profiler at the FBI, yet you don't have answers for those five-thousand bodies. You don't find every killer. There are all these statistics about how serial killer rates have gone down since the boom in the 80's, but they haven't. They just know how to get away with it. Just like Ed Kemper said.

"You guys only find them if they want to be found. That's why Eric Oakley was easier for you to handle. But you didn't even know about Deluca. And the fact is, most of them are probably more like Deluca than Oakley. God only knows how many people are viciously, brutally murdered by monsters that you should be hunting, but instead I am. I cracked Daisy's code. I found the flash drive as well as every lead we have, because I give a damn, and you make a joke about it. And, with the utmost respect, Agents, it pisses me off."

Phillips still held my gaze, but his shoulders curled in a bit. After a moment of silence, likely making sure that I was finished, he said, "You're right. It wasn't funny. I'm sorry."

It wasn't okay, so I wouldn't say that it was. Instead, he got a, "Thank you."

"I'm pissed too, Castle." Gayton leaned forward, propping her elbows on her knees. There was sincerity in her gaze. Sincerity and that same directness I'd heard in her tone a moment prior. "I'm a Black woman who grew up in Philly. Believe me, I know about cops looking the other way. But I'm not one of them. None of us are. We hadn't looked into this case because we didn't know it existed. And you're right. Maybe we should've had some algorithm searching for it. But even if we had, until that little girl got you that flash drive, we wouldn't have had any evidence to form anything remotely resembling a profile, let alone a case. And I'm grateful you have.

"So, in case no one told you so lately, thank you. Thank you for bringing this to our attention, for finding those bodies, and bringing these families closure. But we are on the same team here, and the FBI can't get caught up in a scandal. We have to go in carefully and wait for warrants. That doesn't mean that we are not putting all we got into this. I need you to believe that."

In hindsight, I realized telling a Black woman how angry I was about the broken facets of our justice system was stupid.

"I do believe that." I forced my stiff shoulders and screwed up face to soften. "I wasn't trying to lash out at you. I just want to solve this case."

"So do we," Martin said.

"I think someone else does too," Harper said, nodding behind me.

A glance over my shoulder revealed a familiar face through the window of the hotel lobby. Bentley.

"He's how you got started on this, right?" Gayton asked.

"I haven't let him in on the details," I said. "He's Daisy's family. He just wants to know if we've gotten anything yet, and—"

"We trust you," Gayton said.

"Just make sure nothing gets to the press," Phillips said, standing. "And, for his sake, don't tell him too much."

Chapter 13

Bentley was always difficult for me to describe. Not because he was indecisive or known for contradicting himself. Purely because he was 6'4" tall, with shoulders and arms like a linebacker, but the biggest, dopiest brown eyes. His well-maintained beard tried to distract from the round baby face, but it was never enough. No matter how hard he tried, Bentley always looked like a big puppy dog.

Now, more than ever.

Hands tucked into the pockets of his gray sweats, his big eyes searched mine. The thousand questions he wanted to ask were on the tip of his tongue, but instead, he said, "Hey."

"Hey." I tried to manage a smile, but doubted it looked genuine. "Grace asleep?"

"I told her she needed to, but she looked pretty restless when I was leaving." He swept some hair from his face, revealing deep circles beneath his eyes. "I tried to, too, but I hadn't heard from you yet, and I was worried about you, and about Daisy, and..."

Frowning, I gestured to a set of chairs in the corner of the lobby. "How about we sit?"

He started that way, and I followed. We sat, and I opened my mouth to speak, but no words came out.

Where could I begin? What was vital for him to know? What wasn't?

"I know you can't say much right now," he said. "I'm dying to know more, but I understand."

I reached out for his hand. As our fingers twined together, the words that needed to be said magically appeared. "What do you want to know?"

A hard swallow. Silence set in as he scanned the lobby. It lasted a while. Eventually, he said, "Is she okay?"

"There's no reason to believe she isn't. Our primary concern is him finding out that we unearthed his burial ground. There's a fear that he would run with her, but we don't have any reason to believe that she's in immediate danger."

"Why though?" Shaking his head slightly, his shoulders raised and lowered. "I just don't get it. This guy is a mass murderer, right? I saw those tractors they were moving up there to dig. If it were only a body or two, they'd just use a shovel, wouldn't they?"

Yes, and no. Sure, if we believed it was only one body, we wouldn't have wasted time towing tractors up that mountain. Any Police Department that had easy access to one would prefer it to a shovel, though.

But that wasn't his question. Not really.

"We don't have an exact number yet, but we're certain Daisy's not one of them."

"I get that, but why?"

"Well, the most recent body we discovered only has a few weeks of decomposition. She doesn't have—"

"No, I'm not asking how you know it's not her," he said. "I'm asking why he hasn't killed her too. I'm asking why Daisy is still alive and all those other girls aren't."

I knew that was his question. I just hadn't wanted to answer it.

"Because Daisy's smart." That seemed like a cleverer way of putting it.

"And all those other girls were dumb?" His face screwed up in confusion. "You're reading her journal, Maddie. You know how she survived, and that's what I want to know."

A deep breath escaped my nostrils. "I believe he was going to kill her the night that he abducted her. But she told him that she was pregnant. I don't know why, but that stopped him."

His expression told me he still didn't understand but was beginning to. "He wanted the baby."

"A family, to be specific," I said. "I haven't made it into the several months of her disappearance, but at this point, I know he mostly kept her contained in the beginning."

"But is the baby okay? If she didn't have any prenatal care, that could have really messed her up."

"It seems like she did have prenatal care." I pressed my lips together, searching for a way to continue. "Not with a hospital or registered OB/GYN that we know of, but we're looking at all the possibilities."

"What do you mean?" he asked. "What prenatal care did she get then? Just prenatal vitamins, or CBC testing, or GCT, or what? There's a lot that goes into pregnancy care, and if she didn't get all that, the baby might not even be healthy, and—"

"I don't know, Bentley." Doing my best to keep my voice soft, I twined my fingers with his. "I still have a lot to read. And I'm sure there's a lot that she didn't write."

"What *did* she write?" His eyes were pleading. "How has she survived for this long? Did he keep all the others for this long? What *do* you know?"

Not much. I only knew half of her story, if that. But that wasn't what he wanted to hear. None of this was what he wanted to hear. He wanted to hear that we had found her. That she and her baby were safe. That I was on my way home to him with them in the backseat.

But I couldn't give him that. Not yet.

"I know they stopped at a motel on their way here," I said. "Daisy thinks the guy has some connection to the owner. That Deluca had been there before. She thinks he took many of his victims there, meaning they have some sort of agreement. A look the other way kind of agreement."

"Do you know what the hotel is? Can we go question—"

"Dylan's on it. If he can't figure it out, and the case goes cold here, that's the first place I'm running to. He said it was gonna take a while to track down, if he can track it down at all, and I'm waiting on that call. If he can't track it down, I'll drive back and forth from Columbus to Lancaster myself until I find it. Then I'll go in guns blazing and get the guy's name. But until I have that hotel name, my energy is best put toward the evidence I have in front of me."

Bentley's Adams apple bobbed with another hard swallow. "What evidence is that?"

"The witnesses at the library." I nodded to the agents outside. "Tomorrow morning, we're dividing and conquering. I know, if it were up to you, we'd be knocking on their doors right now. But we're in a small town. We go knocking on doors asking about a missing girl, word can get back to Deluca. Then he might run. That's why my priority right now has been reading the book and gathering as much information as possible before we storm in."

Another deep breath escaped his nostrils. Still, his shoulders stayed stiff.

"That makes sense. I'm sorry. I'm sure dealing with me is just slowing you down right now, but it felt like we had something for the first time, and I know you're busy, but I just wanted to know what it was."

"If only there were more hours in a day." With a soft smile, I reached up for his shoulder. Massaging the deep knots between there and his neck, I shook my head. "You don't need to be sorry. And I think you're right. We do have something. She's out here, somewhere, and I have the feeling we're gonna find her. I just might not be able to keep you posted on every little update."

Finally, Bentley's stiff posture eased. There were still a thousand knots in his neck, but he was the slightest bit calmer. "It's okay. I know how these things go."

"Is there anything else you want to know specifically?" I asked. "I might not have a concrete answer, but I can try to give you something."

Dropping his elbows to his knees, he rubbed a hand over his scruff. "I know she's smart. But what do you mean? How is that helping her survive?"

"Essentially, she's pretending that she has battered woman syndrome when she doesn't. She is well aware that he is her captor. But she's letting him believe that she's happy to be there, that she loves him."

He furrowed his brows. "And that's working?"

"Seems to be, yeah," I said. "From what I read earlier, she and the baby share a room. It's not a torture chamber. He has a nice house—a remodeled Victorian—and he's trying to emulate a normal family. She's well fed, she's not on drugs, and for the most part, she's safe."

He was quiet for a moment. "For the most part?"

Was I supposed to tell him the truth? That the guy got off on violence? That, by now, he'd likely raped Daisy dozens, if not hundreds, of times?

If Daisy wanted Bentley to know that, she would've told him so in her letter.

"He likes things very clean. Like I said, I haven't made it far enough to know everything, but he keeps his house spotless." By now, Daisy may have been the one keeping his house spotless. "I don't think he'd like blood splattered across it."

Bentley winced.

"I'm sorry." I stopped massaging his shoulder and found his fingertips instead. He squeezed, and I squeezed back. "I don't know if that helps. I'm just trying to give you a prettier picture in your mind than the one you've got. Physically, she might be the healthiest she's ever been. That's all I'm trying to say."

Biting his lip, his eyes stayed on the ground. "It does. I keep picturing every horror movie I have ever watched. Then that cabin that you and Grace were in."

"It's not that."

Swallowing he nodded. "But they're similar, right? This guy and the Country Killer."

That whole profiling thing wasn't my favorite topic. Didn't mean it would hurt Bentley to hear. "I don't think so. The Country Killer got off on scaring the public. This guy doesn't get off on fear. Eric was a narcissist, and I'm not sure about Deluca. Eric treated his victims like props. Deluca, in some regard, loves his victims. The burial ground was like a cemetery. Not just a dump.

"He's messed up, obviously, but I think he sees himself as a sort of savior. He got these girls off the street. He cleaned them up. I think that's part of his goal. It's not just about the kill but about helping them better themselves. Or I'm completely wrong, and he just views people in that demographic as easy targets. We might not know for sure until we catch him."

"You said before that Eric was a sadist." He met my gaze, and his eyes were big. Not wide with shock, but with hope. "You don't think Deluca is?"

No, he was. Otherwise, his violence wouldn't be sexually motivated. He was a rapist as well as a murderer.

But I didn't want to say that. I didn't want that image in Bentley's head.

My phone rang in my pocket.

I had never been so grateful for an interruption.

Dylan's name flashed across the screen.

"I have to take this," I said.

Bentley gestured for me to do so.

"Hello?"

"Yes, I believe I found something," Dylan said. "I'm still formulating the list of wealthy men in a fifty-mile radius who own their homes on many acres. Any information you could give me that might help me narrow that down could help. But the hotel. It took some time on Google Maps, but I narrowed down a few different highways people would take between Columbus and Lancaster. Route 70 seems the most likely. It's a direct shot from Columbus to Pennsylvania. While I didn't find any hotels on that highway that match the description you gave, I did find one on Highway 22 running through Pennsylvania."

My heart skipped with excitement. Putting the phone on speaker, I swiped into my notes app. "I'm ready when you are."

"The Sunset Stay," Dylan said, following with the address. I recognized the county, but not the town. "I know you said you were in Lancaster, so it wouldn't be a bad idea to send someone else there to speak to the owner. By the time you get there and back, your leads may run cold."

"That's what?" Bentley asked, squinting at my phone. "Half an hour from our place?"

"More like forty-five minutes." I'd already typed the address into my maps app. "That's great though. Do you have the owner's name?"

"Yes, Nathaniel Cooper," Dylan said. "Who's with you?"

"My boyfriend, Bentley," I said. "Have you done any sort of background check on Nathaniel? Do you have any other information on him?"

"It's nice to meet you, Bentley. I'm Dylan, Maddie's half-brother." Sometimes, I appreciated how direct he was. Others, it was an inconvenience. "Yes, of course I did. Several arrests for drugs and sex crimes. They all had to do with violence against prostitutes. I can send you the details over if you'd like."

Bentley flinched.

"Yeah, please do," I said. "Any way you can access his tax records?"

"Difficult, but possible. It might be easier for me to access his bank account," Dylan said. "Which I will do, but only under the assumption that you will, Bentley, assure me you heard nothing of this conversation."

"Nope, not a peep," Bentley said.

"Perfect. I'll work on that next. Do you have any information that might narrow down my search for the fifty-mile radius?"

"May not be a bad idea to widen that to two hundred," I said. "But it will be in Pennsylvania. This guy kidnaps the girls from other states. He was careful because of state laws and jurisdictions. I guarantee you, he's not in Maryland or West Virginia."

"Noted."

"He drives a newer model Mercedes SUV. Somewhere north of six feet tall with size eleven shoes. The house is also an old Victorian. I don't know how old. It's been remodeled, though. Judging by the style, I'd say sometime in the last ten years. There's also a turret, if that helps."

"It does, yes."

"And possibly stained glass. It would've been installed sometime in the last fifty years. He broke it a couple months ago though, so it's either been restored or replaced. To be specific, a decent sized stained glass piece in the living room with artwork of a hummingbird."

"That might be too oddly specific to help me," Dylan said.

"Yeah, could be," I muttered. A beep sounded on my phone. Sam's name lit up the top of the screen. I clicked the end call button. He could wait. "I don't know. Dude has an odd fascination with birds. Maybe a birdwatcher?"

"Also may be too oddly specific to help me, but noted. I'm gonna get back to work. But if you think of anything else—"

"Yeah, one other thing actually," I said. "Birth records from May of this year. Specifically, home births. Her name would be Isabella. I don't know if you'll find anything, but I don't think this guy would want his kid undocumented in the system."

"Still a two hundred-mile radius?"

"For now, yeah. If you could categorize them by closeness to the address I gave you earlier, that would be preferred."

"Will do. Good luck."

"Likewise."

Just as I reached for the red X, Bentley's phone rang. He flashed the screen my way. Sam.

"Tell him I'm sorry," I said, gripping the edge of the chair for stability as I stood. "I need to go relay this to Harper."

Chapter 14

"She said she was sorry," Bentley said into the phone at his ear. "She had to go talk to another detective."

"Tell her not to be. I just wanted to check in," Sam said. His tone was gentle, fatherly, just as it had been when he'd called earlier in the day. Bentley appreciated that. "Did she find something? More than she had earlier?"

"Yeah, a hotel." Bentley kneaded his fingertips through his scalp. "We're not a hundred percent sure if it's connected to Daisy, but Maddie thinks it is."

"What do you mean?" Sam asked.

Bentley still wasn't sure. He didn't have the evidence in front of him. He wasn't the one reading Daisy's journal. So he settled for the summary. "Daisy didn't catch the name of the hotel she was at the night that he abducted her, but I guess she gave a description? Maddie gave it to Dylan, and he dug around a while, and he found something."

"That was a year ago though," Sam said. "Even if it is the right hotel, no one's gonna remember a random guy and his girlfriend."

"Daisy thinks the owner has some type of agreement with Deluca," Bentley said, swallowing the acid that burned up his throat at the thought. "Like he pays the guy to stay quiet about what he hears coming from his room? I don't know." A deep, shaking breath. "I don't know, man."

Sam took a moment to say, "It might be better that you don't."

That was true. Bentley knew it was true.

As he'd said to Maddie, there were a thousand scenarios running through his mind. He wasn't sure which was worse. The horror show behind his eyes, or the reality.

Accepting that there was a man as twisted as Deluca was hard enough. Worse, even, than accepting the sick nature of Eric Oakley.

Ever since he had kidnapped Grace, Bentley had tried to understand him. He tried to grasp why the man hated women so badly. What joy or power it gave him to kill mercilessly. To kill for pleasure.

Bentley still didn't understand. He doubted he ever would. The truth was, he didn't want to. What point would it serve to go deep down that man's psyche and dissect it? He was dead. Even if he weren't, why did it matter?

Some people were evil. Worse than animals. Sure, animals killed, but that was nature. It was a means of survival.

Men like Eric were not only surviving, but thriving, and killed for the simple fun of it.

That theme repeated with Deluca. Maddie claimed the man had everything. Money. A beautiful home. Acres and acres of private property.

And now, a family.

That's what Bentley couldn't wrap his mind around. How similar his and Deluca's goals in life were. Deluca had what Bentley wanted. A home, land, enough to not only get by, but to thrive.

But Deluca had building blocks that Bentley did not. He had been born into, at the very least, comfortability. Bentley had been born into chaos.

As he'd aged, he, too, only craved what most people did. Normalcy. A comfortable home and a happy family inside it.

If that was what Deluca wanted, why had he gone about it this way? With money, and intelligence, and the world as his oyster, why had he still chosen to harm? Why had he chosen to seek out the women with the least opportunities, exploit what he could from them, give them a glimmer of something better, only to destroy them?

That was what made Deluca worse than Eric. Eric only hated others. He loved himself, and that was all.

Deluca loved, may have in some sense, respected, the women he killed.

Bentley couldn't fathom it.

"When is she going to check it out?" Sam asked, breaking the long silence.

"I don't know," Bentley said. "It's closer to home than here. The feds are involved now. They're gonna want to go in there with a warrant, and there's not enough evidence to support that right now. Plus, Maddie wants to follow the lead she has here first. Doesn't want to make the trip back out that way until everything here dries up."

"Gotta hate red tape," Sam said. "What's the name of the place?"

"Huh?"

"The hotel," Sam said. "And the owner."

Bentley's heart lodged in his throat.

He glanced at Maddie through the window, speaking with the agents. Her brows were so deep into her eyes, he could barely see them. Even from here, he could see the spit flying from her lips with each word, spewing between gritted teeth. At her sides, her hands clenched. On the ground, Tempest's ears flattened against her head.

Maddie was pissed. Likely because she suggested they send someone out to question Nathaniel Cooper, and the agents disagreed. A concrete lead, bound behind a single strip of red tape.

If Maddie could be in two places at the same time, she would've torn through that red tape with a machete.

It was only that. A single strip of red tape. One she agreed needed to be cut.

The only thing stopping her was the distance between here and there.

"I'm just curious," Sam said, a teasing edge to his voice. "I might be able to ask around. Get us some answers."

"Safely?" Bentley asked. "Without risking your parole?"

"I'm a lot smarter than I was twenty-five years ago, kid."

His heart was still in his throat, but it loosened when Sam said that single word. *Kid.*

While college-educated, a father to a preteen, and checking off a thousand other boxes that signified adulthood by the standards of society, Bentley heard that word more often in a condescending tone. *Kid.*

But it sounded different when Sam said it. It sounded like he was an elementary schooler who had just witnessed his father beat the hell out of his mother, only for another poor bastard to walk in, and return the favor. It sounded like the hope, the safety, Bentley felt as a little boy when he watched his father's blood roll onto the kitchen's linoleum as Sam wiped a few speckles of it from his cheek.

Bentley had cowered in the corner, and Sam had squatted before him, offered a hand, and said, "It's okay, kid. Everything is going to be okay."

Bentley had hated his father. He'd never hated Sam.

Sam was, like his daughter, a vigilante at worst and a hero at best. He was the muscle with a heart big enough to match.

He wanted the hotel owner's name not to help Bentley, but to right a wrong. To cut the red tape that, this time, Maddie was tied up in as well. This man acted on a moral compass different than society dictated was correct, but that didn't mean he was wrong. The systems they lived and worked within were.

"The Sunset Stay," Bentley said. "Nathaniel Cooper. That's the owner's name."

"Spelled how it sounds?"

"I think so."

"Cool. I'll keep you posted on anything I find." Bentley was about to remind Sam not to risk himself for this, but Sam continued before Bentley could. "And don't tell Maddie. This is between me and you, alright? It's better for everyone that way."

Bentley did not like keeping secrets, especially not from Maddie. The last time he had, he wound up with her pointing a revolver at him. "Sam—"

Silence.

The call had ended.

Chapter 15

Nathaniel Cooper wasn't number one on their to do list. Nor was The Sunset Stay.

Yes, it was possible that was the hotel Daisy talked about in her journal, the agents claimed.

But it was several hours away. They wanted to prioritize whatever was here before we chased the lead that may only be just that—a lead. Not evidence. Not a witness. Just a possible lead.

I understood that. I agreed. I wasn't jumping in my car to race across the state either.

They were the FBI though. Surely, they had connections. Surely, they could send someone to that area to question Cooper.

They said they may. For now, they were going to have their analysts investigate Nathaniel Cooper and the records of The Sunset Stay.

I stomped away from that conversation, met back up with Bentley, and followed the advice the agents gave me. Get some rest. We had a long day ahead of us.

Bentley showed me to our room. It was a suite, but nothing extravagant. Grace was passed out on the pullout couch, HGTV blaring away. Bentley showed me to our room through the door that separated the spaces. Again, nothing special. A king bed, a TV, a small desk, and a window with a gorgeous view of the parking lot.

Before cuddling up in the blankets, it was best I took a shower. Putting aside how much the hot water would help my knee and injuries from my last case, I'd spent most of the day outdoors. Bentley didn't say so, but a raise of my arm reminded me how badly I stunk.

After a quick shower, I stepped into a clean pair of sweatpants and a clean hoodie. Normally, I slept barefoot. But, in case we got a lead in the middle of the night, and I needed to rush into action, I slept with socks on. The sweatpants and hoodie were a better option than the pajamas I'd packed for the same reason.

When I made it back to the bedroom, Bentley was already passed out.

Stress had a way of exhausting the body.

For some people, anyway. It kept me wide awake.

After I pecked his cheek, I took a fistful of ibuprofen for the ache in my knee that adrenaline had treated all day and crawled under the blankets beside him. I shut my eyes, but sleep didn't come. It didn't take long for me to realize it wouldn't.

I grabbed my phone off the nightstand, swiped open the word document, and resumed reading.

Over the Next Few Months

The following week looked a lot like that first day. When I wasn't in Deluca's sight, I was tethered to that bed.

Much of the time, I was tethered to that bed.

So much so that I was getting rashes around my wrists and ankles. He took me into the kitchen for breakfast, lunch, and dinner. Each morning and night, he took me to the bathroom for a thorough bathing. Throughout the day, he took me to the restroom as well.

But when he noticed those rashes on my wrists and ankles, he tied me back up. A few minutes later, I heard the roar of a car engine. A few hours later, he returned.

I heard him go up the stairs. I heard power tools. I heard bumping and banging, but nothing I could make out clearly.

I missed lunch and dinner that day.

My bladder was ready to explode, but I knew better than to make a mess in his bed.

Shortly after nightfall, he returned to the bedroom. After releasing my ankles and wrists, he took me to the bathroom and apologized for how long I'd had to wait. I told him it was okay.

Doubted my kidneys agreed.

He took my hand, then, and led me up the pretty, winding wooden stair-

case. There were at least half a dozen doors up here, but he led me through the first one on the right.

The room smelled of fresh paint, walls a pale shade of pink. It was the corner of the home, so there were two windows on two walls, catty-corner from one another, with a rounded perch between them—the turret. They opened to the same view I had from Deluca's king bed.

Only difference was the bars that covered them.

To my right was a closet. Fresh clothes—my size—with the tags still on were stacked in neat piles on the shelves. No hangers, no rack. The drawers below the shelves had been removed, creating more space to stack clothing, but removing anything I could use as a weapon.

Below one of the windows, facing the other, was a full-size bed. A closer squint showed the bolts that held the platform frame to the wall and floor. No slats I could use as a weapon.

Plushy white carpet cushioned my toes as I stepped closer. Only a single blanket lay atop the mattress. At the corner where it met the headboard, I squinted at the sheet. A small padlock.

It took a moment to realize. Not a normal set of white sheets. They wrapped the whole way around the bed and zipped shut. Where the two zippers met, Deluca locked them together.

That way, I couldn't pull the sheets off and use them as a noose.

Apparently, he wouldn't allow me even that choice.

But I guessed that was the point.

I wasn't a person to him. I'd had that feeling many times throughout my life, but it was different to realize that someone you would've once given everything for didn't see you as human.

In Deluca's eyes, I was property. Maybe a pet. Perhaps a toy.

But not a person.

After showing me the memory foam mattress he'd gotten me, pointing out where he planned to put the crib when the baby came, he gazed around in wonder, all while smiling. "It's yours. This is all yours. Do you like it?"

I hated it. But I had a role to play, so I played it.

Over the coming weeks, he added more personal touches. One weekend, he built a small bench that wrapped around the turret. That was after the results came back, proving the baby was his, and that she was a girl.

"When she's big enough, she can look out these windows and pretend to be a princess in a castle," he said.

Once we had those results, his energy shifted entirely. There weren't any fancy dinners or extravagant dates—not outside of the house, anyway—but he started acting like the man he was when I met him again. Instead of that cold, distant killer, he was human. Almost loving.

Each morning, he came to my room with an herbal tea. I'd drink it, and he'd sit in the bed beside me, and we'd watch the birds outside the window. He pointed out each one that flew by. Whether a robin or other obscure bird, he knew them all.

Afterward, we'd go downstairs, and we'd cook breakfast together. Farm fresh eggs were a staple. Another thing he was passionate about. Healthy eating. He once insisted that I would love flax seed pancakes. I didn't, but I wouldn't admit it in fear of shattering his fantasy.

If it was nice out, we'd go for a hike in the woods. If it wasn't, we'd put a movie on or binge watch an old TV show.

No matter how hard I tried to lose myself in the entertainment, anytime he'd open Netflix or Hulu, my stomach would twist. There was Wi-Fi in this house. An internet connection. Something that could get my story to the outside world. An opportunity for freedom.

It was right there, all around me. What I wanted most, what my daughter and I needed more than anything, floated all around me. But I had no conduit. I had no way to connect to it.

Even if it was my favorite TV show, all I could think about was the fact that the Wi-Fi was all around me, and I had no way to tap into it.

After we watched TV for a while, he'd make lunch. Before he started the stove or reached into the fridge, he'd pass me a crayon and a notebook. "Write me a story," he'd say. "We'll read it together later."

So I would.

It was my only respite. I could never write what I truly wanted to. This document, this journal, that's what I wanted to write. But I could only do so in code.

A fantasyland with an evil warlord. All the townspeople were trapped within four beautiful walls of gold, and all they wanted was to see the ocean on the other side. But that evil warlord, he would only let them see it from their rooftops. No matter how badly they wanted to smell the salt in the air, feel the sand between their toes, they could only see a vague glimmer of what the evil warlord kept from them.

Most of my stories were written that way. Some type of allegory for what he was putting me through. Deluca wasn't a dumb man. I'm sure he knew I was writing about him.

But each time I finished the story, then read it to him while we ate, he applauded me for it afterward. Then we'd talk about art. How fascinated he was by an artist's mind. Specifically writers. We could create entire realms from letters arranged across a sheet of paper, and it acted as a portal to that other dimension.

"That's what I love so much about you," he said. "You create entire worlds from absolutely nothing."

Maybe that was why he didn't kill me. He preferred to use me as his personal entertainment.

Maybe it was the baby. Maybe it was because I played the perfect part in his sick fantasy.

I didn't know. Doubted I ever would.

Every couple of weeks, that nurse came back. She took my blood. She performed ultrasounds. She gave me more prenatal vitamins, all of which Deluca distributed to me.

The week or so immediately following the positive DNA test felt the way the beginning of our relationship had. But within a month or so, he'd begun to change again. It started small.

My tea was cold when he brought it to me. He stayed silent as the birds flew by. I'd ask what kind the one that had just passed was, and he'd say, "How the hell am I supposed to know, Daisy?"

The sun would be shining, the sky would be blue, but he wouldn't want to go for our pre-lunch hike. He'd want to watch TV instead. I'd try to make conversation as the movie played, and he'd tell me to shut up.

No crayons or notebook at lunch. No story afterward.

Dinner would be premade or takeout, even if I offered to cook.

Sex was like clockwork after dinner and bath, but before bed each night. I'm not sure if you'd call it sex, considering I wouldn't consent to it in any other situation, but the fact remained. It was a part of the routine.

But instead of gentle lovemaking, he became rougher and more aggressive with me. I'm sure you can imagine what I mean. No need to describe the details.

Gradually, he was becoming the monster I'd met the night I wound up in the trunk. So much so that, one night, when we were cleaning up dinner, I didn't scrub a plate well enough. There was still a piece of mashed potato stuck to the ceramic.

Again, without going into details, I wound up with my back to the refrigerator door and his hand around my throat. When I cried, probably when my face turned blue, he dropped me to the floor. I collected my breath there on the white oak floors. As soon as I did, he snatched me by my wrist, hauled me up the stairs, and locked me in my room.

A few minutes later, the roar of his car engine sounded. I didn't catch the plate, but I saw the headlights through the dust cloud from the gravel road.

He didn't return until midday two days later.

I had a bucket to use for emergencies whenever he did happen to leave, two bottles of water, and a single box of protein bars. Those got me through it.

But as those days passed, I went over every possibility in my mind. Was this how I would die? Dehydration or starvation in this bedroom? I wasn't sure if that would be better or worse than dying in his hands. Better, perhaps, because then, he wouldn't get to watch the light leave my eyes and rejoice in it.

When he returned, I saw him through the window carrying a big pink box with a bow on it and a red gift bag. He didn't immediately come to my room, however.

I heard him in the kitchen, and then his footsteps up the stairs, and rustling in the neighboring room. Things banged and clanked, and then power tools again.

It was a few hours before he came to my door. This time, instead of tea, a coffee, that big pink box, and the gift bag.

I knew this routine. Kevin had followed the same one, almost to a T.

Fight with me. Beat me.

Then a bouquet of roses, big dopey eyes, an apology, all wrapped up in a, "I didn't mean to. It'll never happen again." Don't forget the big hug and the "makeup sex."

The coffee, he explained, wasn't good to drink during my pregnancy. But, considering everything, he felt I deserved a treat. Inside the pink box were a dozen different pastries. Croissants, meringue, cookies, cupcakes, brownies. All my favorites. All high-end. Not the kind of sweets you could pick up just anywhere. He'd gone somewhere special, just for me.

In the bag? Lingerie, of course. Pretty nightgowns. A nice silk robe. Oh, and a diamond pendant on a gold chain.

I always preferred silver. Went better with my skin tone. But he liked gold, so I wore the gold.

After I took a shower and put on the lingerie, I did what I knew he wanted, relieved at how much gentler he was this time, we lay there in the bed watching the birds. He told me he was sorry, that he would never put his hands on me again. Obviously, he would. That's how men like this worked.

I told him what he wanted to hear. That it was okay. I forgave him. I just wanted things to go back to how they were. The same lines I had given Kevin.

They worked. Especially when, with tears in my eyes, I told him how afraid I was that he would never come back.

He hugged me tighter than ever before at those words. Like they meant everything and more to him. Ask a psychologist for me if that's why he did this to me. Because he wanted someone who would never leave him.

Supposed most of us could relate to that. I sure the hell could.

And that was the most screwed up part of it all. I'd wanted him to come back. I didn't want to die alone in this room. This wasn't much. It wasn't a life at all. But at least I was alive. At least my story hadn't ended yet.

Worse than that, even, was how joyous I became when he explained what he was doing in the other room. The one across the hall had a powder room attached. He promised that, next time he left for a while, he'd leave me there. He would turn the water off, so I wouldn't be able to flush, but I'd have a toilet to use. Next time, instead of a couple bottles of water, he'd leave me a couple cases as well as a selection of snacks to pick from.

He turned the water off so I couldn't flood the second floor.

Which was insulting for the obvious reasons. The less obvious one, though, was the fact that I wouldn't. Even if the flood somehow managed to damage the floor or wall enough for me to get past the lock, where the hell was I gonna go?

We hiked these trails together every day the sun was shining. Sometimes, from sun up to sun down. We'd never made it to a road or other sign of civilization.

I wasn't getting out of here. I knew that.

Just would've been nice if I didn't have to sit in a room that smelled like shit for however long he decided to disappear for.

His next trip was the following day. This time, he was gone for a week.

But he kept his promise. I was in the room across the hall. I had two cases of water, more snacks than I could eat in a month, and a toilet. The room smelled like shit, but at least I could shut the powder room door.

At the end of that week, I woke in the dead of the night to tires crunching on gravel. But with the view from this window, I couldn't see outside.

I could only hear.

What did I hear?

A woman screaming.

That's when the dots connected.

I wasn't the one he wanted to hurt. I was carrying precious cargo, after all.

But he needed an outlet. He needed someone to hurt. So he got her instead.

Chapter 16

SAM WAS ON HIS THIRD ENERGY DRINK.

The clock on the dashboard read 6:42. Sam had been at the corner of the street since 11 PM the night prior. Luckily, he had a few empty plastic bottles laying on the floor of his truck. They were full now, and he dreaded opening them.

Aside from that awkward shimmying to empty his bladder inside the vehicle, he hadn't moved from the spot once. When his eyes got heavy, he just cracked open another energy drink. They never left that small, ranch-style house on the rough side of town.

Then again, most sides of town were the rough side here in the country. No one had money, and Nathaniel Cooper's home showed it.

Half fallen-off brown aluminum siding. All the windows were intact, but at least half a dozen gray shingles were missing from the roof. There were a dozen other houses on the street in similar condition. Farmland lined the road up and down, stretching for miles with only a few homes in between.

Police response time in this area was half an hour, minimum. Once he was done, he'd have plenty of time to get away.

So, why hadn't he gone in yet?

When Nathaniel had made it home around midnight, a young girl in a miniskirt and fishnets was at his side. Sam knew guys like this. That girl was just a means to an end. A bit of fun, and a goodbye.

She'd yet to say goodbye. Sam had been watching both the front and back doors all night long, and she hadn't left. A quick scroll through Nathaniel's social media made it clear that he didn't have a partner. That told Sam that she was paid to be there or was there for the drugs he surely had lying around inside.

She wasn't the problem. She didn't need to see what he was about to do.

Couldn't see what he was about to do.

Sam knew what the inside of the house looked like. After searching for Nathaniel, then finding his address, he ran a quick search on it. It didn't take long for the realtor listing to pop up from five years ago. Along with pictures of the interior.

A small living room. Smaller kitchen. One bathroom, attached to the only bedroom.

While looking through Nathaniel's social media, he found pictures of his pit bull. A pretty girl with black and white markings. She would be Sam's primary obstacle. That's why he had a few hours-old fast-food hamburger in the passenger seat.

Nathaniel might've been a piece of garbage disguised as a human being, but that puppy didn't deserve to see what Sam was about to do to her dad. And Sam didn't deserve a hole in his leg.

6:51. The front door swung open. That young woman walked out in the same clothes she had been wearing last night, counting dollar bills on her way to her car.

Sam waited for her to pull out.

When her taillights disappeared down the road, Sam put his car in reverse and backed down the nearest alleyway. He worked in construction, after all. He wasn't out of shape. This plan required anonymity. That could only be attained if his truck wasn't visible.

Once he was there, far from Nathaniel's line of sight, Sam grabbed the paper bag of fast food and the ski mask from his passenger seat.

The sun had yet to rise completely. No one was out on the street. Still, Sam was cautious as he stepped from the truck. After tugging on a pair of leather gloves, he grabbed the crowbar from the floorboard, slid it up his sleeve, and gripped the hooked edge with his fingers. His steps were like that of a cat as he walked to the door.

Initially, his plan had been to enter through the kitchen window. He'd seen it open all night. But that would require climbing, which would make more noise.

The young girl who'd just left, likely while Nathaniel was still sleeping, provided Sam his in. All he had to do was walk through the front door.

That pretty pit bull ran to greet him with a roar of barks.

"Shut the hell up!" Nathaniel called from the bedroom.

Without saying a word, Sam showed the barking dog a hamburger. Tiptoeing across the blue carpet toward the kitchen door, Sam wiggled the burger. The dog's eyes followed it. At the kitchen door Sam tossed the burger to the floor. The dog ran to it.

Gently, Sam gripped the kitchen door handle and pulled it closed. When it clicked shut, he lowered the crowbar. The hooked edge jutted inches from his fingers.

On the tips of his toes, Sam returned to the front door. He clicked the lock shut.

Just as quietly, Sam returned to the only other open door in the house.

The curtains were shut, but the light of the TV glowed onto the bed across from it. There, the slimeball lay. Sam couldn't make out his face, but he didn't need to. No one else had been here, and only two people had walked into the house last night.

As Nathaniel snored, Sam walked around the bed. Once he was only inches away, within arm's reach of the man, he let out one calming, grounding breath.

Sam pounded the crowbar through the lamp on the nightstand.

Nathaniel shot forward with a gasp.

Sam pointed the crowbar at his face. "Wouldn't move if I were you."

"Who the hell—"

Sam bashed the crowbar into Nathaniel's leg.

Nathaniel wailed in pain.

Sam dropped his hand over Nathaniel's mouth, muffling a scream. "Here's how this goes. I ask a question, you answer it. That's the rule. You break it, I hit you again. Got it?"

Grasping his leg, trying to regain his composure, Nathaniel nodded.

"I'm looking for someone," Sam said. "Late forties to mid-fifties. Male. Italian. Wealthy. He frequents your hotel, and you have a, 'look the other way,' policy with the guy."

"What?" Nathaniel asked. "I don't know what you're—"

Sam raised the crowbar again.

"No! No, no, no," Nathaniel begged. "Please. I'll tell you whatever you want. Just don't hurt me."

Sam gritted his teeth. "Take it you have a policy with a lot of guys like that."

"No, it's just—"

Sam lifted the crowbar.

"I run an hourly motel!" Nathaniel squealed. "Nobody comes to my place for a vacation, man. It's for drug deals and sex with who—"

"Finish that sentence." Sam brought the crowbar over Nathaniel's face. "I dare you."

Even in the dim light, Sam could see the terror in Nathaniel's brown eyes.

"Just—just give me more," Nathaniel said. "What else do you know about him?"

"He's got a thing for brunettes," Sam said. "Young. Barely legal. And they don't look like your typical clientele. He likes them cleaned up."

Nathaniel swallowed hard, eyes shifting back and forth in deep thought. "Wait, are you talking about The Crow?"

Ironic, given what Sam had just smashed through Nathaniel's leg. "Who's the Crow?"

"I don't know. I—I—"

Sam slugged the crowbar into Nathaniel's leg again.

Nathaniel screamed out.

Sam grabbed his face, squeezing on either side so his lips pursed forward. "See, that's not a good enough answer. You do know. You know something I don't, and you're going to share it with me, or I'm gonna hit your other leg. Then each arm, and then your face. As many times as it takes for you to start remembering."

"I don't know his real name," Nathaniel sobbed. Common enough. Where nefarious means were involved, few people used their real name. "We call him The Crow because of his tattoo. It's on his back. Takes up the whole top half. A friend of mine did it for him in the nineties."

That was something. "Who's your friend?"

"Leo Wilder. He's a good guy, man. Please don't hurt him. He'll tell you anything you wanna know."

Sam hoped he wouldn't need to. "How'd you and The Crow meet?"

"He was around back then," Nathaniel said. "I was friends with his girl."

"You got her name?"

"Rowan. Rowan Palmer, but you're not going to be able to question her," Nathaniel said. "She fell off the face of the planet."

"Around the same time she was dating The Crow?"

"I guess, but—"

"Never occurred to you that those two things could be connected?" Sam snapped. "Or did you just not care?"

"We weren't really friends, it was just—"

"She was just another whore you didn't care about?"

"I sold to her, alright?" Nathaniel said. "I was dealing back then. She was just a customer. That's it. People like that, they vanish."

How tired Sam was of hearing that phrase. "What were you dealing?"

"Ice. That's what she was on. Claimed to hell and back it helped her study."

Since it was a more intense version of the legal drug college students were well known for abusing, that sounded believable. "What do you know about The Crow? What's your deal with the motel?"

"He gets a room in the back, and I don't put any customers on that side of the building when he's there," Nathaniel said. "A day or so before he stays for the night, he brings a car and parks it in the lot. He comes back in a different car. When he leaves, he takes the one he parked there before he came and leaves the other. I don't tow either of them. Eventually, he comes back for the car he left behind. That's it. That's all I do."

"That's all, huh?" Sam dragged the crowbar closer to Nathaniel's face. "Never hear anything suspicious coming from his room? Never see him loading something strange into the trunk of the car?"

"I told you," Nathaniel said, "his room is in the back. I can't hear anything back there."

"And you never thought there was anything wrong with it? Never found it suspicious at all, asshole?"

"It's an hourly motel. Nobody comes with good intentions. There's drugs, and prostitution, and—"

"Kidnappings. Murder." Sam's jaw was so tight it ached. "How does he give you the money? And how much?"

"Five thousand each time. He pays in cash."

Valuable intel.

And probably as much as Sam needed.

"Anything else I should know about this guy?" Sam asked.

"Nothing I can think of, man," Nathaniel said. "He's more of an acquaintance than anything. I didn't know he was into all this—"

"Sure you didn't. Just like you don't know anything about a guy in a ski mask with a crowbar."

Nathaniel's throat bobbed with a swallow.

"Tell anyone about this, and I'll be back." Sam aimed the crowbar at his face. "We understand each other?"

Nathaniel nodded.

"Good."

With that, Sam headed for the door.

Chapter 17

Apparently, I was wrong. Stress exhausted my body as much as it did Bentley's.

At some point while reading, I'd passed out. The last thing I remembered was the scream Daisy described coming from Deluca's car upon his return.

Then it was all black, and my phone was ringing.

Harper flashed across the screen. The time in the upper right corner said 7:15.

"Hello?" I answered, stifling a yawn.

"Hey, we're all down in the lobby. Breakfast first, then questioning the four witnesses. Me and you are going with Torres. If you're in. Are you in?"

"Yeah, let me get dressed." Stretching, I freed myself from Bentley's grasp and sat forward. "Just grab me a coffee and a breakfast bar or something and meet me outside."

"Will do," she said.

As I stood, ending the call, Bentley shot forward. "Did they find something?"

"Not yet. Just going to question those witnesses now. But if we get something, you'll be the first to know."

He nodded, still blinking hard against the crust that lined his eyes.

I leaned down, touched my lips to his for a few heartbeats, then leaned back and ran my fingers through his hair. "Go back to sleep. When you wake up at noon, go get breakfast with Grace."

He only grunted in response.

"Can't pour from an empty cup and all that." Another kiss on his forehead. "Just get some rest."

"I'll try," he said.

Walking to the door, I snapped my fingers for Tempy. She'd lain in the corner of the room on a pile of blankets Bentley had formed into a makeshift bed, but the moment I snapped my fingers, she was at my side. As I reached for the handle, Bentley spoke again.

"Maddie?"

I looked at him over my shoulder. "Bentley?"

"I love you. For who you are, and for everything, really, but I don't think I've said that enough lately. I don't think I've told you how grateful I am for all you're doing here. Beyond words, I'm so grateful for you."

"I know." I smiled. "And I love you too."

* * *

All I did was brush my teeth and throw my hair in a bun. Suffice it to say, I was quite the looker next to Harper in her perfectly pressed slacks, shiny leather shoes, tailored blazer, and full face of makeup.

In our line of work, I thought it was silly to look pristine all the time. Sure, it was professional, but also a waste of time. Why did I have to look pretty to talk to a criminal?

But it was Harper's thing. Probably did make us look better when we were walking up to people's doors. If it were just me and Tempy, they might've thought I was gonna slam through the entry and rob them.

I guess it came down to the fact that I valued sleep more than appearances.

The first witness was only fifteen minutes from the hotel. Still, that was fifteen minutes of reading time. Time to find more clues or insight.

I debriefed Harper on what I'd gathered before falling asleep, discussed it a bit, then opened my phone to find the Word document. But the moment the screen came to life—like everyone in this day and age—I scrolled down the top bar to check my notifications.

A new text from an unknown number. *814-555-9876*

Rowan Palmer, State College PA

Crow tattoo, done by Leo Wilder in the 90s

–a friend

"What's the matter?" Harper asked. Apparently, I was taking too long to open the document.

I repeated the text aloud. "Does this mean anything to you?" I asked her.

"Not that I can think of. You don't know who it is?"

"No idea." Didn't mean it wasn't worth looking into.

I swiped over to Google and typed in that exact message.

Rowan Palmer, State College PA, had some hits. Nothing about the crow or tattoo artist Leo Wilder.

I clicked the first article.

As soon as I saw the image, I knew this was about Deluca. The picture at the top of the headline was a near spitting image of Daisy.

Missing college student

April 13, 1994

Rowan (Rory) Palmer, a nineteen-year-old English major from Potter County, was last seen with friends at a bar on 4/9/94. She left in her green Toyota Corolla and never returned home. Her roommate reported her missing the following day.

Police are offering a $500 reward to anyone with any information that could lead to the young woman's whereabouts.

"Shit," Harper murmured. "They never found her?"

"I bet money that Rowan was his first victim," I said, already googling the state college PD's phone number. "The night he kidnapped Daisy, he called her Rory."

Harper nodded slowly. "Everyone he's killed since then has been a surrogate."

This was big. Maybe the biggest development we had in the case since the flash drive. And of course, instead of being immediately connected to someone who could tell me more about Rowan's disappearance, I sat on hold the whole drive to the first witness's house.

"I'm sorry, ma'am," the officer on the other side of the phone said. "Who was it that you were wanting to speak to?"

"I'm not sure, actually," I said. "I'm a private investigator here with Detective Ashley Harper from the Pittsburgh PD. We're helping a department in Lancaster on a missing person's case. We think it might be connected to a case you guys worked on in the 90s."

"Missing persons?"

"Yes, sir," Harper said.

"The disappearance of Rowan Palmer," I said. "R as in red, O as in orange, W as in Walter—"

"No shit, the Palmer case?" Amusement touched his tone. "The thing's an urban legend around here."

"Why is that?" Harper asked.

"I was only ten years old when it happened," he said. "But rumor has it they know who did it. They just couldn't convict him."

"Who?" I asked. "Who was it?"

"Ah, hell," he said. "I can't remember the guy's name, but it was her boyfriend. The detective who was on that case, he still works here. He's out right now, but he should be back in an hour or so. You got a number? I can have him give you a call back."

"Yeah, of course," I said, followed by my number, then the generic, "Thanks for your help. Have a good one."

Clicking the end call button, I groaned my annoyance.

"You know how these things go, Maddie," Harper said. "Ninety percent of our job's waiting for someone to call us back."

"It would be nice if once, just *once*, whoever we needed to talk to was ready and available at their desk when we needed to talk to them."

"We can dream." Harper opened the driver's side door. "But hopefully we get something out of this guy."

So far? Most of our leads were helping us. I had faith this one would too.

After stepping from the car, I opened the rear door for Tempy. With a snap, she joined me at my side. Behind us, parked on the side of the road, Torres stepped from his cruiser as well. Exchanging our hellos, gravel crackled under our feet as we started for the house atop the hill.

Nothing extravagant, but nice enough. A farmhouse on the edge of town. There were subdivisions down the road, but this place stood on its own.

It was two stories high, with white siding, red shutters, and a big red door. Off to the left sat a two-car garage. Flowers overflowed from the mulched beds that framed the wraparound porch. As pretty as they were, the smell was a bit overwhelming.

Climbing the driveway, I caught sight of a barn out back. Chickens squawked nearby. That was such a common thing these days, and I'd never understood it. Maybe because I didn't eat enough eggs to see the point, but also because it cost more to keep them alive than it did to buy a whole chicken at the store.

"You think this is going to amount to anything?" Torres asked me.

"I don't think it hurts to check," I said.

"Neither do I, but you've been doing this long enough. You helped find somebody who was just as bad as this bastard."

"Yeah?" I glanced his way to see if his face said something that his words did not.

"I'm gonna go out on a limb and say a good gut played a part in that. So what's your gut saying now?"

"That we're close." I shrugged. "A lot is falling into place. I got another lead this morning. I don't know if it's going anywhere, but it sure as hell could."

"That's what I mean." Torres smirked, shaking his head slightly. "You got one trustworthy gut."

"Hasn't failed me yet."

"What's the lead?"

"Maybe Deluca's first victim," I said. "A girl in central PA who went missing in '94."

"Yeah, I've been meaning to ask you. Why do you call him that?"

"That's the name he gave Daisy. I ran a check on it though. Couldn't find anything. Doesn't match any of the names I'm putting together in this area either."

A quiet harrumph. "Either way though. Could match up with our timeline. Guys like this usually start in their twenties, don't they?"

Harper winced. "I wouldn't say that."

"Wasn't the case with the Country Killer," I said. "But judging by the number of bodies, our guy's been at this for a while."

"Could be something then," Torres replied. "Who are you waiting on to call you back?"

"The detective who worked the case," Harper said. "Speaking of which, what's the body count up to right now?"

It took a moment for Torres to respond. Stepping aside to let me climb the stairs first, he cleared his throat. "Fifty-one when I left this morning."

My stomach ached, and my chest tightened.

No one said anything, but we let out a collective sigh.

This was about Daisy. She was how it all started. Finding her was my primary objective.

But I had to acknowledge that this was so much bigger than Daisy. If we didn't find this guy, he would kill again. And again. And again.

Harper thumped on the door, and we all stood there with that thought fresh in our minds. If we didn't find him soon, Daisy would be next. His daughter might not be far behind either.

The red door swung open.

An older man, probably pushing seventy. Hair stuck out the back of his baseball cap, but nothing near his forehead. I imagined he was balding beneath it. The only telltale of his age were his wrinkles and white beard, however. His shoulders were broad, biceps big beneath his gray T-shirt. In contrast to the usual slump that people got as they aged, his posture was perfect.

"Good morning, officer," he said to Torres, then looked between me and Harper. "Ladies. Something I can help you with?"

"Yes sir, we hope so," Torres said, extending his hand. "Are you Doug Hudson?"

"I am." Doug shook it. "Is this about those unpaid parking tickets? Because I swear, I'm working on it. It's just, when you call down to Penn-DOT, they transfer you to a thousand different people before they tell you to do it online. I don't think I could figure out how to pay a bill online if someone held a gun to my head." He laughed. "I can barely use Facebook."

"No, sir," Harper said, chuckling. "We're sorry to bother you at all. We were just hoping you could spare a few minutes of your time."

"I can sure try." Doug cocked his head to the side. "What's this all about?"

Harper extended the photo of Daisy his way. "Do you recognize this woman?"

He squinted at the photo, leaning his head back to see it better. "Maybe. I'm not sure though. My eyes aren't what they used to be."

"You might have seen her about a week ago at the local library," I said. "Is that ringing any bells?"

"You know what?" Nodding, he pointed at the picture. "Yeah, maybe I did see her. She into any trouble?"

"No, sir," Torres said. "She's missing."

"We got a tip that she might've been there around when you were there last," Harper said. "We're just trying to track down as much information as we can. If she was with anyone, if she tried to talk to anyone, if it looked like she was in any danger."

"Phew," he murmured, shaking his head. "I think she was just sitting at the computer. We didn't talk or nothing."

"Did you happen to see her leave with anyone?" I asked. "Or the car she got into? Really, anything along those lines could help us a lot."

"No, ma'am, I'm sorry," he said, passing the photo back. "I think I've seen her around town a few times. Are you sure she's missing?"

"We are, yes," Torres said. "Where else have you seen her?"

"I don't know. Just around, you know? Small town, we see a lot of the same faces," he said. "I think at the park a month or two ago. Maybe she was pushing a stroller?"

"She was pregnant when she disappeared, so that makes sense," Harper said. "Was she with anyone?"

"Not that I remember." Frowning, he shook his head some more. "I'm not as sharp as I used to be, but I wasn't exactly looking for her either."

There it was again. That collective sigh.

But Doug wasn't our only witness. There were five more people we needed to speak with.

"That's alright. Just, if you think of anything," Torres said, passing Doug a card, "give me a call. Day or night."

"I sure will, sir."

There were a few more pleasantries before we turned and started for our cars. A few more witnesses to question, obviously. But I had another name to investigate on the way there.

Leo Wilder.

Chapter 18

The moment I sat in the passenger seat of Harper's car, I headed to Google. Leo Wilder hadn't shown up in my initial search, which contained the entire text message. Whoever this was, the anonymous tipper said he did tattoos. So I typed in *Leo Wilder, tattoo, State College PA.*

Voilà. There he was.

"You got something?" Harper asked, raising a brow at me. "That's the face you make when you've got something."

"Something, alright." I swiped to Leo's Instagram. *Tattoos_by_Leo.* Of course, that could've been any tattoo artist with the name Leo, but when I swiped to his account—which was public—the location tag said State College, PA.

I searched in his bio for a website that would hopefully reroute me to a phone number. But, as many entrepreneurs did these days, he only linked his other social medias in his account. While his work was beautiful, at least a picture of his face would've been nice. Then I would at least have an idea of who I was talking to.

Not any of those either. Just lots of detailed portraits. Animal works as well. His style was hyper realism, usually in black and white.

Damn good artist. But no website.

To the direct messages I went.

Hurriedly, I typed,

Hi Leo

My name is Maddie Castle. I'm a private investigator working on a pretty heavy case. Your name came up in it. I looked for a phone number, but this was the only way I could think to get in contact. I'd really appreciate it if you could give me a call. I just have a few questions. And the feeling that you could help me solve a 30-year-old missing person's case.

"You think that's a good idea?" Harper shifted the car into drive. "I mean, what if he's responsible for it?"

"All the more reason he'll give us a call." I pressed send. "Try to prove his innocence and all that."

"Or block you and run to Mexico."

I shook my head. "This man isn't Deluca. I don't have pictures of his face, but Deluca's hands aren't covered in tattoos. This guy's are."

"We're not even sure if this guy is connected to Deluca."

"We're not sure he isn't either," I said. "But come on. Deluca called Daisy Rory. Rory is short for Rowan. Rowan disappeared in 1994. Going off our estimates, Deluca would have been in his late teens or early twenties then. He may have gone to college with Rory. Rowan was an English major. That's what Deluca loves about Daisy. She looks like Rory, and she loves writing like Rory."

"Yeah, I know," Harper said, making a left onto the highway. "It's a good hunch, but what are you going to do if this guy is friends with Deluca? What if you tipped him off?"

"What if the feds tipped him off?" A tone I hardly recognized came out of my mouth. "What if digging up his cemetery tipped him off? We're in a race against the clock, Harper. One way or another, he's gonna realize that we know. Until he does, I'm going to exploit the hell out of every lead I get my hands on. Because that's the best damned chance we have at saving Daisy and Bella."

Silence. She only cast a glance my way with an arched brow and set jaw.

"What?" I asked. "Am I wrong?"

"No," Harper said, her tone quieter. "Everything you said makes sense."

"Then why did you look at me like that?"

"I think it's obvious, Maddie," Harper said. "You're too close to this."

I rolled my eyes. "If I weren't, no one would've found that field."

"And I'm glad you did," she said. "But you need to prepare yourself for the worst. You're convinced we're gonna find them. There is no guarantee of that. He could've already realized we were on to him, grabbed them, and run. Or worse. You know this."

"Of course I know that. That's why I'm trying to work as fast as I can instead of arguing with you."

Eyes on the road, she raised one hand in surrender. "I'm just saying, Maddie. You need to be prepared for the worst."

"And I'm just saying, Harper. We need to bust our asses until the trail goes cold."

Another raise of her hand. "I'm doing just that."

She was.

I was too, and so was Torres, and so were the FBI agents. We were all doing everything we could.

And yes, there was a chance Daisy would never come home. There was a chance we would never catch Deluca, that he was already packing his bags and plotting a new cemetery halfway across the country.

But believing that all hope was lost was not an option. I still had the last half of Daisy's journal to make it through. I still had five witnesses to question. I still had Nathaniel Cooper, and the Sunset Stay, and...

The Sunset Stay.

That's why State College sounded familiar when I opened that text. It wasn't that far from Nathaniel Cooper's hotel.

Someone was already hot on Deluca's trail. They had to be, or they wouldn't have sent me that information.

But who? Who would give me valuable intel with nothing in exchange?

A friend, they called themselves.

What was the chance that it was Deluca, attempting to send us in the wrong direction? Supposed that was for the police officer whose phone call I was awaiting to confirm or deny.

For now, I had to hang on to hope that they were what they claimed to be. A friend.

Harper cleared her throat. "Is there still more to read in Daisy's journal?"

"A good bit, yeah."

"Thirty-minute drive to the next witness's," Harper said. "Read while we drive?"

The first night, after I heard the screams, I heard sobs. Violent, heart wrenching sobs.

For hours, I heard her sobs.

She cried out for her mom. She cried out in pain. She cried out for God, even for Deluca. But she called him Decesare.

The screams came from below. Lower than the main floor. The basement, I had to imagine.

For a few more hours, she screamed for help.

I crouched in the corner of my room, unable to stop my own sobs.

In those moments, there was nothing I wanted more than to help her. I wanted her name so I could write about her in case I did escape. I wanted her to know that whatever he was doing to her down there, I was here. She wasn't alone. I couldn't help her, but I wanted her to know she wasn't alone.

It was only then that I realized just how powerless I was in this house.

For months, I told myself it could be worse. This was bad, but it could be worse. So long as I was sweet, so long as I manipulated him into believing I loved him, it was okay. He thought he was in control, but I was the one with the power. I was the one lying to him to keep myself safe.

That night, I realized just how much worse it could get.

He screamed back at her. He told her to shut up, and to be quiet, and that he would make it hurt so much more.

She just kept screaming.

I couldn't stop crying. For her, for fear that I was next, even for my baby.

I don't know how loud I cried, if I'd alerted him with my sobs, but I know shortly after he told her to be quiet, he came for me. Each thump of his boots up the steps was like the boom of lightning before thunder cracked. The clap that draws your attention, that tells you to seek cover.

There was no use in seeking cover. I had no refuge here. He was the lightning, and he was soon to strike.

The sound of his keys jingling with the lock outside the door was the silence before the storm.

As he cursed himself and fumbled with the metal against metal, I hyperventilated. This was it. It was the end. I was next. He was done with me, he was done with our daughter, and I would be dead within hours and never found.

But he swung the door open, and his eyes met mine. They were wide, forehead pinched upward in pain. He dropped to his knees before me.

Involuntarily, I shimmied closer into the corner, still gasping for breath.

"Little bird," he whispered, voice so gentle, eyes no different.

"Please don't hurt me," I gasped out between sobs. "Please don't hurt me."

Deluca's mouth fell open, head shaking. His hands reached closer, and I braced for their impact. They were soft on my shoulders, softer still as they slid down my arms to my hands. "I won't. I'll never hurt you."

He already had, and he would again. But the way he hurt the girl in the basement...

There was no stopping my cries. Probably a panic attack, in hindsight.

In those moments, all I knew was that the fate of my existence lay in that man's hands. Hands that held mine, stretching out for me, cradling my entire body. He pulled me into his lap, hushing my sobs, rocking me side to side, kissing my forehead, yet all I could do was cry.

I couldn't run. So badly, I wanted to run. But he soothed me into silence. He was the sun that dried up my rain, and it made me sick.

Lying in his arms, tucking my head into his chest, I found solace, and I found hate. Hate for him. Hate for myself.

God only knew what he'd been doing to her down there heartbeats prior, and now, I found comfort in the fact that I wasn't her.

That only made me cry more. He didn't know the difference between those desperate sobs.

Eventually, in his arms, the panic subsided, and the tears ceased. When they did, he kissed my forehead, extended his hand, and told me to come with him.

My limbs lost all feeling, all control.

What choice did I have?

He told me to, and if I didn't, I would be the girl in the basement.

It was all flashes from there. A blur of walking down the steps with my hand in his. Flashes of walking through the living room and out the front door. A jumbled, pixilated view of the field ahead and the trees that lined them.

My vision was crystal clear when we made it to the cellar door around back.

"No!" Squealing, terrified that I was soon to join her, I yanked against his grasp with all I had. "No, no, no! Don't hurt me! Please don't hurt me!"

He grabbed me by my shoulders, shaking me so my eyes met his. Once I sobbed some more, going limp under his hold, he took my face in his hands. "I'm not hurting you. You're everything to me, my little hummingbird. I just need you for a minute, and then we'll go back to your room."

I'd already fought. I'd pulled as hard as I possibly could, and now, his hands were inches from my throat all over again.

I'll never compare what he put me through to what he put the girl in the basement through. But I never had a choice either. I was lucky, am *lucky, that he saw something in me he didn't see in the others. But I didn't have a choice.*

So I stopped crying. I held his hand as he opened the cellar doors. My bare feet smacked against the cement stairs with each step. Desperately, I wanted to shut my eyes. I knew what I was about to see would never leave my memories, so I tried to shut them. Until I stumbled into his back.

He helped me find my footing.

By then, we were in the cellar.

Four walls, with two more within them. Two cement ones came to a corner. Two more, constructed from iron bars like that of my bedroom windows, made another.

She stood at that corner, only inches away from me.

For a heartbeat, we stared at one another like we were staring in a mirror. Not only because we looked similar with the same shade of blue in our eyes, and the same white skin, and the same dark hair, but because we were a few steps away from trading places. I could've been her, and she could've been me.

Our statures were similar. Petite. She had the same bad teeth that I did. Thanks to meth, I imagined. Her eyes were a little bigger than mine, her lips a bit smaller, but if we stood side-by-side, a stranger would call us sisters. We even wore the same white babydoll nightgown.

Only difference was, hers was covered in blood. One of those blue eyes was swollen shut. Even swollen, her lips were smaller. Our noses, I couldn't compare, because hers was disfigured and purple.

Across her chest were streaks of red between sliced, torn flesh. Not enough to kill. Only enough to maim. Around her throat were bands of black and blue in the shape of the hand that held mine.

"See?" Deluca said, stepping closer to her. "See why I told you to be quiet? See who you woke up with your screams?"

That may have been the worst moment of my life.

The moment I became the nurse. The moment I became the privileged one. The moment I betrayed another innocent woman.

How could I help her when I couldn't help myself? It may not have been on my own accord, but the fact remained. Her suffering was my peace.

"My wife needs her rest," he said. "You're going to shut up, and you're gonna let her get it."

"You're helping him?" She grasped hold of the metal bars between us, only looking at me. "How the hell can you stand there beside him? How can you let him do this?"

I couldn't stop it. I knew I shouldn't have said a word, but I couldn't stop them from leaving my lips. "I'm sorry. I'm so—"

Deluca spun toward me. He raised his hand and slapped my cheek so hard that I dropped to the ground. "You're sorry? You could be her. You could be down here with this bitch. Is that what you want, Daisy?"

I crawled onto my knees, shaking my head. "I'm sorry."

Those were the only two words I could form.

"After everything I've done for you!" Genuine shock bellowed from his throat. "The day we came here together, I could have brought you here. I didn't. I took you to my bedroom. I made you two more upstairs. And that's *what you say? You're sorry for her? You ungrateful little bitch."*

"I'm sorry," I said again, sobbing now, eyes on his. "I'm sorry. I'm sorry, I'm sorry—"

"Holy shit!" the girl on the other side of the bar said. "He's ruined you, hasn't he?"

"I'm sorry." I just kept saying it, sobbing it, as if it were my final plea. "I'm sorry. I'm sorry. Don't hurt me. Please don't hurt me. Please don't hurt our baby. I'm sorry. I'm sorry."

He grabbed me by my arm. He yanked me to my feet. I screamed it over and over, sure that this was it. Sure that this was the end. Sure that I was going to get tossed in that cell right alongside her.

He pulled me up the stairs instead, then around the house, into the living room, up the stairs, and back to the bedroom, all while I screamed that I was sorry.

Chapter 19

I clicked my phone off and stared out the windshield.

That was all I could do.

Daisy had done nothing wrong that night. She did as anyone in her situation would have. There was no way she could have saved that girl, just as there was no way she could save herself.

But the weight of the girl's words—*how could you*—the sound of her screams, the absolute helplessness they both felt, was a burden I could not imagine carrying.

Simply reading the story had punched a hole through the center of my chest. Imagining—not even *knowing*—how that must've felt brought tears to my eyes and solidified a lump the size of a fist in my throat.

All I could do was stare out the window at the trees ahead on the back road.

We were parked now. The next witness lived at the top of the driveway thirty feet to my left. Torres told us he was stopping for coffee on the way here, that he'd grab us some, and I had never been so grateful for the delay.

What I wanted more than anything was to find Daisy.

But if I spoke right now, moved, looked at anything besides those trees that framed the blacktop, I would crumble. I would fall apart.

This was worse than Eric Oakley. Deluca was more prolific, more volatile. Even more sick and twisted. Evil.

That wasn't what made it worse.

This was worse because there was written proof of exactly how the victim felt through her experience. This was knowing, practically *watching*, the worst moments she had likely ever lived through. It was knowing that she was real, that she was human, and she was still out there.

It was knowing that every day, she feared she would be the girl in that cell.

It was knowing the fate of the girl in that cell.

A case was an envelope of evidence that pointed us to the perpetrator. This case was so much more.

Harper had said I was too close to it. My question was, how could I not be?

A few minutes ago, while the chapter had still been playing, Harper had put the car in park. She'd sniffled and cleared her throat a few times.

How could she be any farther from this than I was?

Bentley was my obvious physical tether to the case. I wouldn't deny that.

But no one with a heart could read through this book, this moment-by-moment account of torture and suffering, and stay far from it. Anyone with an ounce of decency who read these words was close to this case.

There were two problems with getting too close to a case: One, failing to see every angle of it; and two, grieving the victim as if they were your own friend or family, should you lose them.

The former was not a problem. I had not overlooked any pieces of evidence. There was not a single document, a single word, that I had overlooked.

The latter... well, maybe this was why I was better as a private investigator than a cop. Maybe this was why Harper had her detective shield, and I never would.

I would always get too close to a case. I would always feel for the victims who deserved justice and do this job with my heart forward, because it wasn't just a job to me.

It was a mission to correct the wrongs of the world we lived in, to fill in the gaps our justice system created. I *was* this job. It was not about a paycheck, or a title, or a power trip.

The world was dystopian, and we were taught to shut our eyes to all its atrocities.

I would face them with my shoulders held high, tears in my eyes, and a knot in my throat. If everyone else needed to stay objective, to ignore the suffering of the innocent, all because they wanted to sleep better at night, so be it. But I would not be one of them. I would not ignore the pain and abuse these victims endured just so I could stay comfortable.

The beaten down, the neglected, the ones the world had failed, they deserved that. At the barest of minimums, they deserved someone to mourn their suffering, and their death, when it came.

They deserved someone who would, if nothing else, listen to their stories. Even if I couldn't fix the broken world, I would listen, feel, and lend a shoulder to the broken.

The rumble of Torres's SUV brought my attention to the rearview mirror. As he stepped from the vehicle with a tray of coffee, I reached for the door handle.

"Do you need me?" Harper asked with a clearing of her throat, unable to meet my gaze. "I just, uh... I need to get myself together."

Maybe that was the problem with the justice system. Maybe that was the problem with the whole world. The task was in front of us, something that might save innocent lives, but we needed to get ourselves together. We needed to prioritize our mental health and our comfortability.

"No." I pulled the handle, stepped out, and opened the rear door for Tempest. As I snapped, and she joined me at my side, I said, "I don't need you."

I shut the door before she had time to respond.

Walking closer to Harper's car, Torres squinted inside. "She alright?"

"Probably not. We just got to a really rough part of Daisy's journal."

"Shit," he said, extending the coffee. "What happened?"

"Thanks." Accepting the cup, I nodded up the driveway. "Let's walk and talk."

I summarized Daisy's account of that night. Torres shook off some chills, took in a few sharp inhales, then shook his head. We were almost to the witness's front door by the time I made it to the end.

This witness, Victoria Bowman, was the one who'd lent Daisy her login for the library computer. She lived in a double wide on a small plot of land outside of town. The beige vinyl siding desperately needed a good power washing, but a glance told you this woman did her best. A few flowerbeds lined the exterior, filled with sun-bleached mulch, framed by plastic weather strips. All the flowers were small, likely picked up from the discount section at the local department store. No fancy bushes, no expensive shrubbery.

Chalk artwork lined each sixteen by sixteen paver that led to the plastic steps at the front door. The same plastic steps I had. The cheapest available porch option for a trailer.

Perched against the front door were a few bicycles, a scooter as well as a big wheel for a toddler. Only one car was parked out front.

The saddest part, as I looked at the front yard of someone who I was sure financially struggled, who I knew had been affected by some tragedy or another in her life but was still doing her best, was the fact that this was Daisy's fantasy. A life like this was all she'd ever wanted. Parents who may not have had a lot but did as much as they could.

I understood that desire, because I'd had the same one all my life.

What a shame it was that Daisy had yet to experience this.

She might never.

"Sick son of a bitch," Torres murmured. "That explains at least one of the bodies, though."

"Yeah?"

"Yeah, give Alex a call if you want more details," he said, "but they let me know the fifth body they found had lacerations like that. Across her chest, I mean. A few other stab wounds, too. Which was weird, because most of the victims have been beaten. Lots of overkill specifically on her though. They're putting her time of death about ten months ago, based on decomp, but even the bones were fractured from the stab wounds. She's the only one like that." He inhaled sharply and muttered, "So far, anyway."

"Because Daisy had altered his routine," I said, my brows furrowing. "He probably has a schedule he sticks to. Daisy was going to check off one of his boxes in his usual timeline, but he kept her alive instead. It threw him off."

"You said he'd lashed out at her before he left to hunt again," Torres said. "Because he needed to kill. Had to get back into his routine."

A deep breath. "Probably, yeah."

Torres nodded and cleared his throat. "Another thing. Each body they've found so far, they're all holding one of those raven figurines. None of them have serial numbers, so we're looking at local ceramic shops. That's probably where he gets them."

"Hopefully that amounts to something."

"Hopefully."

He grew quiet, and so did I.

We were almost at Victoria's door anyway.

Tempy led the way, I came in second, and Torres stayed at the foot of the steps. After a knock, a woman on the other side called, "Coming!"

We waited.

Eventually, the plastic door filled with foam insulation swung inward. I'd had the same one when I moved into my trailer. I'd replaced it because it took practically no force to break down.

The woman in the doorway was around my age. Late twenties, early thirties, with jet black hair, light skin, and pale green eyes disguised beneath a pair of thick-rimmed, black glasses. Her hair was in a messy bun, but the clothes of the toddler on her hip were spotless.

Looking between us, noting Torres's uniform, she furrowed her brow. "Can I help you guys with something?"

"We hope so." Extending my hand, I offered a smile. "My name is Maddie Castle. I'm a private investigator. This is Sergeant Javier Torres with the local police department. We were hoping to ask you a couple of questions."

Cocking her head to the side, she looked between us some more, then down at Tempest. "I mean, go ahead. I don't think I've done anything though."

"No, ma'am, we don't believe you have," Torres said, passing me a photo. "But we believe you may have seen this woman."

I handed it off to Victoria, and she nodded. "Yeah, that's Daisy."

My heart skipped with excitement. "You two are friends?"

"I don't know if I'd say that, but we've seen each other around." Victoria passed the photo back. "Why do you ask? Does she have warrants or something?"

"No, nothing like that," I said. But I didn't want to say the rest yet. If they were on a first name basis, they'd had at least a handful of conversations. In some regard, Victoria cared for her. The moment I told her that Daisy was being held captive was the moment her mind would jumble. She'd forget key details that may help us. Instead, I asked, "How did you two meet?"

"At the park a few months ago. My daughter saw her baby and asked what her name was. Then at the county fair last month. A few times at the park, once at the ice cream shop down the road. Just around."

"Are the two of you in contact?" Torres asked.

"No, we've just talked a couple of times," Victoria said, still squinting between us. "My daughter is three, and she's obsessed with babies. When she sees Daisy, she wants to see the baby."

Made sense. They were practically passing ships. I just prayed it wasn't a wall we were running into. "Did she ever mention where she lived? You don't by chance have a dash cam or anything like that in your car? Any pictures that you've taken with Daisy or the baby or—"

"What the hell is going on?" Face screwed up in confusion, she looked at me, then down a Tempest, and back at Torres. "If she's not in trouble, why do you need to know all this stuff? Is this a drug dog?"

"Ma'am," Torres said, "if you could just answer our questions—"

"She said she was from Columbus, but she lived up in the mountains now with her husband. I don't have a dashcam, and I never took any pictures with Daisy or the baby. There. Answered your questions. Now could you please answer mine?"

I took a deep, calming breath. Torres didn't speak, so I took the hint. He was letting me take the lead on this.

"Daisy Miller has been missing for a little over a year. We believe she lives locally, but that she's being held against her will."

Slowly, Victoria's expression changed. She grew more confused, forehead creasing, mouth dropping open. Then her eyes widened ever so slightly, and her jaw dropped further. "Oh my God."

"Was she usually with a man?" Torres asked calmly, extending another photo. This one from the security camera at Nature's Pantry.

I handed it over.

Victoria clapped a hand over her mouth. She nodded quickly.

"I'll take that as a yes," Torres said.

"Every time." Swallowing hard, she continued nodding. "He was always there. The only time he wasn't was at the library a week or two ago. She didn't have the baby that day either."

"Did you guys speak that day?" I asked.

Another nod. "She asked for my login to use the computer. Said that she forgot her library card at home or something? So I logged in for her, and just told her to make sure she logged out before she left."

That made sense. There was only one thing that didn't. If Daisy was able to slip the bag with a jacket and the flash drive into that ceiling tile, why wasn't she able to pass Victoria a note? Of course, she would be worried if Deluca had her baby. But she could've written a simple message.

Call 911. When they get here, tell them not to come inside until my boyfriend comes back. Wait until my baby is in my hands. Then arrest him.

Daisy was smart. Smart enough to pull off something that simple.

I was missing something.

"When we showed you that picture of her boyfriend," I said, "you panicked a little bit. Can I ask why?"

"Not panic," Victoria murmured, shaking her head. "It's just... My ex is in prison right now. It took him trying to kill me for the cops to do anything. I went before to the precinct, with pictures of the marks he left on me, and the most they gave me was a PFA. Which is jack shit, you know?" She looked past me at Torres. "No offense."

He lifted his hands in surrender.

"And after you've lived through something like that, you see signs." Victoria nibbled her lower lip, shaking her head. "The fact that he was always there. Right behind her, or right at her side. This look in his eyes. I know that sounds crazy, but there's a look with men like that. You can see something, and I swear I did. I swear I saw something in him."

"That doesn't sound crazy," I said.

"The one day, when my daughter was leaning over the stroller to see the baby, I tried to talk to them. The guy, he tried to take over the conversation. Said that he couldn't wait for his baby to be as big as mine, how old was she, a bunch of stuff. But I don't talk to strange men, you know? Especially when his girl is standing right there. I'm gonna talk to her before I talk to him. Just a respect thing, girl to girl."

"Girl code," I said. "We all do it. We don't want anyone to think anything suspicious, so when we're talking to a couple, we talk to the girl."

"Right, but he kept trying to get my attention. She was really quiet at first. Then, it was like—Hell, I don't know." Tightening her lips to a line, she gazed around, as if searching for the words around her driveway. "She looked at me the way I probably looked at a woman on the street who wasn't going through what I was going through with my ex. Like she hoped I could help her. I tried to get her number, make plans to get the kids together, but he butted in."

"Said he was looking forward to seeing you guys around or something like that?" Torres asked.

Still biting her lower lip, Victoria nodded. "Something like that, yeah."

"Have you ever taken a picture at the park that Daisy's car might've been in?" I asked. "Even if it's just in the background."

"I take thousands of pictures of my kids at the park," Victoria said. "So maybe. I'm pretty sure I saw them get into a big black SUV. I can look through my pictures for something like that."

"That would be great," I said, reaching into my hoodie pocket. I came out with a business card. "If you think of anything else, day or night, call me or go down to the local PD."

"Sure," she said, voice quieter now. As we turned and started for the driveway, she spoke again. "She was trying to tell me something, wasn't she? Every conversation we had, she was trying to tell me she needed help."

Looking over my shoulder, I frowned. "Like I said. If you think of anything else."

Chapter 20

There was an ache in the pit of my gut while we descended that driveway. I couldn't put my finger on it, but something wasn't adding up.

"He wasn't there," I said, not sure if I was thinking out loud or waiting for Torres to bounce an idea back.

"Didn't exactly expect him to be here," Torres said.

"No, at the library." Squinting at the gravel beneath my feet, I shook my head. "It doesn't make sense. He left Daisy at the library, alone, because he had the baby."

"What—Are you wondering why she didn't ask Victoria for help?"

"In part, yeah," I said. "It's not adding up."

"He told her he'd kill the kid if she told anyone."

"But are we sure that would give him enough incentive to leave?" I asked. "Daisy's not stupid. He *knows* Daisy's not stupid. Yeah, he might be convinced that she has Stockholm's, but then why would he take the baby?"

"He wouldn't, unless he was unsure he could trust her," Torres said. "Or because he needed to take the baby somewhere. Doctor's appointment, maybe?"

"Then she'd be in the system," I murmured. "The library said Daisy was logged into Victoria's account for almost two hours."

"Most of my kids' doctor appointments don't run longer than thirty minutes, but wait time is usually half an hour too," Torres said. "I mean, we could look into pediatrics within a thirty-mile radius."

"HIPPA is gonna have us waiting on warrants for days, and a thirty-mile radius isn't big enough. The appointment could've run five minutes. Possibility there was no wait time. We have to do at least an hour for that possibility."

"We can still get started on them," Torres said. "Around here, there won't be that many pediatricians to search through. So much of this area is rural."

"It's worth looking into, but this guy's got money. He's got resources. Nobody asks for ID when you take a kid in for a doctor's appointment. Especially if their parent is paying in cash."

"You think he'd do that? Use a fake name?"

"I'd like to think that, as a man of privilege, he'd want to pass that onto his daughter. But I also think he'd be cautious to avoid using Daisy's real name. Not unless he genuinely believed he had warped her mind and made her forget or forgive everything he's done. If that were the case, though, would he still have a lock on her bedroom?"

"Doubt it," Torres replied, folding his arms. "But it's possible, right? He wants control. Otherwise, he wouldn't have a torture chamber in the basement."

That, I wouldn't argue. He did like control. Contrary to Deluca's belief, control was his one true love.

"Right," I said.

"About the latter? Or the former?"

"Your guess is as good as mine. But on the slim chance that he had gone to a doctor's appointment that day, I know a guy who can track that down."

"A guy who can get around the warrant we need?"

Feeling my cheeks flush, I smiled. "You know what, sir?"

"Hmm?"

"Not something you need to worry with."

I swiped open my phone and shot Dylan a quick text. As soon as it went through, he read it. Then replied with an eye rolling emoji and a thumbs up. While I had my phone in my hand, I swiped down the notification bar at the top.

Instagram direct message.

Tattoos_by_Leo

Yeah, I can give you a call. Is now a good time?

Hurriedly, I typed back, *Yes, ASAP would be great.*

Seconds later, my phone was ringing. I held it in Torres's direction. "Sorry. I gotta take this."

"Your hacker works that fast?" he asked.

"What hacker?" Another smirk. "No, this is about that lead I got earlier. Someone from the town that girl disappeared from."

"Deluca's first victim?"

"That's the one." I gestured to the phone again, as if to say I needed to answer it before it went to voicemail.

Torres raised a hand.

"Hello?" I answered, patting my leg for Tempest to stay at my side. Of course, she did.

A man with a deep, husky voice answered. "Yeah, is this, uh, Maddie Castle?"

"It is, yes," I said. "And this is Leo Wilder?"

"Sure is." There was a touch of something I had a hard time placing in his voice. Amusement? Hope? "This is about Rowan, isn't it?"

"I think it might be, yes." At the foot of the driveway now, I leaned against Harper's car. It gave my knee a much needed rest. "And maybe about a tattoo you did? The Crow?"

He snorted. "The bells are ringing."

"You do know what I'm talking about then?"

"Wish I didn't, but sure do," he said. "What do you want to know exactly? Anything I can do to help, I will."

An unfair question. I wanted to know all of life's, the world's, and even the universe's greatest mysteries. Today, I would settle for The Crow.

"To be blunt, whatever you're willing to tell me. I'm looking into a missing person's case that I believe is connected to Rowan's. I got an anonymous tip that said, 'crow tattoo done by Leo Wilder.'"

"So you don't know shit, basically."

I huffed. "Not about this, no. Care to enlighten me?"

"The Crow is a person. Rowan's boyfriend, to be exact. I don't know his real name. Never did. Even before I did the tattoo, he called himself The Crow and Rowan, The Raven."

Interesting. That's why he buried his victims with ravens. They were all surrogates for Rowan.

"When was this?" I asked.

"I met Rowan at a party in—I want to say '91? Maybe '92. She was a freshman at Penn State, and I was a sophomore. We were just friends. Hung out in the same circles, smoked together, drank together. Usual college stuff."

Phone pinched between my shoulder and ear, I found a receipt and pen in my hoodie pocket and started jotting down notes. "Got it. And The Crow?"

"I didn't meet him until late '93, maybe '94. I don't remember the exact date, but it wasn't long before Rowan disappeared. He was a weird dude. Girls liked him. A lot. But he never vibed with any of us guys. You ever meet someone, and they're just off?"

In this line of work? "More often than I'd like to."

"That's how he was. The kind of guy you look at, and you just don't trust," Leo said. "But Rowan didn't see what we did. We noticed things, you know? He started an argument with a guy who made a drink for Rowan. We were all friends. The kid wasn't flirting. But this guy, he just flipped out. Me and Rowan had to split it up."

"Possessive and controlling," I said. "Kind of figured that. Were there a lot of occurrences like that?"

"Too many, yeah. We'd all be hanging out at a party, Rowan would be there, then he'd show up, and they'd have a screaming match outside. They'd only been together a couple months, but he was always convinced that she was cheating on him with one of us. We never saw anything, but we all had our suspicions."

"You thought he was abusing her?"

"Never could prove it. It was the '90s. Rowan was artsy. She liked dressing kinda provocative, and that changed after he entered the picture. Like she was covering stuff up."

Either because he didn't want her wearing it or because there were bruises she didn't want anyone else to see.

"No proof, but plenty of signs."

"Yeah, pretty much."

"Now, where did the names come from?" I asked. "The Raven and The Crow."

"I think that was Rowan. She was obsessed with Edgar Allan Poe. He was her favorite author. The Raven was her favorite poem. I'm not sure when he started calling himself The Crow, but Rowan was eccentric. Goofy. She went a little wild with drugs. It wouldn't surprise me if she gave him the nickname."

And he'd decided to make it his entire personality. Like any stalker would. Most of them genuinely did believe they were in love with the object of their obsession.

"Do you mind if I ask which drugs?" I asked.

"Mostly party stuff, but she really liked ice. It was a problem between her and The Crow. He'd have a few drinks, but he wasn't about that life. Looked down on her for it. Looked down on all of us for it. But wherever Rowan was, he was, so he put up with it, I guess."

"This is really good information." Granted, most of it was filling in details I already knew and understood. But this added a bit more depth to it all. "Is it possible they met in writing class or something like that?"

"Honestly, I have no clue. I cared about Rowan. We were good friends. But that was girl talk. Dudes don't ask questions like that. It was a big campus. I can tell you that *I* had no classes with the guy."

"Right," I murmured, nibbling my lower lip. "So when I was talking to the local PD, they said it was him. The cops knew it was him, but they couldn't convict him. Do you feel the same way?"

"Hundred and ten percent," he said. "I was there that night. The night she disappeared, we were all drinking together. And that bastard kept calling her. I don't know what he was saying, but she went outside to talk to him on the phone, and even with the music blasting, we could hear her screaming. I don't know why she didn't just dump the guy. She wouldn't though. We kept telling her to, and she just wouldn't. Even that night, she came in, all upset, and we tried to get her a drink. She wouldn't take it. Said she had to go meet up with Crow. He was pissed about something. Wouldn't tell us what, but what did it matter? The guy was always pissed about something."

"So that's where she was going when she left the bar," I confirmed. "To meet up with him."

"That's where she said she was going, yeah. No one ever found the car. No one ever found her. She just dropped off the face of the planet. And that guy, Crow, he had money. Back then, he was driving a real nice car. I don't remember the make and model, but I think I got a picture of it back home."

"Is he in the picture? Or maybe the license plate?"

"He might be, but I don't remember. The picture was taken from the front, so I don't think the license plate is in it."

Damn it. "Do you have any idea where his money came from?"

"I think his parents had just died, if memory serves. Life insurance money, maybe?"

That was good. Very good. Dylan could track that down.

I hoped.

God, I hoped.

The only question I had left to ask was why the cops hadn't caught him. But he would give me the generic answer everyone in his situation did. *They're crooked, man. They didn't care about her, dude.*

I already knew that wasn't the case. They hadn't had enough evidence to convict him. But they'd known his name. The moment they gave it to me, I could track him down and show up at his door.

"This has all been really helpful," I said. "I don't think I have any more questions at this moment, but if any more come up, do you mind if I give you a call?"

"Yeah, no problem. Anytime. If I can help in any way, I want to."

I knew the feeling.

Just as I ended the call with Leo, the phone rang again.

State College, PA.

I prayed to hell and back that it was the police department.

Chapter 21

"Yeah, is this Maddie Castle?" the man on the other end asked.

"Yes, sir," I said, gesturing for Torres to come back. As he jogged in my direction, I said, "Do you mind if I ask who's calling?"

"I'm Detective Hank Walker with the State College PD. You're a PI, right?"

"Yes, sir," I said again. "I'm working a case right now, and—"

"*The* Maddie Castle? The one who worked the Country Killer case."

A deep breath. "Yes, sir. Now—"

"Wow, I feel like I'm talking to a celebrity." He chuckled. "You didn't catch the guy, right? But he took you, and you escaped."

Torres cocked his head to the side, obviously wondering why I called him back here.

Rubbing my eyes with my thumb and forefinger, I said, "That's correct. Lennox Taylor, he was the officer who made the shot. But—"

"Yeah, I knew it was something like that. Real hero he was, getting that guy off the street. Did you guys know each other?"

"He was actually my ex-fiancé. But—"

"I'm so sorry. I know he went down doing it, and my condolences are with you."

"Thank you. I'm getting through it," I said. "I'm actually calling because—"

"Back when I was out in Harrisburg, we saw too many things like that. Lost a lot of good guys to pricks like him. Well, maybe not quite as bad. I did work a serial case, but it was drug related. Less exciting than what you did. Either way though, I know that pain. Losing someone you love to this job, it ain't easy."

"I'm sorry for your loss too," I said, my words falling out in a tumble. "Definitely a tough job. At the moment though—"

"Sure is. Been at this for forty years, and it don't get any easier. That private investigator stuff though, I thought about it. How long have you been doing that? My wife wants me to get out of this place, but once you're in, it's so hard to get out."

Not much different than how hard it was to get out of a small talk cycle with a near retirement-aged detective. "I've been at it a couple years, and right now, I'm working on a case similar to one you worked in '94. I'm hoping you can help me out."

"Of course," he said, finally. "Why didn't you just say so?"

I gritted my teeth.

Torres chuckled.

"What case was it?" Detective Walker asked. "Our old files, they're not all digitized yet, but I can try to tell you what I know from memory."

"Rowan Palmer," I said.

The first time Walker went silent throughout the whole conversation. I expected him to chime back in, to go on a tirade about what he knew.

Instead, he only said, "Been a long time since I heard that name."

"And I only heard it for the first time this morning," I replied. "I looked online, but all I could find were a few articles about her disappearance."

"Because we never had much," he said, his voice quieter now. "That one still haunts me."

Usually, the cases that haunted us were the most grotesque, the bloodiest. But they'd never found Rowan. So I wasn't sure what about that case would keep him up at night. "Why is that?"

"Unsolved missing persons are always rough. A lot of the time, they're just misunderstandings. Someone stayed at a friend's house instead of coming home. Couple got into a fight and one of them gets out of town for a couple days. But we all knew that wasn't the case here."

"The officer I talked to earlier, he said you all believed it was the boyfriend?"

"Still do. But never found a damn thing to back it up."

"Why did you assume it was him? And did you ever get his name?"

"Sometimes, you meet someone, and you can just see it. You can see the violence in their eyes. The danger, you know? This kid, he was sharp. Smart as a whip. Talked clever. Articulated his words perfect. Didn't show an ounce of remorse or care when we asked him about his missing girlfriend though. Not a droplet."

"What—" *was his name*, I was about to ask again.

"It was the damnedest thing. We did all the reading we could, grabbed every bit of information possible on Rowan. She was a good kid from a bad background. Alcoholic mother, absent father, but she got good grades. Made it to Penn State on a full scholarship.

"But a week before she disappeared, she'd gone to the doctor. Turns out, she was pregnant. Her teachers and friends all said she wanted to be a journalist. Travel the world, write books about conflicts all over. She would've graduated that year, summer of '94. But then she got pregnant. She didn't want to keep the baby."

That was why he clung to Daisy. Daisy wanted their baby. She was his new and improved Rory.

The FBI may have found this information vital, maybe more so than his name. They'd say that it'd helped us better profile him.

And fair enough. It gave a better narrative. That would definitely help in a courtroom. That's what juries loved most. A good story.

This was a good one. At least, for Deluca's team. They'd tell the jury of how Rory planned to get rid of the baby, whether through abortion or adoption, and Deluca lost his mind. He spiraled. He killed her in a moment of rage, disposed of her body, then kept searching for the woman he loved. It wasn't right what he did, of course, but her act made him lose his grip with reality. It was Rowan's fault that he killed somewhere around a hundred women.

I could already see the trial playing out, and it was making me nauseous. I just *knew* his attorneys would make a plea of insanity to evade the death penalty.

"Never could find a damn thing though," Walker continued. "We had witnesses place Rory at the bar Friday night. They told us she was arguing on the phone with the boyfriend, and that she left to meet up with him. Probably at his apartment. We go to his apartment, we question the neighbors, and one of them remembers Rory's Corolla parked out front.

"So we've got enough, right? We can make an arrest. Might not be enough to charge but enough for an arrest. We get the warrant, we bring him in, and he won't say a word. The second he sits down, he says he wants a lawyer. Law says we have to, so we let him call. Lawyer comes in, says the same stuff they always do.

"'My client hasn't seen Rory since Thursday morning.' That's the last time the two of them were seen together. They were at a coffee shop where they had breakfast. Where they *argued* at breakfast. This wasn't far from the campus, and Rory went on to school. Rory was home with her roommate Thursday night. Told her that she and the boyfriend were arguing about the baby. She didn't know what she wanted to do yet, but she knew she didn't want it, and he wanted her to keep it.

"We say we have witnesses that can place Rory's car at his apartment complex. We know she made it there. We think he killed her and got rid of the body. The guy says speculation. We have no evidence. This goes round and round. Lawyer kept asking if we're going to charge his client. Judge won't sign off on it. Tells us we need to get more evidence. Gives us a warrant though. We can search his apartment, his car, even a cell phone, but we can't arrest him. We don't have enough.

"Lawyer keeps pressing, we keep telling him that we have seventy-two hours to hold him before we charge him. Those seventy-two hours, we keep fighting the guy. He's emotional, crying, but we can't even go that hard on him. His lawyer's telling him not to answer questions, that we're abusing our power, that he's gonna sue us if we keep talking to his client instead of him. Blah, blah, blah. Same old, same old.

"Seventy-two hours pass. We ain't got a choice. We searched his home, his car, his phone, and we came back with nothing. Nothing concrete. Yeah, we find Rory's belongings in his home, but no blood. It was his girlfriend. No shocker that her belongings were in his apartment. We've got motive, we've got means, we got opportunity, but we don't have a body. We've got no tangible proof that he killed her. Only the fact that he lawyered up as soon as we brought him in.

"We release him. Two days later, that witness, the one who saw Rory's car in the parking lot, she disappears too. She was the only evidence we *did* have. The only thing we could start to build a case from. Then she drops off the face of the planet. Just like Rory did. We keep trying, keep looking for evidence, but we can't find a damn thing. Eventually, the guy leaves, and we never see him again either."

All of that might help somewhere. Certainly formed a better story. But I still didn't know who the hell this guy was. "And what was the boyfriend's name again?"

"Deangelo." he said. "Salvatore Deangelo."

The phone was already on speaker, and I was sliding over to Google.

"At that time, did Deangelo have any connection to the Lancaster area?" I asked.

"I'd have to pull up the files to make sure, but I do think he came in from out of town," Detective Walker said. "Most folks around here do. It's a college town. He was an English major at Penn State, though. I'm pretty sure that's how he met Rowan."

But they hadn't searched the property in Lancaster because, as Leo had informed me, Deangelo's parents had recently died. That likely meant the deed was caught up in litigation. When they searched for him, they didn't know that it was his second address.

A quick search on Deangelo amounted to nothing. No social medias, no news articles, no immediate hits. I was working fast, so I may have missed something, but next registry was the DMV. There were fifteen Salvatore Deangelos in Pennsylvania, but only two over six feet tall, and only one in the age range we were looking for.

Looking at his picture was surreal. He easily matched Daisy's descriptions. Dark hair, medium brown skin, attractive, masculine facial features. He looked like the photo from Nature's Pantry security footage as well.

What made it surreal, though, was that I saw what Victoria and Walker did.

It could've been my years in law enforcement. Interact with enough shitty people, and you can feel their hideous nature from a glance. But maybe it was deeper than that. Maybe it was some ancestral memory, some instinct that women developed throughout history. One that whispered, *No matter how handsome he looks, no matter what your body says when you look at him, listen to me. Listen to this little voice in your head. Listen when I say: run. Run like your life depends on it.*

Only problem was, the Salvatore Deangelo listed his address in Harrisburg. Maybe he owned a home out there, one we needed to search, but he wasn't that far. He was right under our noses. I just knew it.

I hopped over to a software I used to look up addresses. All I got was a PO box for a borough one town over.

I flashed the screen to Torres. He nodded quickly.

"This has been a lot of help," I said. "Thank you, Detective. I think this Deangelo guy might be responsible for a kidnapping I'm working on. If we get him, we'll be giving you a call back."

"Anytime," he said. "Day or night. If it means catching this guy, I'd give my left foot. If you need anything else, just give me a ring."

"I sure will. Thanks again."

Walker started to say something else, but I had already ended the call.

"PO boxes," I said to Torres. "You have to show proof that you live in the borough you've got the PO box in. The post office has to have his physical address."

Torres was already jogging toward his car. "Follow me."

Chapter 22

Tempest was faster than me hopping into Harper's backseat. While I limped around the vehicle, she rolled down the window. "What's going on?"

"We got his name," I called, hoping the adrenaline would kick in on the way there. "His address is listed as a PO box."

"You can't do that for a driver's license, can you?" Harper asked.

I sat in the passenger seat and swung the door shut. "His ID says he's in Harrisburg, but we know that's not true. That's why we're heading to the post office."

"Is it close?"

"Pretty sure it's a good distance away."

"Next chapter?"

I was already opening it up. "Next chapter."

* * *

The First Murder

He left me in my room all night, the following day, the one after that, and the one after that. Seven consecutive days. He slid my prenatals under the door though. Then, he instructed me to take them, his words muffled by the door between us.

I did.

For seven days, I heard that girl scream. For seven days, I tried to drown out the sound with pillows pressed to my ears, humming to myself, plugging my ears shut, eventually singing aloud. For seven days, I feared that at the end of them, I would be next.

At the end of those seven days, he came to my door. He instructed me to shower and get dressed. Of course, he'd already laid out my clothes. Black sweatpants and a black hoodie.

It was jarring compared to the usual white nightgown. Like he wanted to prove a point. Like he wanted me to be a guest at a funeral.

He always was a poetic son of a bitch.

After I was finished, he tied a black ribbon around my eyes. He guided me outside. I thought, This is it. This is the end.

So I stayed quiet. I wouldn't give him the satisfaction of my screams. I would not beg again. I would die quietly, giving him no joy, no relief.

But he didn't lead me to the cellar. He led me onto the gravel. The beep of a car sounded, as though he had double-clicked the unlock button. Then the clunk of the door handle. He told me to step up, to have a seat, and I did.

The car was already warm. It was crisp outside–October, I believed—but the vehicle was warm. He'd already started it.

He strapped me in, saying, "Don't even think about moving, little hummingbird."

When he'd first called me that, it was sweet. Unique. Baby and sweetheart were overrated. Little bird, little hummingbird, they were different.

Now, every time he says that, I have to fight an eye roll. It sounds ridiculous. It doesn't even roll off the tongue right. Baby and sweetheart are popular because they sound endearing. Little hummingbird sounds creepy.

Which make sense, with everything considered.

I stayed still as the door swung shut. When a few minutes passed, then a few more, I peeled the ribbon up just enough to get a look inside the vehicle. Leather seats. Moonroof. A high-end, fancy dashboard. The navigation wasn't open, but a car like this would have it. I noted that. If I got nothing else out of this, I would find out where the hell we were.

But I didn't have time. Not then.

The rear hatch clicked, then thudded open.

I acted as though my blindfold hadn't moved. He wouldn't have been able to see that it had anyway. It was only the slightest slit along the bottom where it met my cheek. Just enough of a crevice for me to get a peek around the vehicle. Just enough for me to see that the windows were blacked out, so he wouldn't see me move within the vehicle again.

Weight shifted the rear end downward.

The faintest hint of iron touched my nose.

Chills stretched up my spine, and tears burned across my eyes.

I took a deep breath. A deep, calming breath.

If he were going to kill me, wouldn't he have taken me to the basement? That's what I had to cling to. The possibility that I still had a chance.

The rear door slammed shut. A few heartbeats later, a gust of cool wind blew in from the front left. The driver's side.

"Tuck your chin to your chest," he said. "For the entire drive, keep it that way."

I did so. Usually, he got a, "Yes, sir." Not this time. I only did as he said.

We traveled for ten to fifteen minutes on a gravel road. The speed was slow, but bumpy. Now that we've done this more often, left the oasis, I recognize it as the driveway. I don't know if it amounts to a mile, or more, or less, but I suppose without the precise numbers, there's no way for you to tell that either. I just hope you find it relevant.

Once we were on to a paved road, we drove for at least another thirty minutes. It may have been closer to forty-five. I know that's not precise, and I'm sorry. I wish I had more to give you. But in that situation, when your vision is obscured, when you're trying to remember the turns—left and right and so be it—it's nearly impossible. I don't remember how many left and right turns, or in which order.

Another thing stuck out to me as we drove. A prominent thump and rattle coming from the rear. Not inside the vehicle, but below it? As if something was wrong with the car?

All I remember is that, after some time had passed, hearing that weight shift around in the cargo area, my hands trembled like leaves on autumn trees when we approached another gravel road. This one was a sharper incline. It shifted my weight backward in the seat. Sitting forward, keeping my chin to my chest, was like warring with gravity.

It was just as bumpy as the driveway.

When we made it to the top, when we plateaued, he shifted the car into park. Again, he told me not to move.

But I knew. The moment the door slammed shut, black tinted windows would camouflage me. He wouldn't be able to see me move.

Once that driver's-side door shut, I opened my eyes and lifted the blindfold. Just enough to see that he was walking around the car to the rear.

I pulled it down again.

But silence followed. He didn't open the rear hatch.

Then I heard it again. That thump and rattle. Like metal on metal. But it wasn't beneath the car, it was behind it.

It wasn't wise to disobey him. I didn't know how much time I had. But I had to take the chance.

I lifted the blindfold and whipped my head around to look out the rear glass.

A trailer was attached to the back of the vehicle, hauling a small tractor on top. Deluca crouched down beside it, fiddling with a tiedown.

Heartbeats. That was all I had, and it was all I needed.

Carefully, I released my seatbelt, looking over my shoulder to make sure he was still kneeling beside the trailer, and stretched for the dashboard. He had a playlist open through a music application. I clicked the home button, then the navigation, and the dropped pin of my current location appeared.

That's how I got the coordinates. I recited them to memory as if my life depended on it. Suppose it did.

At least, I hope it did.

Repeating them aloud to myself a time or two, I clicked back to the music and carefully sat back down so he wouldn't see the vehicle shift from my movements inside.

As he continued to fiddle with the trailer, I repeated those numbers a thousand times, praying I didn't mess one of them up. I'm still praying I didn't mess one of them up.

Until he opened the door on my right, I repeated those numbers over and over in a whisper. I recited them again in my mind.

He said to get out.

I did.

Holding my elbow, he guided me to the trunk. Another beep of the vehicle. I heard the struts on the lift as the hatchback raised. A rush of heat from inside the cabin floated toward me.

Deluca yanked my blindfold down.

There, sprawled out in the trunk, laying atop a blue tarp, was the girl I'd seen in the basement. Her pale skin was now as blue as her eyes, her lips no different. They were parted, as though she had gasped for breath in her final moments. One of her eyes was still swollen shut, now with a big red slit across it, as though all the pressure inside had ripped the skin apart. The other couldn't get any wider. Her eyelashes reached her eyebrows.

That single blue eye stared at me with hate. Hate that I hadn't helped her. Hate that I'd known what was happening to her and did nothing.

I pinched my own eyes shut, spinning to look the other way.

"Look at her!" Deluca grabbed the back of my head. He shoved me toward her. "Look at her, damn it!"

I did.

I did, and I saw my future. I saw my fate. No longer did I see the hate she must've felt for me as she was tortured to death in that cell.

When I looked at her now, I saw where I would soon be.

"This will be you," he said, as though he could read my thoughts. "Show them sympathy again, and it will be you."

Them.

I held my breath. If I didn't, I would cry. I would not let him see me cry. I told myself I'd never let him see me cry again, but that would prove to be a lie.

In that moment, it was for me. Keeping my pain inside was for me.

"I tell you to do something, and you damn well do it, Daisy." He yanked my head back, wild brown eyes burning into mine. "You understand me?"

Somehow, I managed to hold on to my composure. "Yes, sir."

"Good. Now help me load her into the bucket."

The bucket of the tractor. The very thing he would soon use to dig a hole and dump her into.

He wouldn't even carry her to the grave himself.

But he made it clear. If I didn't do as he said, I would be next.

So I helped him load her into the bucket.

Soon, the nurse would chastise him for that. At my stage of pregnancy, I shouldn't have been lifting anything more than fifty pounds.

At least the woman had given me that much.

While he dug the girl's grave, he made me sit beside her in the grass. It couldn't have been less than forty degrees outside. I had a hoodie, and I was in sweatpants, but I had never felt so cold in my life.

Sitting in that soil, watching him dig her grave, unable to look at that innocent young woman, I lost all hope. For the first time, those bedsheets, the ones Deluca kept padlocked shut, sounded rather appealing wrapped around my neck.

I wanted to scream, I wanted to cry, I wanted to run, but I could do none of those things. I was frozen atop that grass, just as the dead woman beside me was.

Going on, continuing to live, felt useless.

A fight with Deluca would have ended it all. But it wouldn't come quick. It would last seven days. That's how long it took for this woman. Seven days of physical torture were not something I could endure. If he blew my brains out, I would've accepted that fate. I sat as he buried her and watched as he arranged her in the grave. I watched as he pulled something from his pocket and tightened it between her palms. He kissed her forehead.

He treated that corpse exactly how he treated me.

Once he emptied the dirt back into the grave, he told me to sit in the car while he put the tractor back on the trailer. I sat then too, not moving a muscle.

I didn't lift the blindfold on the way back to the oasis. Instead, I watched those numbers play out against the back of my eyelids. I repeated them from the moment I sat motionless in the car to the moment he took me back to my room.

It was dusk by then. I smelled food cooking downstairs. I wasn't hungry, and I dreaded the moment he'd arrive at my door for dinner.

I wrote the numbers into the carpet beneath my bed. It was only carpet. There was no pen nearby. But forgetting those numbers would be forgetting the only bit of hope I had left. Even if I didn't have it now, I needed to cling to a time when I did.

When Deluca arrived at my door, he knocked. That was the first time he'd done this. Not once had he knocked before.

"I'm sure you're tired," Deluca said. "I know I am. But you haven't had a real meal all week. You need to eat."

He said it like I was the one holding the key.

"I—I am hungry," I said. I wasn't, but I was trying to be cooperative.

The sound of the keys in the door.

It swung open.

A plate of steaming food atop a box wrapped in shiny red wrapping paper.

Deluca gave an almost meek smile as he walked across the room to me. Like he had seven days ago, he sat on the carpet. "Homemade pizza."

"I—it—it smells good," I managed to get out. That wasn't what I wanted to say. But it was like my mind and body worked as two separate entities now. "Thank you."

"Open your present first." He lifted the plate of pizza onto the carpet and set the box wrapped in red paper onto my lap. "I really think you're gonna like it."

With shaking fingers, I opened it.

A laptop. I'd always liked Bella's Mac operating system. This was a weird, off brand, bottom barrel, basic computer. A glance at it told me so.

Which was so ironic. He showered me with expensive lingerie and silk robes, but the one area I would've appreciated a nice gift, the one thing that I would've wanted the most, was a decent laptop. Instead, he gave me the glitchy piece of shit I am writing on now.

"This way, you can write your stories faster," he said, voice teaming with excitement. "Do you like it?"

It was like someone else possessed my body. I was smiling, telling him how much I loved it, how appreciative I was, how grateful I was for how well he treated me.

My hands were still shaking, but my voice didn't. I sounded sincere.

It worked.

Until that moment, he had no trust in me. When he gave me that laptop, something shifted. It was like he realized now that I was under his complete control.

What he didn't know was that he gave me what I hope will be my way out.

In the box, along with the laptop, was a flash drive. A bonus gift, of sorts. A bonus gift I hope you're reading, Maddie.

Because even if you don't find me, I hope someone knows my story. I hope someone knows what happened to me. I hope I'm not a distant memory. I hope everyone I knew didn't forget me. I hope telling my story will help you find this bastard so that he never does it to anyone else.

That flash drive, it was one of the only two things that gave me hope since I arrived here. Those coordinates and the flash drive were the only reasons, before my daughter was born, that I didn't tear that sheet apart and hang myself from the doorknob with it.

Chapter 23

The post office was within our line of sight. Just another few blocks down the road. The sign for it was all we could see so far.

I hoped like hell we'd get our answer in there.

For now, for those last few blocks, I paused the narration.

Like I had when I finished the last chapter, all I could do was stare out the window. There was a lump in my throat, a few tears in my eyes, but I had hope. This wasn't over yet.

I prayed this wasn't over yet.

"How much is left?" Harper broke the silence.

Another block down the road now.

"A chapter, I think," I said.

She shook her head. "But there's so many more questions."

"Daisy didn't write this to answer our questions." Face screwed up, I swiveled to see her better. "This wasn't about us. Don't you get that?"

"She just said she wanted us to find Deluca."

"Of course she does. She gave us all the hints she could," I said. "But the story isn't about him. It was never about *him*. She wrote it so that, if she doesn't make it out, her story will. To prevent another little girl from thinking that her golden ticket in life is a man who might pay her way while killing everything she has inside of her."

Again, Harper quieted.

Over the years, she'd made a habit of saying I was cold and distant. That wasn't fair. It wasn't true either.

I felt immeasurable empathy for the wronged, for the injustices faced by those less fortunate. Never would I truly understand their pain, not unless I endured exactly what they did. But at least I understood that it wasn't about the villain.

He was the bogeyman. The monster was never the protagonist.

Only a few dozen yards from the entrance of the post office now, I unclipped my seatbelt. The building was like every other small-town business. Four walls of brick, nestled between a doughnut shop and an antique store. A big blue drop box sat beside the glass doors. A green awning perched over the doors, a nice contrast against the red brick.

Torres tore into the parking space before the front door. All the others nearby were taken.

"Let me out here and meet me inside?" I asked.

Harper agreed, slowing to a halt in front of the entrance. I stepped out, opened the rear door for Tempest, and thanked God for the rush of adrenaline that numbed the pain in my knee.

Torres was already walking to the front door.

Managing a slow jog, I caught the handle before it swung shut. Tempest waited for me to pull it open for her, and in we went. At the white Formica countertop, Torres rang the metal bell repeatedly. While I walked that way, sneakers squeaking on the linoleum, he didn't stop tapping that bell.

"Did you call Gayton on the way here?" I asked.

"Yep. They're on their way." Squinting behind the counter, then down the hall, Torres kept tapping the bell. "Learn anything new from the journal?"

"Just that the laptop and flash drive were gifts he gave her," I said. No one was around, but I still lowered my voice. "That girl, the one in the basement, he made Daisy help him dispose of her body; she had to sit beside the grave while he dug it. That's also when she got the burial location. She memorized the coordinates from the navigation screen of his car."

"Just a minute!" The voice carried from the far left of the counter where a door led to the back of the building.

"If the DA doesn't insist on capital punishment for this one, one of us is gonna have to do it ourselves," Torres said under his breath, still tapping the bell.

Couldn't say I disagreed with that one.

"Nothing else?" he asked.

"Nothing that will help us find him," I said. "Just her explaining what she went through."

"At least she's got a concrete report written for us already."

"Amen."

A woman came through the doorway at the end of the counter. Mid-thirties to forties, blonde with a few grays sprinkled throughout. She wore a blue shirt with a USPS label and a name tag that said Kathy. Her blue eyes narrowed at first but widened when she saw Torres in his uniform.

"Is there something I can help you with, sir?" she asked, approaching the counter.

"I need the address of one of your PO box owners," he said. "Salvatore Deangelo."

Blinking with confusion, she looked from him, to me, down to Tempest. "I—I'm sorry, but I don't know if I can do that without a warrant."

"Are you the manager?" Torres asked.

"No, but—"

"Then get them on the phone. Now."

"She's on vacation right now, and she—"

"We are investigating the murders of dozens of innocent women. We have good reason to believe this man is responsible. Also that he is holding a twenty-one-year-old girl and her three-month-old baby hostage. So we can do this the easy way, or we can do this the hard way." He let the words hang in the air for a moment. "Get your manager on the phone."

Kathy opened her mouth to respond, but her cheeks were a bit flushed, and nothing left her lips.

"Now." Torres leaned over the counter. "*Quickly*."

Kathy nodded, unblinking, and scampered off back the way she had come from.

A gust of wind blew in behind me. Gayton walked through the door, a bit winded. "We got a location yet?"

"Not yet," I said. "Your analyst couldn't find anything?"

"Working on it, but this is probably faster," she said. "Did you get anything else from the journal?"

I rehashed it all, ending with, "So this is our best hope."

"Then why do you look like that?" Gayton asked.

"Look like what?"

"Like you're already mourning," she said, eyes flicking carefully over my face. "Do you know something I don't?"

"What? No. Of course not." Aside from the anonymous friend's text message. But I wasn't legally obligated to share any tips I received anonymously.

"You had hope last night," she said. "You look defeated now. What's going on in that head of yours?"

Shaking my head, I bit my lip. "I just think we're missing something."

"Like what?"

"Something we've seen already, but didn't tie to the case."

"When did you start feeling like that?"

"She—she approved it," Kathy said, powerwalking to her computer on the other end of the counter. "She just asked that you give her a call later to go over the details. If there's any paperwork she needs to sign off on, I mean."

"Will do," Torres said. "How long is it going to take to pull that up?"

Kathy tapped away on the keyboard, eyes racing around the screen. "Not long. I just have to go into our PO box registry, then—Salvatore Deangelo. Got it." The printer beside her hummed. "Looks like he lives at 1234 Nature View. It's on the ridge—"

"Let's go." Torres had already spun around and was reaching for the door handle.

I was slow, but not far behind.

Chapter 24

Thirty-one minutes.

That was all the time it'd taken. The GPS said thirty-one minutes to Deangelo's home.

Now I understood Daisy's hatred for the Wi-Fi. All along, the tether she'd needed to the outside world was right there floating around her. It was practically within arm's reach. But she didn't have the password. The one piece of information she needed to access it.

The same way that, until we found that PO box, we didn't have that one piece we needed.

At least, that was what my rational mind said.

One piece of evidence. That was all we were missing. We had it now. We were headed there. We were on our way to save her, to save them both.

So what was that feeling in the pit of my stomach?

Racing through the vegetation-covered backroads, flying sixty miles an hour in a thirty mile an hour zone, I should have been full of hope. I should have been bursting at the seams with it.

On any other case, I would have. At this point, on the precipice of justice and freedom, I was usually riding the adrenaline high. I knew we were close, and we were about to solve it. The answers we were looking forward to were right around the corner.

The adrenaline was different this time. Not because it was Daisy. Not because of my personal connection through Bentley.

Even when Eric had taken Grace, I hadn't felt like this.

In that investigation, I had flipped every stone. I'd known I wasn't going to catch him until he'd wanted us to. I had done all I could.

This was different. I was missing something. What the hell was I missing? Why did I know, as we peeled tire onto Nature Drive, that I had missed something?

"You coming in, Castle?" Torres asked in the driver's seat.

I was in the back with Tempest. Harper was up front. Her car wasn't equipped for as fast as we were tearing up this mountainside.

"I'd like to," I said. "As long as you're cool with that."

"That's where I want you," he said, touching thirty miles an hour on the gravel road. "You bringing in the dog?"

"I can after we clear it," I said. "No use in bringing her in immediately."

"It's a plan," he said. "You get any further in that book?"

"No, sir."

"You're telling me we had a twenty-minute drive, and you weren't reading the whole time? Like you have been since you found the damn thing?"

"That's what I'm telling you."

"Why is that?"

Because I had a bad feeling. Because while I read the journal, I got to know her. I cared for her now. There was one chapter left, and when I finished it, there may never be another new word written by Daisy Miller.

"Just trying to brainstorm our entry," I said instead. "If this is the place Daisy described, we should go in the front door, but we need someone to cover the cellar and the rear doors."

"Where do you want me?" Harper asked.

"Us three, we're taking front," he said. "Phillips and Gayton are getting the rear. Martin and one of my guys are getting the cellar door."

"Hopefully he doesn't have someone down there," Harper said. "You secure the warrant?"

"Judge is working on it, but as long as Daisy was telling the truth, and there are bars on the windows—"

"Qualifies as plain view," I said. So long as there was enough evidence of a serious crime to raise suspicion, we could legally go in without a warrant. "Not worried that's going to interfere with the trial?"

"The latest victim, Jane," Torres said. "During the autopsy, they found DNA. Semen, to be exact. We match it to him, and nothing else matters. We're going to get this guy."

I hoped. God, I hoped.

"You do a deep dive on him yet, Mads?" Harper asked.

"Salvatore Deangelo?" I asked. She nodded. "No. I ran a quick search, but no social media popped up. I could've found more, but I have no signal."

"With an eyewitness, they won't need much for a conviction."

"They're going to do everything in their power to discredit her," I said, shaking my head. "She's got a record. A drug problem. Really, there's no concrete proof that he was holding her hostage. Just her word against his. We have to prepare ourselves for the possibility that a judge will throw out everything she says. Even if they don't, we still need physical evidence. So yeah, that semen inside the strangled corpse is going to be important."

"The guy's gotten away with murder before," Torres said. "Eyewitness account wasn't enough. As it is right now, we don't even have enough for an arrest warrant. We're hoping to see something bad enough that we can pull him in for, then build the case and get a warrant."

"That's going to be another thing we should arrange as soon as we get Daisy," I said. "She's going to need protection. Otherwise he's going to do to her what he did to the witness in the Palmer case."

"We'll cross that bridge when we get to it." Torres's shoulders broadened with a deep breath. A clearing appeared ahead. "This might be the house. Once we get Daisy and the kid to safety, then we worry with the trial."

If there would even be a trial.

I pushed that thought from my mind as quick as it came. As worried as I was, it wouldn't help me find her.

Craning around to see between the driver and passenger seat, the clearing came into full view. The field like Daisy had described. That was all I could see for now. Only the field. Every bump of the vehicle, every breath I took, seemed to move in slow motion. It was right there, only a few dozen yards ahead, yet still felt so far away.

Ascending through the aperture of foliage, I rehashed every moment in this case from start to finish.

Bentley told me Daisy had disappeared. I discovered her fictional writings. One of them featured Mr. Deluca, a sexy, older man she'd met while dancing, and he'd offered her the world. The story ended with the two of them running away together.

Next came the poem. Bird in a Cage.

He called her his bird because of his obsession with the woman who started it all. Rowan Palmer adored Edgar Allan Poe, particularly *The Raven*. Deangelo had nicknamed Rowan "Raven," and she'd nicknamed him, "Crow." She'd gotten pregnant with their kid, decided she was going to get rid of it, and he'd killed both her and his unborn child.

Daisy's experience with Deangelo mirrored Rowan's. They were both smart girls from bad backgrounds, they both loved poetry and language arts, and they both got pregnant with Deangelo's kid. Killing Rowan had most likely been an accident. But he'd enjoyed it and continued to do it, replicating the *events* of his first love, as well as the *woman* he'd first loved.

He kept Daisy alive because she was a good replacement for Rowan. Daisy gave him the child and family he had wanted with her. She had also been a "project" of his, taking her out of her life of drugs and prostitution, and promising her so much more.

What was I missing? I was missing something, damn it, but what the hell was it?

Maybe Harper was right. Maybe I was too close to it. Because now, after rehashing the case, I kept clinging to Daisy. I kept clinging to the emotion, and I was falling away from the fact.

There was a fact in here somewhere that I was overlooking.

She was a damn good writer though, because this was exactly what I imagined.

A white Victorian, perched high in a circle of grass, surrounded by trees and rolling hills that stretch on for miles. Stone stairs lined the way to the big, blue door. Beside it was a wall of windows with a two-by-eight stretch of stained glass, displaying a hummingbird flying through a field.

Even the turret was exactly what I'd expected. Including the bars that lined the windows.

"Looks like the place," Torres said.

It did.

So why was my stomach in knots?

Only a couple of yards from the front door, Torres slammed the car into park. Scratching Tempest's head, I told her, "Stay."

She froze in place.

Torres and Harper were out of the car before me. I was right behind them. The moment I closed the door, I released the safety on my gun. Holding it out before me, muzzle aimed at the ground, I walked slowly behind them. Torres took the lead, Harper at his flank, and I stayed at hers.

I heard the others arriving, saw them in the corner of my eye walking around the house, but I kept my eye on that blue door. I glanced up at the bars on the window, then steadied my gaze on the door again.

We stayed in those exact positions. Only when Gayton, and then

Martin, sounded over Torres's radio clipped to his breast pocket, did we advance.

"Police!" Torres called, banging on the frame. "Salvatore Deangelo, come out with your hands above your head."

Silence.

He rapped on the door once more.

Still silent.

"Mr. Deangelo, if you don't come to the door right now, we're gonna have to take it down."

When no response came, he checked the handle. Locked.

Torres lifted his walkie-talkie from his chest. "No one's answering. We gotta go in."

Did the bars on the window justify this? The court could decide when and if Deangelo decided to sue.

* * *

Over the next ten minutes, six officers came to the door with a battering ram. A few pounds of it later, and the door swung open.

The place was pristine. Exactly as Daisy described it. White oak floors. High-end luxury sofas. Carefully sourced artwork. A cozy kitchen with old but refinished cabinetry.

Down the hall from the kitchen was the master bedroom. The same dressers Daisy described. The same view into the bathroom from the bed. The same skylight. The same camera pulsating in the corner of the room.

Up the winding staircase that Daisy described in detail were half a dozen doors. Two of them were padlocked shut. We knocked on the door, we called for Daisy, and only silence sounded. With a pair of bolt cutters, we went into those rooms as well.

Exactly how Daisy described. The bed was bolted to the wall. White carpet. Pink walls. Closets with the metal racks and drawers removed. Even the same settee around the turret.

The only difference was the cradle. Instead of only women's clothes in the closet, there were stacks of diapers, onesies, sleepers, baby blankets, even cans of formula.

In the bedroom across the hall, there was a powder room, just as Daisy said there would be. Another bed, this one also bolted to the wall. Instead of a cradle, just a small bassinet on wheels. A few cases of water. Some protein powder. A closet full of snacks. All labeled as GMO and preservative free, of course.

And don't forget the bars on the windows.

The basement? Also how Daisy described. A cement room, half quartered off with steel bars. Beyond those steel bars was a metal table. Forensics quickly found traces of blood all over it.

Was it Daisy's?

No idea yet. DNA would take at least a week to come back.

Standing in the living room, watching the forensics team sweep every inch of the place, I crossed my arms and nibbled my lip.

"This doesn't mean she's gone for good," Harper said at my side. "We know he takes her out in public. It was only a week ago when he last took her to the library, right?"

I nodded. "Something like that."

"All the cop cars are up here by the house," she said. "Torres has one of his guys watching in the woods. If anyone pulls up this driveway, we're getting them."

I took a deep breath and shook my nose. "He's gone, Harper."

"You don't know that," she said. "The big mystery all along was his name. We have that now. We're gonna find him."

I wished I could believe that.

I wished I could respond to Bentley's text, asking how my day was going.

I wished it weren't over. But damn it, he ran. He ran and forced her to come along.

Or it was her blood in the basement.

Across the room, Torres's eyes met mine. He was speaking with another officer but frowned at me. He gave the other man a pat on the shoulder and headed my way. "Find anything?"

"Just exactly what Daisy told me I'd find," I said. "You?"

"There's an APB out on his car," Torres said. "Working on getting roadblocks up all over the county."

"That's not gonna make a difference if they left two hours ago. Two hours from Virginia, only three from New Jersey and Maryland."

"I'm sure he has already contacted all the neighboring states," Harper said.

"I have." Torres pressed his lips together. "We've got a shit ton of evidence now though. The padlocks on the doors, the jail cell in the basement. We catch this guy, there's no way in hell we aren't getting a conviction."

"He's evaded the authorities for decades." I squinted at that hummingbird. "If he figured out we were coming two hours ago, then he's long gone, and we're never going to see him again." I looked between Harper and Torres, both their frowns staring back at me. "We need to get into the security camera in the bedroom. It's the only one I've seen, but it can give us a timeline of how long they've been gone."

"I'll go talk to Gayton," Harper said. "We'll get a tech on that."

If not for the fact that all the other cops were already here, I would've gotten Dylan on it. He would've worked faster.

"If we find out that he left only thirty-five minutes ago," Torres said, giving a half smile, "you gonna cheer up?"

He wasn't trying to be an asshole. I knew that.

He spoke without thought. I opened my mouth to say that I wouldn't "cheer up" until Daisy and her baby were both safe, followed by some other choice words.

But before I could speak, the walkie-talkie on his chest beat me to it. "Sarge, we've got the car."

My heart skipped.

Torres lifted the radio to his mouth. "Black Mercedes SUV, license plate B as in boat—"

"You are breaking—" Static. "—sir. It's the car." Static. "Dropping you—location."

Torres was already racing to the door, and I was like a bat out of hell behind him.

"Do you have the girl, Anders?" Torres was usually faster than me, but the high of adrenaline numbed any pain in my knee. "Where's the baby? Do you have the baby?"

"No, sir, no baby." The man on the other end—Anders, apparently—sounded clear now that we were out of the house. "The girl—It don't look good."

Chapter 25

Grace hadn't liked the look on her dad's face yesterday. The way Maddie had run out of the hotel room this morning wasn't much better.

What if it didn't turn out okay? What if she and Maddie were wrong? What if, for a second time—for the last time—Grace would lose Daisy?

She didn't want that to be true, but didn't she have to be prepared for it? Especially after reading Daisy's letter.

Mostly, it was full of sweet things. How much Daisy loved Grace, how grateful she was that Grace had cracked her code, sweet little anecdotes about her little niece. Cousin, technically, but Grace would think of her as her niece.

In the last paragraph, though, Daisy told Grace that as much as she wanted to come home, if she didn't, Grace needed to cling to her father. The whole paragraph, she talked about how miserable she had made Bentley's life. The ways she'd harmed Grace, even if Grace hadn't realized it at the time.

That letter should have given Grace hope. Or closure in the worst-case scenario. When she'd finished it, though, she just kept thinking about the last few months. How angry she'd been at Bentley for things that were not all his fault. The way she'd blamed him for Daisy's disappearance, for moving on so quickly.

Lying on that pullout bed while Bentley tiptoed to the coffeemaker in the kitchen, Grace's heart grew heavy.

Bella's death had shattered him. Taking care of Daisy, fighting to keep her, to protect her from the system, had been a failed attempt to put himself back together. Daisy's disappearance? Well, it was his final straw.

Bentley was a sensitive guy. Grace knew that. If he hadn't had Grace, would he even be alive? The pain of those tragedies back-to-back had to have been paralyzing for him. All he had left was Grace.

And she'd been nothing but cruel to him for months.

She didn't even know why.

Although she had been awake for hours now, she finally sat up in the bed, yawning dramatically.

"I'm sorry, kid," Bentley said. "I didn't mean to wake you up."

"It's okay." She stretched her arms all the way into the air. "What time is it?"

"One, I think." He pressed the button on the coffee machine, and the lid popped back up. Cursing under his breath, he tried again, only to have the same outcome. "Late, I know that."

"Looks like that's giving you some trouble," she said, stepping from the bed.

"I don't get it. I don't get why everybody has to be so fancy with a damn coffee maker." He shut the lid down again, only for it to swing back up once more. "The old-fashioned ones work just fine. Water in the back, grounds in the filter, press on. There you go. You got coffee."

Grace laughed. "Okay, boomer."

He shot her a look over his shoulder. "I'm a millennial."

"Not much better." She propped her hands on her hips, giving a teasing smile. "I saw a cool coffee shop down the street when we were on our way in. Want to just go there? Maybe get lunch or something?"

Accepting his defeat with the coffeemaker, he arched a brow at Grace. "Wow. You want to go out with *me*? I'm honored."

"Poke fun, and I'll rescind my offer."

Bentley walked past her and roughed up her hair. "Let me get dressed."

* * *

Since the coffee shop was only a few blocks from the hotel, Grace and Bentley walked. While they did, they talked. It was the first time in a long time that they had talked.

Of course, they spoke to one another every day, but this was different. It felt like it used to. They talked about how, even though there were plenty of hills around here, it wasn't nearly as mountainous as back home. Grace had grown up in Ohio, but she liked the mountains better. Bentley said he did too. It was nice to be able to see for miles, but there was something cozy about being tucked between two mountain peaks.

They talked about the electives Grace was going to take this year. For the first time, she had the option to take a cooking class. It was only for one semester, but she was excited about it. She knew, of course, that she would ace the class because she had far more experience in the kitchen than the average eighth-grader, but it would be fun. An easy class.

When they made it to the coffee shop, they talked about the artwork that hung on the walls. Most of it was modern abstract. Bentley hated modern abstract. He explained that, in his opinion, it was pretentious and wasteful. Artists used to spend years, decades, perfecting their technique and drawing the perfect human face. Art existed to mirror what people were incapable of documenting any other way. After all, they didn't have cameras back then.

"Art exists because *people* exist," Grace said, sipping her caramel macchiato. "Yeah, rich people had their portraits painted so the generations that came after them would know what they looked like, but artists make art because of who *they* are. Even if that painting doesn't make sense to you, it made sense to the artist."

Bentley only smiled at her.

Grace's brows furrowed. "What?"

Still smiling, he shook his head.

"Are you making fun of me?" She wiped the edge of her lip. "Is there something in my teeth?"

"No," Bentley said. "It's just weird. Watching you grow up. You have your own head, and now you're forming your own opinions, and it's weird. Cool, but weird."

"Well, yeah, that's usually what happens. It's not like I could stay a little kid forever."

"I used to wish that you would." He spun his spoon through his black coffee. "Not so much these days."

"No? Why not?"

"Little kids, they're fun and everything." Bentley shrugged. "But the older you get, the more unique you get. The smarter you get." He stared down at his coffee cup a moment. "And the more like your mom you're getting."

Grace didn't know why, but anytime anyone said that, it embarrassed her. Not because she didn't want to be compared to her mom. That was the greatest compliment. But because it made her feel stupid. She hardly remembered her mom, and without the same source material, how was she supposed to participate in the conversation?

All she could think to say was, "Yeah? How so?"

"This whole conversation." Bentley laughed and pointed at the white canvas, covered in blue paint splatters. It matched the theme of this coffee shop, but he saw no artistic depth to it. "Me and your mom, when we were in college, we went to an art museum. She kept showing me pieces of art that she loved, and a lot of them looked like that. And eventually, I just said it. I didn't see stuff like that as art. A toddler could do it. And she said almost the exact same thing you just did."

That, Grace remembered. Most of the memories Grace had of her mom were painting together, or drawing, or singing, or dancing. She didn't remember much else, but she remembered all of that very clearly. "Really?"

"Really. Her coffee order was the same as yours too. Large caramel macchiato with extra caramel, extra milk, and extra vanilla."

Grace didn't remember that one bit. Such a silly thing, really, but it made Grace's heart warm. "You're kidding."

"Nope. Exact same order." He arched a brow at her. "And when did you start drinking coffee anyway?"

"When Maddie got me some."

A half laugh. "Of course she did."

"Have you heard from her today?" Grace asked. "I know she left this morning, but I didn't even get to talk to her last night."

Lips flapping together in a trill, Bentley shook his head. "Not yet. But she told me that was probably gonna be the case. They have a lot going on. A lot of leads that they're looking into. She's just really busy. But once she has something, she'll call."

A lump thickened in Grace's throat. "What if she doesn't?"

"I made sure to plug in her portable charger last night," he said with a smirk. "Her phone's not dying on us this time."

"No, I mean—" Grace's voice cracked. She cleared it away before she continued. "What if she doesn't find her? What if he realizes we're close and kills her, Dad?"

There went Bentley's smile. His lighthearted, silly tone vanished just as quickly. "Don't think like that, kid."

"We should be prepared for it though, right? I mean, it's not like this is a simple case. It's a mess. The whole thing is a mess, and they're chasing a bunch of leads that are barely that. The only evidence they have so far are the bodies, and—"

"Grace—"

"I'm just saying, Dad." Grace frowned. "It's possible. We might not ever see her again. And if we don't, that's not your fault."

He had opened his mouth to respond, but now, he cocked his head to the side with confusion.

"I was angry about the way you handled things," Grace admitted, "but then I read her letter. And I don't know. I just—it's not your fault. I realize that now. And it's not Daisy's fault either. Whoever did this, this Deluca guy, it's his fault. It's not yours, and it's not mine, and I'm not gonna blame either of us for it anymore. I'm sorry I've been such a bitch to you lately. You don't deserve that."

He frowned. "Language."

Grace narrowed her eyes. "Way to ruin a moment."

Bentley tried to smile, but it didn't reach his eyes. "I hear you, kid. And I appreciate it. I get it. You've been through a lot, and considering it all, I can't blame you. But thank you. Thank you for saying all that."

On the table between them, Bentley's phone dinged. Grace squinted at it just before he grabbed it. A text from Maddie.

We think we found her, but she's not doing good.

Chapter 26

Two Hours Ago

Daisy's heart had been in her throat since she'd put that flash drive in the library bathroom ceiling.

It was a typical morning. Daisy slept in her bed, waking periodically when the baby fussed in the cradle. Once she got her back to sleep, she lay back down. Shortly after sunrise, Deluca came to the door with her tea. He moved her to the bedroom across the hall, where she drank the tea while the baby slept. Then she did as she always did with him.

Afterward, they lay in bed watching the birds outside the window. He pointed out a piping plover this morning, then explained little details about its flight patterns and breeding rituals that Daisy couldn't begin to remember now.

Sometimes, Deluca offered valuable information. She learned a thing or two from him.

But most of the time, he was a pompous prick with his head up his ass. When he talked for an hour about a bird, with such authority and knowledge, as though the rest of the world were idiots for not understanding its intricacies, she just nodded along. It wasn't like he really cared to hear her opinions anyway.

She was just relieved that their routine was back to normal. Relieved, and disgusted with herself for feeling it.

It had only been a handful of weeks since he'd killed Jane.

That's why he was back to normal.

In another month and a half, maybe two, he would be less than agreeable again. She'd have to tiptoe around every move he made, every word he spoke.

She would try to keep him happy, try to keep him calm, so that he wouldn't kill again, but it would make no difference. He would always kill again.

After their time in bed, Daisy woke the baby and got her ready for the day. A bath in the kitchen sink, followed by a gentle combing of her little black hairs, some lotion, a fresh diaper, a onesie, a pair of pants, and a little cardigan.

It was nearly ninety degrees outside. The baby did not need so much clothing. But that was how Deluca wanted her to look. Always perfect, always pristine. That was how she looked in the bouncer at Daisy's feet while she continued writing the sequel of *Moonlit Whispers* from the sofa.

Bella was a beautiful baby, with big blue eyes trimmed in thick lashes, chubby cheeks, and perfect red lips against her ivory skin. Feature by feature, she didn't look much like Grace, yet Bella reminded Daisy so much of her little cousin.

Daisy remembered when Grace was this age. She'd practically lived in a diaper with just a sleeper because of how frequently three-month-olds peed and pooped. It was just about useless to dress them because of how frequently they needed to be *un*dressed.

Deluca clearly had never been around a baby in his life. He never wanted to see a booger beneath her nose, a dribble of milk on her chin, or a drool covered bib. That was the purpose of the bib. To catch the drool.

So when Daisy noticed it was wet again, she set her laptop on the couch cushion, grabbed another bib from the diaper bag beside her, and switched them out.

Behind her, Deluca's phone rang.

He kept it on him every moment they walked around the house, but never when they lay in bed. He fell asleep in bed sometimes. That would give Daisy the opportunity to grab it and call 911.

She could think of a thousand times she'd debated grabbing it from his jeans pocket, but never did. She simply gritted her teeth when she heard him answer it. Which was seldom. He had strong feelings against them. This generation was too reliant on their phones, blah blah blah. Not to mention the radio waves that were interfering with our brains.

It took everything Daisy had not to roll her eyes at that. Maybe there was some truth to it, but if he was so worried, why did he still carry one? Or was he unbothered, and the tirade about their dangerous nature was just a way to justify why she wasn't allowed one? If she'd asked, that was what he would say. They both knew the real answer, but he would claim it was to protect her.

The hypocrisy of that statement was not lost on Daisy.

"Hey, I was just thinking about you," he said in a casual, content tone. "What's going—" A pause. "What? How?"

That lump in Daisy's throat thickened.

Was this it? Had someone found her? Had someone found *him*?

"The library—Ah, shit."

Daisy's stomach turned. She looked at him in the reflection of the windows. Her eyes dare not meet his. They'd give her away. If he didn't know already, he would know the moment he looked at her.

Matching the thump of his footsteps, he paced the kitchen. His hand was in his hair. Breaths short, uneven, he spared her a glance, then nodded quickly.

"Okay. Okay, yeah. We'll meet at the cemetery, you guys take Bella, and we'll meet back up next week when things die down."

What?

Daisy lifted Bella from the bouncer. She brought her close to her chest, practically holding her breath.

No. No way in hell was anyone taking this baby. Not Deluca, not whoever he was on the phone with. Daisy would die first. She would kill herself, kill them both, before she let this baby go.

Perhaps it sounded extreme, but she couldn't allow it. She could not let this man raise her baby. That was why she took the risk. That was why she'd left the flash drive in the ceiling. She knew it might get her killed, but it was her baby's one chance at a normal life. Bella's only opportunity to get away from the monster who shared her DNA.

"Yeah, okay," Deluca said. "It's gonna take me at least an hour to get there, but I'll see you soon."

He stomped toward the sofa. Daisy had the baby in her arms, but she still braced for an impact. He'd never hurt her while she held their child. She hoped that wouldn't change now.

He only grabbed the diaper bag, shoving every toy and diaper he saw within arm's reach into it. "Get your shoes on."

Out in the world. That was her best shot. If they were attempting to do an exchange of some kind in public, she'd have a chance to get away.

She hoped. Dear God, she hoped.

* * *

For the first time in all the time she had been with Deluca, he left her unattended in the living room. He never left her unattended there. She could run.

She didn't run. Where would she run to? The car? The one he was about to lead her into anyway? The one *he* had keys for?

She had no keys. She had nowhere to run.

She only sat there in the living room with her baby in her arms, staring out the window, preparing for what came next.

At a cemetery, Deluca would hand Daisy's child to someone she did not know. Or perhaps to the nurse. The one who had assisted in Bella's delivery and all of Daisy's prenatal care.

Aside from the women he'd killed, that was the only person Daisy knew was close to Deluca. It was the only person she'd seen him make physical contact with. But he was gone often. He would leave for an hour or two in the morning, maybe an hour or two in the afternoon, whenever he liked. She never knew where he went. Not unless he came back with a victim.

It had to be the nurse.

Right?

If it was the nurse, she could make a run for it. If it was the nurse, Daisy could fight her. If it was the nurse and Deluca, Daisy could...

Daisy didn't know what she could do.

Threatening to hurt Bella, that might be enough for him to let her go. Maybe.

But she couldn't do that. She couldn't threaten to hurt her own child.

If she had to though, if she had to risk Bella's life for the possibility of a better one, then she had to.

He came down a few moments later, duffel bag dangling from his shoulder. With panic in his eyes, he told her to get the baby in the car. She did. No blindfold this time. It was the first time they got in the car, and she didn't wear a blindfold.

Deluca came out heartbeats later, started the car, and didn't even buckle his seatbelt before he tore down the driveway. Didn't check that she and Bella were strapped in either.

He flew faster down that driveway than he ever had before. Daisy hadn't known what it would look like, but she imagined it was something like this. A gravel road surrounded by trees and foliage. She kept waiting for a street sign, or an identifying marker of some kind. None came. He didn't even notice she was looking.

Every two seconds, he picked up his phone and checked it again. Cursing under his breath, he slammed his fist into the steering wheel.

Daisy winced.

The baby cried.

"Where the hell is her bottle?" he snapped.

"I'm getting it, sir," Daisy said, voice sheepish.

She stretched for the diaper bag at her feet. A bottle of water, the powdered mix, and the bottle itself. Assembling it, glancing out the window, she waited. She waited to see something. Some sign of hope. Instead, only the mouth of gravel emptying onto a strip of asphalt.

The baby kept screaming. As Daisy shook the bottle, she only screamed louder.

She couldn't think. Daisy couldn't think.

This was the best opportunity she'd ever had. Someone knew. Maddie, Daisy hoped. Bentley and Grace, they knew she was alive, and they were looking for her.

That had to be what was happening. Someone around town had recognized Daisy, and they named Deluca. They were headed to his home. That's why they were tearing out of here so suddenly.

It had to be.

It had taken Daisy months to develop this plan. It had taken her months to find some semblance of hope. She could not let this slip away.

No one was taking her daughter. She could not let them take her daughter. Even if, as Deluca said, they would reunite in a week or so once things calmed down, that was the very problem. If Daisy disappeared with this man again, she may never have another opportunity.

She was so close to freedom. She could see it now. Her eyes were uncovered. The blindfold was gone. She could see hope. She could see life again.

She couldn't just sit here, feeding the baby in the backseat, waiting for this bastard to rip her away.

But what could she do at this moment?

As they drove faster through the winding, wooded back roads, she searched for a street sign. A business. Someone she could roll down the window for or break the glass and shimmy out the window to.

But for miles and miles, at least fifteen minutes of driving, there was none of that. A handful of homes, spread too far apart for her to access, even if she were to break out of the car.

How the hell was she going to get out of the car?

For another ten minutes, totaling somewhere between twenty and thirty since they'd left the house, her mind spun over that very question.

Her only opportunity to get out was now.

A few moments before, Bella's eyes had drifted shut. Deluca was still checking his phone. For what, Daisy didn't know, but what the hell did that matter?

He was distracted. In the year Daisy had known him, in the year he had made her life a living hell, she had never seen him distracted. She had never gotten an opportunity to escape.

Judging by how fast they were whipping around the bends, Daisy knew they had to be going at least fifty miles an hour. Maybe close to sixty.

She needed him to slow down.

Swallowing that lump in her throat, she found more courage than she knew she had. "Where–where are we going?"

"If you needed to know, I'd tell you."

"But I heard what you said," Daisy managed, voice cracking over every word. "Who was that? Who are you giving Bella to?"

"It's none of your god damned business, Daisy." He shot her a look in the rearview mirror. More of a warning than a simple expression. "She's my daughter, and I'll do as I damn well see fit."

Looking at her in the rearview mirror, he slowed the car. Just a bit. Maybe thirty to forty miles an hour instead of fifty to sixty.

It was working.

Daisy grabbed the nylon belt between Bella's legs and pulled.

Her eyes fluttered open.

Daisy wanted to apologize. She knew it was tight. She knew it probably hurt.

But it was their only shot. This was their only shot.

Edging back into the seat, Daisy clicked her seatbelt into place. "She's my baby. She's not leaving my side."

"Excuse me?" He turned. He turned just in time to see Daisy fastening the center belt tight at her waist. The car slowed, no more than thirty miles an hour now. Daisy was sure of it. "Keep on. Keep arguing with me, and—"

Daisy lunged forward. The seatbelt kept her range limited, but hopefully would save her life. Daisy prayed like hell it would save her life.

She wrapped her fingers around the back of his head.

He screamed. Profanities, at first, telling her to stop.

Bet he's regretting that he likes my nails so long now, she thought.

She tore deep into his cheeks.

He stretched up to push her hands away, to free himself from her grasp.

But to no avail. When he got one hand away, she only dug the other nails in deeper.

And she rejoiced in it. She rejoiced in the sounds of his screams, his pain, his terror.

She may die. Everyone in this car could soon die. Daisy knew that. Daisy didn't want to die herself, or to kill her daughter, but she would not let someone take her baby away. She would not let Bella grow up with this monster as a father. She'd rather they all die than sentence her baby to the same hell she had endured.

When Deluca shoved her hand away again, and Daisy's hand returned to his face, something wet and mushy sloshed beneath her fingernail, like dipping a spoon into a cup of jello.

He screamed louder than ever before.

The car spun.

Tires squealed.

Daisy smiled.

Bang!

Chapter 27

PAIN.

Pain ripped through Daisy's head. Sharp and aching and throbbing all at once.

Screaming.

No, crying. The baby was crying.

Daisy's head hurt so badly she couldn't open her eyes. When she tried to, something seeped into them. Hot and sticky. The faintest glimmer of daylight, and then red.

Banging. Thumping. Someone, or something, was thumping beside her head. A voice. An unfamiliar voice.

"Are you okay?" Another thump. "I can't get the door open. Are you okay?"

Lifting her eyes was like lifting a tank. With enough effort, she managed.

Through the tinted glass, a figure became clear. A man in a red flannel with wide eyes. He smacked on the cracked window a few more times, nodding as Daisy gripped the door for stability. "There you go. Help's on the way. Just stay put. Just..."

His voice faded into the background as Daisy turned her stiff, aching neck toward the front seat.

Groaning, Deluca grasped the steering wheel for stability, then the seatbelt that held him in place. She could only see his profile. Just enough to spot the blood rolling down his cheek.

But he was moving. He was alive.

She needed to get out. She needed to get out while he was injured, because she wouldn't have another chance.

She stretched across the back seat for Bella. Despite the glass that coated her fuzzy pink blanket, there wasn't so much as a nick on her. She squealed and squealed, but no blood drained from her skin.

Freedom was so close, Daisy could taste it.

She turned to look at the man who had been at the window, but he was gone now.

Daisy's heart dropped.

With shaking, aching hands, she unclasped the baby's straps. The ones that buckled at her chest, the ones that buckled at her groin, and lifted the baby into her arms. Her arms were weak, throbbing, but she had her baby, and the rear passenger window was shattered. Remnants stayed between the frame, but with the baby in her arms, climbing into the car seat, she almost had enough leverage to reach the door handle from the outside.

The child locks were enabled. They could only be opened from the outside.

Glass scratched her forearm as she stretched farther. Deluca was moving but only shifting as he groaned and grumbled. She had enough time to get out of the car. If she could just grab the handle, if she could just pull it open, if she could just—

She got it.

The rear passenger door clicked open.

Holding the baby in her right arm, keeping the door handle open with her left, she lifted her knee. Pain ripped through it, but she didn't stop. Not until she shimmied it the rest of the way open.

"Help's coming, sir," that unfamiliar voice said.

"No," was the only word Daisy could speak.

Daisy was already dropping out of the car, cradling the baby close to her chest.

Her shoulder smacked pavement.

Her stomach ached. She looked at the baby. She was still crying, screaming, but nuzzled close to Daisy's chest. The impact of falling from the car jarred her, but she was okay. The car seat had kept her safe. That was the hope Daisy needed to cling to.

"Shit, are you okay?" That unfamiliar man again. He was getting closer, extending a hand to help her. "The 911 operator—she said to stay where you were. She said—"

"Run," Daisy said, struggling to sit forward. When she couldn't, when her back proved too weak, she extended her child to him. It was all she could think to do. "Run."

"What?" He didn't accept the child. He reached, instead, for her hand. Daisy took it, shaking her head furiously, no matter the pain that ripped down her arms when she did. "The ambulance is going to be here soon. Just—"

"We need to run." She gripped the child tighter, yanking the man's hand until he was only inches from her face. "We *have* to run!"

Face screwed up in confusion, he gestured behind her. "Let's sit in my car until help gets here, okay?"

Daisy looked behind her, taking in the crash site, the road they'd been driving on, for the first time. To her right was a cliffside, stretching high toward a mountaintop. To the left, a patch of trees, framed by grass and bushes. That's where she stood, on a patch of grass torn apart by the SUVs' tire tracks. A large strip of concrete with two yellow lines down the middle. Half a dozen yards back, a blue Honda Civic parked facing the crashed SUV with its hazard lights blinking.

That blue car, that was freedom. "We need to go. We need to—"

Thunk!

The hand holding hers slammed downward.

Daisy swung back around.

The nice man in the flannel lay at her feet.

Behind him stood Daisy's worst nightmare. Deluca holding a large piece of metal. A crowbar, an ax, she couldn't be sure. Thousands of scratches lined his cheeks. His left eye, or what remained of it, rather, hung against his cheek, eyelid practically swollen shut.

No matter how much it had all hurt a moment ago, her body was electric now. She spun around, and she ran. Quickly, quicker than she thought she could. Her only chance at freedom was that car.

That man, he'd said the cops were on their way. Deluca had only hit him in the head. He would be okay. Maybe he would be okay.

She prayed he would be okay.

Every footstep was like an earthquake pounding in her ears. If she could reach that car, if only she could reach that car—

A yank of her hair.

She collapsed backward.

The air siphoned from her lungs.

She opened her mouth, attempting to breathe in, attempting to stay alive, but no breath came. It was like someone put a cap on her lungs. No air was coming in, none was going out, and pain ripped up her spine, through her limbs.

But her arms were still locked around the child. Bella screamed, wailing for help, for comfort, but Daisy couldn't breathe.

And then he was there.

He was over her, reaching for the baby.

Daisy gasped in a breath and clamped the child closer to her chest. She used all the strength she had to roll toward the side, but he grabbed her wrist. He yanked her arm from the child's back.

Daisy screamed. Words, perhaps. Profanities, probably. She didn't know. She didn't know what left her lips, only that she would not go down quietly. She would not let him steal the baby from her arms and—

He grabbed her. He grabbed Bella from Daisy's forearm.

A strength unlike anything Daisy could ever imagine she possessed washed over her in a wave. She was on her knees in heartbeats, grabbing Deluca's leg. She used it as leverage to stand. Something bonked her in the cheek, but she didn't stop. Even when he whaled her with it again, and again, she advanced, reaching desperately for the baby in his arms. She couldn't register what he was saying, how bloody she was, how beaten she was.

All she could think was that he had her baby, and this couldn't be for nothing. She hadn't taken such a risk, she hadn't gouged his eye out, for nothing. This could not be for nothing.

The baby's eyes were on Daisy.

That hunk of metal intercepted her view.

Daisy ducked.

From this angle, crouched beneath Deluca, she did all she could think to do. She slammed her fist into his groin.

He only grunted.

Then it was flashes. That piece of metal, slamming into her face, then her arm, then her stomach. She was on the ground again, and all that strength had vanished. She lay sprawled on the concrete, helpless, watching that same hate in his only remaining eye as he plunged his foot into her stomach, into her chest. On his hip, curled against his chest, wrapped in that fuzzy pink blanket, squealing in terror, Bella must've felt the same hopelessness.

It was Daisy's job.

Protecting Bella was Daisy's job.

The risk Daisy had taken was for her. For the life that Bella would never know. It was for safety, and normalcy, and that was gone now.

All Daisy had wanted was to protect her daughter.

She had failed.

Chapter 28

SHE WAS ALIVE, SHE WAS INJURED, AND SHE WAS HYSTERICAL.

That was all the information we had for the thirty-minute drive to the site of the accident. Paramedics were en route, and four officers were on site. None of them could give us good information about Daisy's state. Probably because they were busy trying to calm her down.

From what we gathered in the chaos over the radio, Deangelo wrecked his SUV, a bystander called 911 and tried to help, only for Deangelo to knock him unconscious and get away with the baby.

As soon as we figured out that much, I asked Torres if I could contact Bentley. He was our best shot at getting her to calm down long enough to explain what happened. Torres agreed. Bentley was meeting us there, Grace would stay in the car, and Torres told his officers not to let him in until we arrived.

The roadblock had traffic backed up half a mile. With the siren and lights on, we whizzed by them all.

The site was what I'd imagined.

Deangelo's SUV was wrapped around a tree off the winding, forest-covered road. That SUV was the reason they'd all survived. Cars like that were tanks.

Sunlight barely trickled through the dense foliage overhead. Flares and cones quartered off a fifty-foot radius. A cruiser blocked the road in each direction. An officer on each side of the road leaned into every vehicle in the fast-forming lines, likely informing them to turn around and go a different way.

Daisy wasn't in my line of sight when I hopped from Torres's cruiser and jogged toward the SUV. But her screams were what led me to her.

Only context clues confirmed she was Daisy. She didn't look much like the girl in the photos. She didn't look like much of anyone. Swelling and bruises obscured most of her face. Blood flowed from a gash down her hairline. More dribbled from her lip, dousing most of her pink top and black yoga pants.

Hugging her knees, she rocked back and forth in the mud beside the totaled vehicle.

Officer Grant, the first cop assigned to this case, the one who was at my side when I'd unearthed the field of bones, sat beside her on the ground. He was a foot or two away, speaking softly in her direction. She just kept rocking back and forth, sobbing.

When Grant saw me, his shoulders dropped with relief. We exchanged a look. Mine said, *I got this*. His said, *Thank God*.

With Tempest at my side, I approached slowly. Her head was pressed toward her knees. The sobs didn't cease until I sat before her. With her ears back, Tempest sat beside me.

"Daisy?" I asked. "I'm Maddie. Bentley'll be here soon."

Still whimpering, she looked up. I could barely make out her left eye through the swelling, but it was enough for me to know that we were looking at one another. That was all she gave me. Just a bit of eye contact.

"Do you know who I am?" I asked.

She nodded.

"Do you know where you are?" I asked.

Her bottom lip, nearly the size of a sausage, quivered. "Somewhere in Central Pennsylvania?"

"About an hour out of Lancaster," I said softly. "The paramedics are on their way. They're going to take you to the nearest hospital and run some—"

"I don't care about me!" she screamed. "I need my baby. He took my baby. I need to find my baby!"

"I'm going to." Although I expected her to shove me away, I reached out for her hand, and she grabbed mine. She squeezed, and I squeezed back. "I'm gonna find her, and I'm gonna bring her to you in the hospital. Okay?"

Stifling a sob with her free hand, she nodded.

"Okay. But I need you to tell me everything you remember first. Can you do that?"

Daisy swatted a tear away, then grimaced at the pain it must've caused. "I don't know."

"That's okay. Let's just walk through it together, alright?" I stroked my thumb over the back of hers. "You were at the house this morning, weren't you? Deluca's house."

Another nod. "Someone called him. He packed a bag, and he got us in the car."

A partner?

Until now, we had no reason to think there was a partner. This wasn't enough to confirm one. Someone in town may have called after they heard about the field we uncovered.

"Did you hear who was talking?" I asked. "Do you know what he said to them?"

"That we'd meet at a cemetery, they'd take Bella, and we'd meet with them next week after things die down." A sob escaped at the end of that sentence. "It couldn't be for nothing. That flash drive, the story, all that work. It couldn't be for nothing."

I was already piecing the puzzle together. "You fought back?"

Daisy nodded. "He was distracted. He kept checking his phone. I was in the backseat, and I talked back to him. It was enough to get him to slow down, to turn around and look at me. I tightened Bella's car seat, and I attacked him. I think I gouged one of his eyes out."

I wanted to smile. I wanted to tell her she was a badass, because she was. "You caused the wreck."

Another nod. "That man, the one in the flannel. I woke up when he was tapping on the window. I got Bella out of her car seat, and I stuck my arm out the window to open the door from the outside, and I jumped out. I told him. I told that guy that we needed to run. But he didn't listen, and Deluca got out, and he hit him in the head. I tried to run to the guy's car, but Deluca caught up with me. We fought, and I fell down, and he got the baby. And I don't remember anything else. Just him kicking me." Her eyes came to mine. "That man. Is he alive?"

"In and out of consciousness, but yeah." I managed a smile. "The person he was on the phone with. Could it have been the nurse?"

"Maybe?" She wiped some snot from her nose. "I didn't hear them. I don't know if it was a man or woman."

"Has the baby ever been away from you?"

Daisy shook her head. "Not once since she was born. Except for at the library. He took her that day."

So there was no one we could look at who had a history with the child.

"I'm allowed to be here!" Bentley's voice. "They told me to come!"

Daisy and I both looked in that direction.

"That your boyfriend?" Torres called from somewhere behind me.

"Yeah, that's him," I said.

"Let him through."

Bentley appeared around the edge of the cruiser to my left. He ran as fast as he could to us. Daisy started to stand, but I ushered her back down. Given how badly she was beaten, it was best that she didn't move more than necessary until she had some scans done.

Tears covered his face. Even at full speed, all but gasping for air, a smile came to the corners of his lips. A sob accompanied it.

He dropped to his knees beside her, and she collapsed into his chest. The heaving, heart wrenching sobs resumed.

"I'm so sorry," she said between cries. "I'm sorry. I'm so sorry. I'm so—"

"Shh," Bentley murmured, holding her tightly around her waist. He soothed his free hand over her head, letting her muffle her screams into his chest. "There's nothing to be sorry for."

She kept weeping.

It wasn't going to stop. Not until they got their reunion. Not until she came to grips with the fact that this was real. Not until she realized she was safe.

* * *

While Bentley soothed Daisy, Torres, Gayton, Martin, Phillips, and I discussed our next moves. Standing a few dozen strides from Bentley and Daisy, I went over all the missing pieces, first in my mind, and then verbally.

"We need a list of all the cemeteries nearby," I said. "If we can figure out where Deangelo's parents were buried, that is the first place we should look at."

"They may have changed rendezvous locations now," Martin said. "He knows we have Daisy. He knows she heard him say that was where they were headed."

"Why *did* he leave Daisy?" Gayton said, folding her arms. "He could've strangled her. Would've only taken a couple seconds."

"He was holding the baby while he was beating her," I said. "Literally, he didn't have the hands to strangle her."

"But why not load her into the vehicle?" Torres asked. "Maybe because he was injured too? He wasn't strong enough to lift her?"

"She also gouged his eye out," I said. "Doubt you're thinking clearly after that. Even beating her, that's not his usual MO. He strangles. And if you're asking if he thought Daisy was somehow to blame for this, no, I don't think so. Whatever info he got was connected to Daisy, enough that he knew he needed to run with her, but not enough for him to realize she informed on him. But she did egg him on in the car. She caused the accident."

"He lost his temper," Gayton agreed. "Probably heard the sirens coming. He didn't have time to finish her off, or he thought she was already dead, so he loads into the good Samaritan's vehicle and runs."

"If he is still in that car, and he's trying to get out of the county, he won't," Torres said. "I got roadblocks up everywhere. Every way in and out of this county is sealed."

"He knows he's not getting far in a stolen vehicle," I agreed.

"He's not getting far with one eye either," Phillips said. "The only way he's getting out of here is with help. We should be informing every hospital in the area though. He's going to need medical attention."

"Unless he's relying on that nurse," I said.

"That brings us back to whoever called him," Gayton said. She glanced behind me at Bentley and Daisy. "She knows more than she thinks she does. We really need to get back in there. Between the scans at the hospital, and surgeries she might need for any damage he caused, we're not going to have many more opportunities to talk to her."

"What about his phone?" I asked, dodging the question. "Have your analysts tracked it down? There's no way for us to find out who he was talking to?"

"It's going to take hours at least, maybe days, to get any information from the service provider," Phillips said. "Have we swept the car? Top to bottom? If it's still in there, we can try to figure out who he was talking to."

"The front end's smashed in," Torres said. "But we'll do another once over."

"You never responded to what I just said, Castle." Gayton arched her brow at me. "We need to ask the girl more questions."

"What else is there to ask? At the bare minimum, she's got a concussion. But she's just been through something traumatizing and now her baby's missing. The girl's in shock. She can't process even half of what we're saying right now."

"She might know where he could've gone," Gayton replied, not unkindly. "If she has any idea what cemetery he might've been going to. Any and everyone else she's had contact with while in his custody."

"If you've got questions for her—"

"You've already got the rapport," Gayton said. "I can go over there and ask the questions, but she's going to answer better to you. She trusts you because *he* trusts you." She nodded toward Bentley, still sitting on the ground beside Daisy. "If you want me to be the one to interrupt that though, I will."

The point she was making was valid.

I raised my hands in surrender. "Alright. Let's go talk to her."

"I'll lead the questions, but you ask them," Gayton said.

"I'm gonna try to track down the cemetery," Martin said.

"And I'll help look for the phone," Phillips said.

Tempest was to my right, and Gayton was at my flank as we walked across the pavement. Daisy was calmer now. I hadn't heard her scream once since she and Bentley embraced one another. Now they sat cross-legged, facing each other. Bentley must've felt my gaze on him, because he looked up as we drew closer.

"The paramedics should be here any minute now," I said, keeping my voice soft as I joined them in the grass. I stretched my leg out behind Bentley to ease the throbbing in my knee. "We were hoping we could ask you a few more questions while we wait, if that's okay."

Sniffling, Daisy glanced at Gayton, then nodded to me. "Yeah, sure."

"Do you have any idea which cemetery he might've been talking about?" I asked. "Are there any cemeteries he goes to often? Maybe where his parents are buried?"

"He does go to visit their grave on Sundays," she said. "But every time I have been in the car with him, he keeps me blindfolded. He had me come with him a few times. He always puts roses on his mom's grave. But I never saw the name of the place."

"Was anyone else ever nearby?" Gayton asked.

"When he was visiting the grave, she means," I said. "Someone you saw several times, even if you never spoke to them."

She shook her head. "Never. I saw a groundskeeper a couple times, but he never paid us much mind." She used the inside of her shirt to wipe some more snot from her nose. "The only person I ever saw him talk to in any depth was the nurse."

"And you saw her weekly throughout your pregnancy, right?" I asked. "She was around frequently."

"Monthly in the early parts. When I was further along, yeah, weekly," Daisy said. "I don't think I know anything valuable. Everything I've gathered that might help you find out who he was, I gave you in the journal. I don't know much of anything. I don't even think I know his real name."

"Salvatore Deangelo," I told her. "That's his real name."

Her lip quivered. Swallowing hard, she swiped another tear away.

"Does that name mean something to you?" Gayton asked.

Daisy shook her head. "Never heard it in my life. It's just weird to finally know."

I could only imagine.

"Did he ever mention a place you guys would go to if things went awry?" I asked. "Did he ever fantasize about traveling somewhere with you?"

"Or the baby," Gayton said. "Maybe a place he went when he was young? Somewhere special to him?"

"I don't think you guys get it." There was an edge to Daisy's voice now. "You know how in the beginning of a relationship, everything is superficial? You talk about the way one another looks, and how you make each other feel? That's how Deluca—Deangelo is. That's how our relationship has always been. I opened up about my dreams and my desires, but he never did. He just tried to make me *feel* desired. Desired and controlled. He wanted me to know that I was his. He talked to me the way you talk to your pet. '*Oh, you're so beautiful. Wow, look at the weather today. I guess we won't be going for a walk.*' In his eyes, I'm not a person. No, he never told me about things that were special to him. He never told me much of anything. That's how we wound up here."

"But he took you to visit his parents' grave," Gayton said, her brows furrowing in confusion. "That might seem small, but—"

"He took his *daughter* to visit his parents' grave." No denying the attitude in Daisy's voice now. "It wasn't about me. It was never about me. I'm nothing to him. I take care of his baby. That's why he kept me alive."

She was wrong. I didn't need a profile to tell me that.

In his own sick and twisted way, Deangelo or Deluca or whatever his name was, loved Daisy. Mostly because he loved Rowan, and Daisy was a good surrogate for her. But the fact remained. I agreed with Gayton. Deep in Daisy's psyche, she knew things we didn't.

That feeling, though, the one I'd been having for the past few hours, was gone now. Maybe deep in my subconscious mind, I'd known he had a partner. Maybe that was why I felt more at ease now. Because it was confirmed.

When did you start feeling like that? Gayton's earlier question reverberated through my mind.

"Victoria," I murmured.

"What?" Daisy asked.

"Victoria," I repeated. "That girl. The one you saw at parks and community gatherings."

Daisy's face was so swollen, it was hard to make out any micro-expressions. Still, I could tell she was offended. "She's just some girl. She's not working with him. She would never. She's a mom, and all she cares about are her kids. She wouldn't—"

"No, of course not. I know she has nothing to do with all this," I said. "But she let you use her login that day in the library. You trust her, right?"

"Well, yeah. As much as I trust any woman with a bunch of kids," Daisy said. "It's a lot easier to trust a mother than it is to trust a random man."

"But you just used her login," I said. "You could've called her into the bathroom with you. You could've passed her a note and said he was gonna be back soon, and that he was going to take you and hold you captive. I know you don't have Stockholm's. You wouldn't have left the flash drive in the ceiling of the library if you did. You were trying to get out. So why didn't you ask her for help?"

Daisy blinked a few times, then slumped her shoulders. "I don't know."

"You do." I made sure to soften my voice as I said that, placing my hand over hers again. "He said something, or he did something, and it made you afraid to ask anyone for help. It couldn't have just been about the baby, because you're smart. You know there are ways around that. If you had told the librarian you needed help, to call the police, you would've made sure that the baby was in your arms before anyone approached him." I kept my gaze soft as I asked her, "So what did he say?"

Tears gathered in her one good eye. Her voice cracked when she said, "That he had eyes everywhere. If I told anyone, he'd know, and he'd run with Bella, and I'd never see her again."

"We've met him." I looked up at Gayton, my breath hitched in my chest. "It was one of the witnesses at the library. One of the witnesses tipped him off. That's his partner."

Chapter 29

SAM HADN'T WORKED ALL WEEK.

In construction, that was common enough. It depended on when his supervisor needed him at a location, how many guys he needed at any given time, or whether he needed work at all. Last week, they had finished up a big job. His boss had told him he wouldn't need him again until next week.

Yesterday, he had needed that free day. Today, he didn't.

But he had a feeling.

After Bentley asked him to look into Nathaniel Cooper, he had the suspicion he'd get another call. The only way that Maddie could work this case to her usual excellence was if she could be in two places at once. And if she had the same moral compass as her father.

The thing was, at her core, Maddie was better than Sam. Although she was happy to criticize faults in the justice system, she still did her best to work within it. Whether because she had too much to lose if she broke the law, or because a part of her was and would always be a cop, Sam wasn't sure. But that was irrelevant.

Sam had become privy to a case of high stakes. Innocent women murdered en masse. One of whom was still missing, along with her infant daughter.

That and that alone would've gotten him emotionally invested.

But this was for Bentley.

The man his daughter loved. The man who came from so little and had become so much. The man who had given his baby girl hope and compassion while growing up in a household filled with such hate.

The man Sam had known as a little boy, who always took care of everyone else, and so seldom took care of himself.

Sam would not, *could not*, let this bastard who'd caused so much pain get away. Just as he couldn't have let Russell game the system nearly thirty years ago.

So he had stayed close.

Rather than return home after his questionable interview with Nathaniel Cooper, Sam had rented a hotel room near the Sunset Stay. Using a fake ID, of course. As much as Sam had hoped he could return to a life of civility after his release from prison, he knew he was put on this earth for reason. To do good in a world so wrong. No matter how nefarious his methods.

Although he'd paid his debt to the Russell family, he always feared they would come back for vengeance. No honor among thieves and all that. Sam wanted to be prepared in case he needed to run. He still had some connections from back in the day. That was where he'd gotten the fake ID.

Just so happened that the first time he would use that fake ID was to keep a close eye on the place he imagined this monster would use as a rendezvous, as a shield, when Maddie got close on his tail.

He couldn't see the motel out his hotel window or anything like that. It was a few miles down the road. But every hour, on the hour, he drove by the Sunset Stay.

An hour ago, he'd done so. This morning, there had been half a dozen cars parked out back. In contrast to this morning, the last time he had driven by, there were none. Just as Nathaniel said, no other cars were parked when The Crow was coming.

Sam had worried that Nathaniel told The Crow about their meeting. That it was a trap. That Sam would watch for him to arrive and when he did, and Sam barged in, Crow would make Sam his next victim.

It was still a possibility Sam braced for.

But Sam wasn't afraid of this man.

Sam had heard Maddie talk about him for months. He was weak. A privileged, spineless prick who lured young, vulnerable, unarmed women to their torturous, cruel demise.

He doubted the man had ever been in a fair fight. He doubted he knew what the words meant.

What Sam knew for certain was that Crow would stand no chance.

After tying his boots, Sam rolled his neck from left to right. The clock read 2:53 PM. Sunset Stay's check-in for an overnight was 3. It was time he made his hourly round.

He stood, checking himself in the mirror. With the heavy jacket over his shoulders and black baseball cap pulled down over his face, he was almost certain he wouldn't be recognized on any security cameras. A blue surgical mask laying on the dresser was the final piece to his disguise. How convenient a pandemic had been.

Just as he tucked the mask around his ears, completing his look, the burner phone he'd texted Maddie on rang in his pocket. He pulled it out. Although he didn't add names to his contacts, he was good with numbers. Prison had taught him that. By heart, he knew the numbers of everyone close to him. This one was Bentley.

Sam answered. "What's going on, kid?"

"They found her." Bentley breathed out the words like a sigh of relief. "He beat her up pretty bad, but we've got her."

Sam's shoulders softened with relief. "She's okay?"

"I don't know. She was responsive and the paramedics are loading her into the ambulance now. They're worried about internal bleeding. I am too." He paused. "More than anything, I'm worried about how she's going to do mentally. We have no idea where the baby is. He ran with her."

Sam's heart picked up speed. It took a lot of effort to relax his gritted teeth. "Any idea where he could've gone?"

"Not really. But I was thinking about that motel," Bentley said. "The FBI, they can't even prove that the Sunset Stay is the place he took her that night. But Maddie said she got a tip from an anonymous number. I'm guessing that was you, so you were right."

"And you're thinking he might show up at the motel. That makes sense," Sam said, as though he weren't already dressed to return to that very parking lot.

"Yeah. And I thought about mentioning it to them," Bentley said, lowering his voice. "But they don't think he could've gotten out of the county. I don't believe that. This guy's been getting away with murder for decades. He had a backup plan, and I'm ninety-nine percent sure it's that motel."

"So the cops aren't checking it out?" Sam asked, starting for the door. Once in the hallway, he kept his head down, avoiding eye contact with any of the security cameras. "And you want me to?"

"I wouldn't ask that."

'Course not. Bentley never asked anything of anyone.

"But if you could keep an eye out," Bentley said, "if you see him, call the local cops. That would help a lot. If you're nearby, anyway."

"Yeah, I'll keep my eyes open," Sam said. "Any idea what car he might be driving? Or identifying features?"

"His face is pretty screwed up. Daisy scratched the shit out of him," Bentley said. "She thinks she messed up his eye pretty good. He might be wearing a covering over it. No idea what car though. Could be a little blue Honda Civic, but we think he's probably jacked a new one on his way."

"Got it," Sam said. "I'll let Maddie know if I find anything. Just remember what I told you. This is between us."

Before Bentley could respond, Sam ended the call.

Chapter 30

There were six witnesses from the library. We already had each of their names. We knew none of the women were the nurse because Daisy would've recognized her. That didn't rule out every possibility. One of them could have been connected to Deluca in some other way.

But the FBI analyst Gayton spoke with looked at the men first. It took her all of a minute and a half to determine that one of them was married to a labor and delivery nurse, Pamela Hudson. Wife of Douglas Hudson. The older man who was abnormally fit for his age. The house I was at when I got that odd feeling that we were missing something. The first witness I'd questioned with Harper and Torres.

In mere heartbeats, Gayton had an image of Pamela's driver's license on her phone. The paramedics were loading Daisy onto a gurney when we jogged to her, flashing her the photo.

"Is this her?" Gayton asked. "Is this the nurse who helped Deangelo hold you captive?"

Jaw dropping open, Daisy nodded slowly. "That's—that's her."

"Thank you," Gayton told her. Holding the phone to her ear, she spun around and called to Torres. "We need a search warrant for any and all properties belonging to Douglas and Pamela Hudson."

They hollered back to one another, heading to Torres's vehicle. With Tempest at my side, I spun around to join them.

But Daisy said, "Maddie."

Time was of the essence, but she was the top priority. She was the reason for this case. I turned back around. "Yeah?"

Daisy sat forward on the gurney, waving off the paramedic who tried to edge her back down. "How did you find her?"

"Her husband was at the library with you last week," I said. "Best assumption is that she and her husband were both working with Deangelo."

Daisy blinked hard in disbelief, shaking her head. "Why the hell did she do it?"

"We don't know yet." I frowned. "But my best guess is that she is maybe a distant relative or family friend. We're gonna do more digging, and I'm gonna let you know everything I find. But they might have your daughter. I gotta get going."

"Okay. Okay, thank you. But they"—she gestured to the paramedics around her—"said Grace can't ride in here with us. I don't want to be alone right now, but Bentley can't leave her, and—"

"I'll see if an officer can drive Grace down to the hospital and meet you there. How's that sound?"

Daisy forced a smile. "That'd be great. Thank you."

I gave her a smile back. "Hang in there."

"Castle!" Torres called, head tilted out the window of his cruiser. "Are we leaving you here, or are you gonna pick up the pace?"

I limped as fast as I could to his SUV with Tempest at my side. "Don't you dare leave without me."

* * *

In the movies, they never showed this part. The waiting. The drive. Every moment trickled by as we raced as fast as we could, knowing an innocent child's life was on the line.

It was a thirty-five-minute drive from the site of the accident to the Hudson home. We trimmed it down to twenty-five with the lights on, but the fact was unavoidable. Every cop and FBI agent here was all but speechless.

I did my best to find as much information as I could on Doug and Pamela while we drove, but they were from a different generation. While I found Doug's Facebook, I couldn't even be certain it was his. He had a bald eagle as his profile photo and all his settings were private. I couldn't even see his birthday.

My typical Google search amounted to little as well. We already had his address. That's where we were headed.

With nothing else immediately available, I texted Dylan.

We've got the missing girl, and we got a name. Salvatore Deangelo. You can stop looking into the other stuff. But he ran with the baby. We think he has a partner, but no idea how they're connected. Any chance you can try to find one? Other guy's name is Doug Hudson. Accomplice is his wife, Pamela Hudson.

Heartbeats later, Dylan replied, *On it.*

I did learn that Doug owned a construction company as well as a junkyard.

Which cast a wave of chills up my spine.

I had worked a murder case once. Technically, Ox had worked the case. I'd just assisted.

We knew for almost certain that the construction worker had killed his girlfriend. She had cheated, he was the last one she was seen with, and he was twice her size. Motive, means, and opportunity.

After securing a warrant, we searched every inch of his home and vehicle. Sure enough, found blood spatters in the bed of his truck. But no body.

The DA offered him a plea deal. Tell us where her body was, and they'd lower the first-degree murder charge to second. He agreed.

Then he explained that he chopped her body up in a woodchipper, mixed the remnants with cement, and laid the cement as the foundation of one of his customers' homes. We wound up tearing apart that concrete, only to find bone chips.

There was only one other profession so great at getting rid of a body. Morticians with access to an incinerator.

No matter what, we had the wife, Pamela. But what did we have her on? Accessory to kidnapping?

And we couldn't prove a damn thing about Douglas. Based on the size of his home, and his two successful businesses, he would be able to afford a good lawyer. We could try to charge him with accessory to any or all of Deangelo's crimes, but we had no evidence.

No part of me wanted to think the worst. But Deangelo was good. Incredibly good at being disgustingly bad.

When Deangelo had killed Rowan, Doug would've been in his forties. Had he been the reason Deangelo got away with it? Had Deangelo shown up at his friend's door, begging for his help with the body in the trunk?

Did they, together, kill these women?

All the bodies we collected with a year or less of decomposition were Deangelo's victims alone. We knew that because Daisy had witnessed the murders.

But then again, *did* we know that?

Daisy had been locked away on the second floor while Deangelo was in the cellar. She'd heard the girls screaming for help, and she'd heard Deangelo yell at them to be quiet, but no one's voice was quite the same when they yelled as when they spoke. It was possible that she'd heard not only Deangelo in that basement, but also Hudson.

We had no evidence to support that theory. Proving so would be damn near impossible.

But why else? Why else would Doug have helped Deangelo? Why else would his wife?

Was it possible that Deangelo had kept Daisy with the hope that, one day, she would be as loyal to him as Pamela was to Hudson?

"What if she's got Stockholm's?" I blurted.

Torres glanced at me in the rearview mirror. "What?"

"The nurse," I said. "Pamela. What if that's why Deangelo kept Daisy? Because his old family friend, Doug, was just as disgusting as he is."

"I'm not following," Torres said. "We only got another two minutes till we get to the Hudson house, so make it quick, Castle."

"1994." I stretched forward, leaning against the passenger seat to get a better look at Torres. "Deangelo kills Rowan. We're probably gonna find her body soon in the field. If we haven't already."

"Right," Torres said.

"But the murder was executed perfectly," I said. "Most of the time when someone kills, they screw it up. They leave evidence. Deangelo didn't leave any. He even went back for the neighbor."

"Okay, I'm following you now."

"A first-time killer, someone who does it in a blind rage, they're not going to be that smart covering it up. But someone experienced will know exactly how to pick up the pieces. If Deangelo had shown at the door of a killer with a body in the trunk, asking for help, the killer would've told him to make sure to bury her far from where she disappeared."

"If they didn't have access to an incinerator," Torres said.

"Right. Would've told him to get rid of any witnesses too. Like the neighbor who turned up missing."

Torres squinted, gazing out the windshield. "You think Doug taught him how to do it?"

"Why else would he help him?" I asked. "With a single murder, sure. Plenty of people would help a loved one or close friend cover up a blind-rage killing. But why help him hold Daisy hostage? Why have his wife help too?

Getting one person to help cover up a murder, that's gonna be hard enough. Getting two people, one of whom is a woman with no direct relation to the killer? That would be a hell of a lot harder. Add child abduction into the mix, and I just can't see it. I just can't see why they would do this unless Deangelo is Hudson's protégé."

"And his plan all along was to get Daisy to be as compliant as Pamela. He'd seen it done before, so he knew he could replicate it with another girl." Torres rubbed a hand over his forehead. "Shit. This is so screwed up."

"With another girl, it may have worked," I said. "But Daisy's been in and out of the system her whole life. She was in sex work before she was even an adult. It was her only means of survival. She learned to act. She learned to manipulate, because she wouldn't make it on the streets if she didn't. That ability to manipulate men saved her life a thousand times. Just like it did today. I have the feeling Pamela doesn't have that same background."

"My God." Torres ran a hand down his beard, shifting the car into park outside Doug and Pamela's home. No lights were on, and the car that had been parked out front earlier was gone. "Bounce it off the FBI after the raid. We gotta find some evidence before we can try to get this guy for murder charges too."

I planned to do just that.

Giving Tempest one last scratch, I opened the rear door.

As soon as my feet hit the concrete, my phone buzzed in my pocket. Agents and officers flocked all around me, heading for the door.

They didn't need me on the front lines.

I grabbed my phone to check the notification.

That same 814 number from earlier.

An attachment. A drop pin of a location with a message that said, *That's where they're keeping the baby. Bring cadaver dogs.*

—A friend

My face went cold. No way. No damn way did this guy have information this vital without somehow being connected to the case.

Chaos sounded at the front door. The same chaos we'd caused at Deangelo's home. Telling them to come out with their hands above their head, insisting if they didn't that we were coming in, then the sound of the battering ram slamming against the front door.

I typed back, *Who the hell are you?*

The icon to signify that they were typing back showed up immediately.

A friend.

Friend of Deangelo's?

A friend of yours.

Before I could type back, another text came through.

This address belongs to Pamela's mother. She's in a care home. Pamela manages the property. Look it up. It'll check out.

Will this number check out if I have my tech guy look at it?

It's a burner, so probably not. You take the credit. Don't tell the feds about me.

If you tell me where you got this information, I won't.

Wasn't sure if I would hold true to my word on that one, but it was worth a shot.

It's better you don't know the details. Just make sure the girl knows that this bastard's never going to come after her or her baby again.

That *this* bastard.

Whoever they were, they were with Deangelo right now. They'd found him. And they'd gotten this information out of him.

Another text.

If I'm wrong, let me know. I don't think I'm wrong though.

They were torturing him. They were holding Deangelo captive and torturing him, just as he had done to all the women in that field.

And I didn't feel an ounce of sympathy for what Deangelo was enduring if that was the case. I wasn't certain, *couldn't* be certain, but it was the only thing that made sense.

I'd never say so aloud, but I was damn grateful for it.

Daisy didn't deserve to sit through a trial for months on end, detailing all of the abuse she'd endured at his hands. Deangelo didn't deserve a trial. He didn't deserve a possibility of freedom. Bella didn't deserve a father like him.

Half of me considered calling Simeon and asking if he'd had anything to do with this. No guarantee he'd answer honestly. One thing I was certain of: he'd agree it was best I didn't know.

Maybe my "friend" was right. Maybe it was best I didn't know.

Swiping out of my text messages, I went to the software I used to look up tax history on properties. Sure enough, my friend was telling the truth.

The address he'd given me was owned by Candace Johnson. Johnson was Pamela's maiden name.

With the address, I hopped over to my maps app. The address was almost an hour away on a secluded piece of land surrounded by trees. Although I saw the mailbox, the home was out of view behind them.

Much like Deangelo's cemetery.

Was this the cemetery they'd planned to meet at all along?

"They're gone," Torres called from the porch. He smacked a fist against the vinyl siding. "No sign of either of them. We need to search the barn outback, but—"

"What if they ran?" I said, starting toward him on the porch. If I wanted to take credit for this, and I didn't want Torres to know what I believed about my friend, I needed to tread carefully. "Do they have friends or family in the area? It looked like a couple of their parents were still alive when I searched."

Gayton and Phillips walked out the door behind Torres. Phillips said, "Yeah, our analyst told us that they have family locally."

"You got addresses?" I asked, turning to face them. "I can find them, but your analyst probably has a better Wi-Fi connection than I do right now."

Chapter 31

On the way there, Torres tried to get a warrant. Judge said no can do. Candace Johnson had no connection to this case aside from her daughter.

Judge then said to pursue the lead. Bring human remains dogs—which were in hot pursuit behind us—and if they signaled, that would qualify as Plain view. Meaning that we didn't need a warrant, just as we hadn't when we saw the bars on the windows of Deangelo's home. Although that was common enough in some areas, there was no rational reason for the bars on the windows since he lived in the middle of nowhere. That left nefarious means as their only purpose.

If we heard a baby cry inside, we could qualify our barging in as emergency aid doctrine. It would be a stretch. If we tore inside only to realize that the baby crying was not Bella, the owners could sue for any damages caused by our entrance without a warrant. The state police were willing to take that lawsuit if it came. The judge encouraged it as well. We were lucky we made it this far without the press getting involved. Our best course of action was to find the people responsible before they did.

Given that text message, I had the feeling we wouldn't find Deangelo anytime soon. Maybe in an unmarked grave a few years from now, but highly doubtful he was inside this house.

Or trailer, rather.

The trip up the driveway had me questioning mine and Bentley's plans to move our trailers onto a piece of property. That was exactly what Candy had done.

The property wasn't nearly as vast as Deangelo's. At max, it spanned ten acres from the bottom of the driveway, trimmed in trees and foliage, to the trailer atop the hill.

What caught my eye, what caught all of our eyes, was the pathway to the wooden porch. One hundred yards away in a three-hundred-sixty degree radius, more trees framed the property. But everything in between?

Covered in knee-high wildflowers.

Just like Deangelo's field.

Parked in the gravel, just beside the walkway, was a blue Honda Civic. Same license plate as the one that had vanished from the scene of the accident.

Beside it was a gray, nondescript van.

"License plate matches Pamela's," Torres said, unbuckling his seatbelt as we got closer to the entrance.

"We've got a warrant for her arrest," I said. "Charging in there qualifies as—"

"Hot pursuit." Torres slammed the car into park. "Yes, ma'am. You coming in on this one?"

"No way I'm missing it." I gave Tempest a scratch on the head, telling her, "I'll be back."

She panted away in the middle seat, watching Torres descend from the vehicle. I followed suit.

As already established, he was much more agile than me. I was barely out of the car by the time he made it to the front door. Gravel crunched under tires as the agents and other officers flooded in behind us.

Slower, I may have been, but the adrenaline was here now. I wasn't in pain. I held my gun out in front of me, watching for anyone who might sneak around the edge of the trailer.

No one did.

"Pamela Hudson." Torres pounded on the same low quality, plastic wrapped insulation front door that Victoria had on her home. We wouldn't need a battering ram for this. "Pamela Hudson, are you in there?"

Silence.

God no.

There was no baby cry. Babies cried a lot. Especially if they heard a strange man banging on the door.

"Pamela Hudson, I'm Sergeant Javier Torres with the state police of Lancaster County. We need to speak with you." Two more hard knocks. "Ma'am, if you don't answer this door, we're gonna have to take it down."

Silence.

"Son of a bitch," Torres said under his breath. He glanced my way. "Cover me?"

I got closer, gun at the ready, raised, but careful to avoid Torres's body.

Torres slammed his shoulder into the door.

It crumbled.

He stumbled through it, catching himself on the frame.

What remained of the door swung inward.

Gun drawn, Torres took a step inside. I stayed at his flank.

He swung to the right with his gun up while I swung to the left.

And there she was.

The woman in the driver's license photo. The woman Daisy had described. The woman no one would suspect.

She sat in an old brown recliner. One of her eyes was swollen shut. She wore a pair of pink scrubs with red hearts all over.

Nuzzled in her arm was a pink blanket. With her free hand, she lifted a cigarette to her lips.

Whatever lay between those layers of pink fuzz was silent.

It could be Bella. It could be only blankets. From this perspective, there was no way to tell.

"Pamela," Torres said. "I need you to put the baby down."

Exhaling a puff of smoke, she laughed. An odd sound that reminded me all too much of my mother. Reminded me all too much of anyone who'd been smoking for over thirty years.

"He said put the baby down," I said, taking a step closer.

Still holding the cigarette, her hand disappeared into that mound of blankets. The cherry still burned bright, a trail of smoke floating to the ceiling above. Prepared to grab the baby by the neck, maybe? Regardless, it was enough to stop me in my tracks.

"Why did it take you so long?" Pamela asked. Her voice was almost haunted, her eyes no different.

"It's not like you left us a map at the house," I said. "We got here as fast as we could."

She snorted, gaze turning back to the mound of blankets. "I always wanted one, you know. When Salvatore called this morning, I thought it was finally my chance. That I'd get to have a baby."

Maybe they'll give you a doll in prison.

"She's not your baby, ma'am," Torres said, his tone firm. "You know that.

Somewhere, deep down, you know it would be wrong to take her from her mother."

"Would it though?" She lifted the cigarette, taking another drag. When she finished, she dropped it to the floor. "You know how many babies I helped come into this world to mothers like hers? You know how many of them end up in the system?"

"Too many," I said. "She won't be one of them."

"You don't know that." She looked back down at the mound of blankets I still wasn't sure was a baby. "Do you have kids, miss?"

"This isn't about me," I said. "This is about you doing the right thing."

"Humor me." Her eyes came back to mine. "Do you have kids?"

"Not yet. I plan to one day," I said. "Now—"

"That's what Doug and I always said. Around thirty-five, we were ready. I had my life on track, his hobbies had slowed down, and it just seemed like the right time. But we tried for months and months, and nothing happened. Don't be like me. Have one sooner rather than later."

"I'll get right on that. Now, Pamela, I need you to put the baby down."

"If you'd gotten here half an hour ago, you would've gotten us both," she said. "But you just screwed yourselves."

"Because your husband already left?" Torres asked. "Doesn't matter. You don't need to worry about that. All you have to worry about is giving us that baby. If you do, we might be able to cut you a good deal with the DA."

"You're going to cut me a deal with the DA either way." She smiled. "I'll tell you anything you want to know about the bodies buried outside. I'll tell you exactly how he did it."

"If you don't hand us that baby, you won't get shit," I snapped. "You're real close to one of us putting a bullet through your head."

Pamela laughed. That throaty, congested laugh. "You don't have a reason to shoot me."

"You put your hand near that baby's face again, and I've got every reason in the world."

Smiling, she shook her head. Carefully, she tucked one hand under the midsection of the bundle of blankets and the other behind the head. She held it out toward me. "Take her. Give her back to her junkie mother. But you're never going to find them. Either of them. They're gonna run, and then they're gonna pick up somewhere else."

Hesitant as I may have been, I had to take the risk. Slim chance she was handing me a bomb, but I prayed it was what she claimed it to be.

As my hands grazed hers, and the baby inside the bundle of blankets became clear, my heart dropped. A baby indeed, with wisps of brown hair, pouty red lips, and pale white skin.

But her eyes were closed.

I yanked her closer to me.

The jarring movement popped her eyes open.

"She's okay," I told Torres, backing slowly away from Pamela. "She's alright."

"Get her to the hospital." Torres walked past me, cuffs in hand. "Pamela Hudson, you are under arrest for accessory to kidnapping. You have the right to an attorney. If you cannot afford one..."

Chapter 32

Babies were far from my area of expertise. I liked this one though.

Paramedics were already in the driveway, so that's where I took Bella. They told me I could drive with one of the officers down to the hospital, and I said no way in hell. I was not letting this baby out of my sight. One of the officers agreed to bring Tempest to the hospital for me once more officials arrived to relieve him. Harper, who came with the convoy behind me and Torres, said she'd bring Tempy to me if no one else could.

They gave her a quick physical exam, just to make sure she didn't need any immediate medical attention. By all basic accounts, she seemed fine. Since she had been in a car accident earlier today, they still wanted to run some scans when we arrived.

But it looked like a happy ending. A mostly happy ending, anyway.

At the very least, I had accomplished my mission. Daisy and her baby were almost home, and they were safe. Bentley confirmed that when I called to let him know that we had Bella. They rushed Daisy's tests, and all her scans looked normal. She did have a bulging disc in her spine, but she was young. They hoped it could be treated with physical therapy.

Also several broken ribs, a sprained wrist, and a hairline skull fracture. None of which were ideal, as I well knew since my various injuries from my last case were still healing. But all survivable. Within a couple of months, they expected Daisy to be back to normal.

With that ray of hope, I sat peacefully in the rear of the ambulance, holding a beautiful little girl who would surely live a better life than her mother had.

* * *

As I stepped from the rear of the ambulance, holding Bella close to my chest, Bentley came into view. He stood just outside the emergency exit, both hands clasped over his face. Tears budded in his eyes, but as I descended, he laughed and wiped them away.

"How's Mom doing?" one of the paramedics asked him.

"Anxious to see her daughter," Bentley said. Clearing his throat, he walked toward us. "I already talked to the doctors. They said it was fine to bring her up to her mom before they triage the baby."

"Then who am I to argue?" she said. "I'll get my charts to the ER though. Just make sure someone knows where she is."

"Sure," Bentley promised. "Thank you. Thank you all for everything."

They exchanged a few more pleasantries before Bentley led me inside. It was a hospital like any other. White linoleum floors, horrible smell of bodily fluids mixed with cleaning agents, flickering fluorescent lights, and the dreaded sound of beeping monitors.

But with this little ball of warmth in my arms, and with the weight of such a tragedy softening on my shoulders, I didn't even mind.

When we made it to the elevator, Bentley stretched over to touch Bella's cheek. She was sleeping now, looking far too much like a porcelain doll. The feeling of warmth and peace in my chest was unlike anything I had felt in a long time. Maybe it was just some silly biological imperative; maybe it was the relief of knowing this little girl was alive. But I had to admit it. I liked how it felt to hold a sweet little baby.

"Do you need a kidney?" Bentley asked.

"Huh?" I asked, looking up for maybe the first time since I'd walked into the hospital.

"A kidney. If you need one, you can have mine." Smiling so big, cheeks flushed with tears, he shook his head. "I don't know how to repay you for this. For all of this. For taking the case at all, and then actually solving it. Bringing them home. I just... I can't tell you how grateful I am, Maddie."

I laughed. "I'll pass on the kidney, but a decent meal after we get this little one to her mom would be nice."

"Anything you want, it's yours." Stretching an arm around my waist, he pulled me in close and kissed my forehead. "I love you. I love you so much."

I leaned closer, which was the best I could do to show my shared affection with the baby in my arms. "I love you too. But I didn't do this for you, mister." Trailing my thumb across Bella's cheek, I basked in that fuzzy feeling in my chest. "I did it for her. Her, and her mom, and all those women whose names we don't know yet."

"I know. And that's what I love about you."

Maybe the fuzzy feeling in my chest wasn't all because of Bella.

"Just wish I'd put the two bastards in prison while I was at it," I said under my breath.

"That's a problem for another day. For now, let's just breathe."

That had me arching a brow.

It was a bit too calm. Too serene. While I understood his relief, and felt it too, I also knew that two out of the three people we knew to be responsible for this were no longer a threat. Only one remained.

I hadn't shared that with Bentley and didn't plan to unless I had to.

But he wasn't the least bit worried that the man who was obsessed with Daisy was still on the loose? That he could show at this hospital, or at Bentley's own home, to take Daisy and Bella back to their prison? Or to do worse?

Bentley didn't talk much about his underground employment. But that hadn't changed. He was still working for the most powerful drug dealer in Western Pennsylvania. A friend of his, a friend of mine, who'd made a habit of torture and murder.

Finally tearing my gaze away from Bella, I squinted up at Bentley. "You haven't been talking to Simeon during this, have you?"

"No, why?" He spoke so casually, eyes still on Bella.

Bentley was many things, and a shit liar was one of them. I didn't see any of his usual dishonest tells, though. He just looked happy. Relieved.

The light above the elevator door dinged.

The doors opened to a long hallway. One glance told me where we were headed. Two armed guards stood outside of the room on the left, only a few doors down.

Giving Bentley another look, one that I hoped expressed my concern, I continued out into the hallway. "Just curious."

Bentley exchanged a few hellos with the nurses, as well as the guards, while we got closer. Before we'd even reached the door, I heard Grace's laugh from the other side.

What a relief it was to hear her sound like herself again.

One of the guards pulled the door open for us, and I got my first glance inside.

Daisy still wasn't looking her best. She needed a good shower and a few months of rest before she would. But most of the blood was cleaned up. Although her lips and eyes were still swollen, her joy was like a cloud of mist on a spring morning, filling every square inch of the space with tranquility and hope for a sunny day.

Smiling from ear to ear, she sat forward on the hospital bed. Her eyes stayed on that pink bundle of blankets in my arm, hand clasped over her lips. Not a word was spoken, but as I lay the baby in her arms, she erupted in quiet, joyful tears.

Grace stood nearby, tears in her eyes as well. She gazed down at the baby in her sister's arms with such wonder, such adoration.

And I felt just the same. I'd never been happier to solve a case. No, it wasn't over. It wouldn't be over until we got every piece of information out of Pamela possible. Not until we found Doug.

But for once, the people with the worst hand of cards won the game.

When Daisy finally regained her ability to speak, rocking the sleeping baby in her arms, she looked up at me. "Thank you. Thank you so much."

"Don't thank me yet," I said. "Any minute now, a couple nurses, maybe a doctor, are going to come in and take her and run a thousand tests. The paramedic said everything looked good, but with how young she is, it's just best to check."

"I'm still thanking you." She smiled, then glanced at Bentley and Grace. "Hey, would you guys mind talking to the doctors? See if they can bring a bassinet thing in here for her? I know they have to run their tests and everything, but I really want her to be in my room as much as she can be."

Bentley nodded. "Yeah, I'm sure we can work that out."

"And maybe take a trip to the vending machine while we're at it?" Grace asked, starting toward him. "I'm starving."

"Maybe we can ask some nurses for a takeout menu too." Bentley kissed my cheek on his way out.

Grace did the same, but to the opposite cheek.

Chuckling, I looked down at Daisy and Bella. I knew where this was going, and I wasn't looking forward to it. Every victim in a situation remotely similar to this wanted to talk to the cop they felt was responsible for their justice. They wanted to thank them, and make sure they knew how grateful they were, and I loathed compliments.

After reading Daisy's journal, I should've known better than to expect the usual from her.

As soon as the door clicked shut, her smile fell. "So you read it, huh?"

"Everything but the last chapter," I said. "We just found the flash drive yesterday. I made it through most of it while we were following the case, but after we got his name, my main objective was finding you. Figured you could tell us the rest of the story yourself." I smiled. "And, if I'm being honest, I was a little afraid that you were gonna die, and I wanted a new work of yours to read if you did."

Daisy laughed too. "Not my best work, honestly."

"But it was beautifully written." I sat in the chair beside the bed. "What was in that last chapter?"

"A summary of everything that came next," she said. "Not vital stuff that would help you find me. Just details. Like how I communicated with Jane through a vent in Deluca's bathroom. How often he killed. How many he killed since he had me." A hard swallow. "Just summing it all up, really."

"It'll be helpful for the cops," I said, making sure to keep my tone soft. "And for you. It's basically a police report of what happened. Should make all the interviews a lot simpler."

"Right." Taking in a slow, careful breath, she nodded. "You didn't... You didn't tell Bentley and Grace everything you read, did you?"

Frowning, I shook my head. "You told me not to. I agreed that was best."

"Thanks." Daisy still held the baby tight to her chest. "Thanks for everything. I know you're probably tired of everybody telling you that, but I just really appreciate it. Grace explained that the cops weren't really looking into it, but you didn't give up, and that means a lot."

"You're right." Another smile. "I am tired of everyone telling me that. You don't need to keep doing it. I'm just happy you're home."

"Not quite yet." She stroked her thumb down the baby's cheek. "They're probably gonna release me in a day or two, but I don't even know where home is."

"With your family."

A heavy sigh. She looked up, managing a smile, then shrugged. "I can't keep living off of him. My problems have been his problems most of my life, and I need to get out on my own two feet. I want to be close and everything, but I won't leech off of him again."

"He doesn't see you as a leech."

"But I was." Another awkward shrug. "I put him through so much. Grace too, even if she doesn't remember or understand it, and that's just not how I want to live anymore. I want to get a job. A real job. Have my own place and somehow pay off all the medical debt I'm gonna have now and build an actual life for myself."

I understood that. Related to it, even. It was a positive thing to aspire to. "I think if you went out on your own the second you get out of here, it would hurt them a lot more than help them. And the fact is, you're going to need some time before you're ready for that. You've got a lot of healing to do. Physically and mentally."

"Yeah. I know." One more deep breath. "But that's what I have to work toward. I can't get comfortable relying on anyone again. Ever."

"No one should," I said. "And you won't. I know you won't. You're older and wiser than you were when you were making Bentley's life hell. No offense."

She snorted, smiling. "None taken. Grace warned me you were kind of a bitch."

"More than kind of." My tone was playful. "But you were a kid back then. And even if you weren't, addicts screw things up. Lord knows I have."

She squinted me over. "What'd you use?"

"Oxies. Those were my favorite." I gestured to my knee. "I got injured on the job. Left me with chronic pain. I'm not proud of it, but it's a part of my story. I didn't get clean for a good reason though. Mostly, it was spite. But you, you got a hell of a reason right there." This time, I gestured to the baby. "And believe it or not, you have more opportunity now than you ever had before."

"Yeah? The high school dropout, unmarried twenty-year-old with a record a mile-long has opportunities now?"

"More than you did when all this started," I agreed, lifting my hands in mock surrender. "The foster system kept you trapped. You've aged out of it now. And once the news gets hold of the story, it's going to be everywhere. Everyone will be talking about it for years to come. Journalists are going to approach you and offer to tell your story for a publishing deal. But you've already written your story. You wrote it really damn well. If you pitch it to a few agents, considering the publicity it's going to get, you'll get a hell of an offer from a publisher. Enough to pay off the hospital debt, and probably enough to buy your own home while you work on your next book. You don't need a clean record to be a writer."

Daisy shuddered. "That feels gross. Profiting on this. I wasn't his only victim, and I don't want to make money off of their pain."

"So don't." I shrugged. "Make money off yours. That journal, it wasn't about his other victims. It wasn't even about him. It was about you. It was a cautionary tale to all women. Reading that book reminds every woman who reads it that we can't count on a hero to save us. If someone wants to rescue you from your problems, and it sounds too good to be true, it probably is."

She huffed at that. "I guess."

"And let's be honest. The true crime industry is exploitative as hell." Leaning forward, I propped my elbows on my knees. "If you don't tell your story, someone's gonna tell it for you. They're gonna profit off your pain. Why not own it?"

Daisy gazed at the baby in her arms. "Because a big part of me wants to forget it ever happened. And make sure she never knows that it happened."

There would be no wiping this from the Internet. One day, Bella would have questions. She would wonder why all the other kids had a dad, and she didn't. "You have time to figure that out. But even if that is what you want to do, write under your legal name. Daisy Miller. Then change yours and Bella's names. That way, you can have some sense of anonymity."

Her shoulders softened ever so slightly. "That might be a good idea."

"And in the meantime, until you've got some money coming in, we can get you on some assistance. We can also crowd source money for your medical expenses," I said. "You need a good story to raise the kind of money that this is gonna cost, but you have one. And it came with a happy ending."

"For me." Daisy's eyes met mine again, tears forming in the one that wasn't swollen. "Not for all those other girls. And not for whoever comes after me."

That sentence could have two meanings, and I wasn't sure which one she was referencing. My expression must've said so, because she said, "You guys didn't catch them. Either of them. Even if he doesn't come after me again, he'll find someone else. He can't help himself. He's going to kill again."

Deangelo wouldn't.

But if he had been Doug's protégé? I had no doubt Daisy was right. He would kill again.

"One battle at a time," I said.

Silence stretched on for a moment. Daisy only caressed Bella's face, staring down at her with emotions I couldn't begin to comprehend. I could sympathize, but no one could understand what she had been through.

"You're good for him, you know." Another smile, this one the softest so far. "I didn't think Bentley was ever going to move on after my sister, but I'm glad he did with you. You're the type of partner he needs."

"I'm honored you think so." I brought back my playful tone. "But do you mind if I ask why?"

"Why you're good for him?"

"Yeah. I mean, you and I just met, and you could just be saying that because I helped find your missing baby and everything."

"Because he's just a big softy. He needs someone who's gonna take charge. He always wants to be everyone else's hero, but he really needs one of his own. I'm glad he has one now."

"So, because I'm a bitch?"

She gave one more good laugh, then grabbed her ribs. "Shit, I gotta stop doing that."

"I think laughter is the kind of medicine you need right now."

A knock sounded at the door behind me. Daisy called, "Come in."

The door swung open, and in walked a nurse with a wheelchair. "Daisy? And Bella?"

"Yes, ma'am."

"Perfect. We just talked to your brother-in-law, and he said that you really don't want to be separated from her right now. Normally, we don't let the parents come down to the CT and MRI, but with everything considered, we figured you could wait outside while we run the tests if you want to."

"That would be perfect." Daisy gripped the bed frame, using it as leverage to lift her legs from the bed. As the nurse helped her stand, Daisy glanced my way. "You're gonna stay close, right?"

"I'm not going anywhere."

One more sweet, kind smile as she sat in the wheelchair. "Good. I trust you more than the guards outside."

Since they were only security guards? So did I.

Lounging back in the hospital chair, propping my legs up on her bed, I sighed dramatically. "Then I'll get comfortable."

We exchanged a few more smiles, looks of mutual appreciation, before the nurse wheeled her out. When the door clicked shut behind her, I reached for my phone in my hoodie pocket. At the top of my notifications was a text from Torres and another from Dylan. The one from Torres said,

Pamela isn't talking. I don't think she's gonna say anything else until she has a lawyer. The dogs signaled a lot in all those wildflowers though. Looks a lot like Deangelo's cemetery. I think you were right. Deangelo is Doug's apprentice. We're getting Doug's picture on the 9 o'clock news. He was still using his credit cards when we got here earlier. Last transaction was five minutes before we broke down Pamela's door. He couldn't have gone far, and we're setting up more roadblocks. We don't have shit on Deangelo though. We're gonna have to be really careful with Daisy until we find him. Just thought I'd let you know.

Oh, and I've got your dog. She's a sweet girl. Come down to the PD to get her whenever you have time.

A slow, shaking breath escaped my nostrils. All I could manage to text back was, *Thanks for keeping me posted. I'll be down to the station in an hour or so to get Tempest.*

The text from Dylan said,

I can't find much. There aren't any connections at all between Douglas Hudson and Salvatore Deangelo. But I did find a connection between Douglas Hudson and Mario Deangelo, Salvatore's father. It looks like they went to high school together. In their twenties, Mario cosigned for a few of Doug's loans. Also listed as an investor in his business. It looks to me like Doug and Mario were friends. Maybe Doug stepped into a fatherly role for Salvatore after Mario died? I don't know, but I'll keep looking.

I wrote back, *I think that would make perfect sense. Thanks for keeping me posted. And for all your help.*

As soon as I set my phone down, another one rang on the counter in the corner. Bentley's phone, to be specific. I recognized the ring tone.

"Of course." Groaning, I stood and walked across the room to it. "As soon as I get comfy."

I looked at the screen.

An 814 number.

The same number that had texted me today.

It had to be Simeon. It had to be.

And I had to be sure that whoever did this was someone I could believe.

I slid the green bar.

Doing my best to lower my voice and sound masculine, most likely failing, I said, "Hello?"

"Haven't heard anything from you, kid." A voice I knew. One I knew well. But not Simeon's. "How are they doing? The baby okay and everything?"

"Sam?"

Silence for a long moment. Eventually, he broke it with, "Ah, shit."

The door behind me swung open.

Bentley walked through wearing a smile, struggling with a dozen snacks and bottles of pop. "We can go out to eat, or order something in, but—"

"Where's Grace?" I asked.

In my ear, Sam said, "Look, how about you call me back later, and—"

"I don't want to hear another damn word out of your mouth right now," I snapped. "Stay on the line, asshole. Bentley, answer the question."

"In the bathroom." He cocked his head to the side. "What's going on?"

"Great question." I held the phone in his direction, showing the unmarked number. "Let's go outside and talk about what the hell is going on here."

Chapter 33

"You're idiots," I snapped, looking from Bentley down to the phone that was on speaker in my hand. "You're an idiot for doing this, and you're an idiot for not telling me about it."

Swallowing hard, Bentley shrunk into the passenger seat of my Subaru. "He told me not to tell you, and I figured that made sense."

"Because it did," Sam said on the other end. "Look, I had to do what I had to do. If I hadn't, you wouldn't have known the guy's name. You wouldn't have been able to find Daisy, and you wouldn't have found the baby either."

"And you killed our only lead!" I yelled into the phone. "He had a partner, Sam. Doug Hudson. He taught Deangelo how to kill. We thought Deangelo was bad, but we have barely touched the cemetery outside of the Hudson home. This guy could be more prolific, more dangerous, and Deangelo was our chance at finding him."

"Bentley said you got the wife," Sam said.

"Wait, you killed him?" Bentley asked, eyes on the phone as well.

"I—well, I don't know if I should talk about that."

"You better not, dipshit," I snapped. "Ohio doesn't have the death penalty, but Pennsylvania does. They're not going to go easy on a two-time murderer, Sam."

"I didn't say I did it—"

"You told me he wasn't coming back for Daisy," I said. "That's pretty damn close to a confession."

"Or an educated guess," Sam said. "He ran because he knew how much danger he was in. He—"

"Not another word." I rubbed my hands over my eyes. "Not another word from either of you. I need to think."

"What is there to think about?" Sam asked. "I was careful. There's nothing connecting me to any of this. I'm on a burner phone right now—"

"That you contacted Bentley on," I said. "And me. In court, I'm gonna have to explain where my anonymous tips came from. I can say they came from a burner. But if they do enough digging, they're going to see you also contacted my boyfriend."

"But if there's no body, there's no crime," Sam said. "No one can prove you're connected to—"

"I've seen convictions with less evidence." Rubbing my eyes between my thumb and forefinger, I tried not to think about what he meant when he said no body, no crime. But he was right. So long as nobody ever found Deangelo's body, he might get away with this.

Did he *deserve* to get away with this?

Bentley did. All he had done was convey a bit of confidential evidence. Confidential evidence that I had also conveyed to Bentley, which could, at the very least, lose me my license.

At the most? Be used to charge me with accomplice to murder.

But only if they found the body.

Regardless of where I fell morally on what Sam had done, Sam wasn't the only one who would go down for this. We all would.

"The only way to make sure a body is never found is to incinerate it," I said.

"I know." Sam's tone was matter of fact.

In other words saying without saying that he had, in fact, burned Deangelo's body to ash.

He'd only had this information for the past two or three hours. And he already got rid of him? Sam had connections to someone who owned an incinerator?

"Oh my God." I rubbed my temples. "This is insane. This is batshit crazy, dude."

"You're friends with Simeon Gunn," Sam said. "I don't see how this is any crazier."

"You don't see how you killing my only chance at finding a mass murderer is insane, Sam?!" I yelled. The moment I did, my stomach sunk. I looked around to make sure no one else was nearby, but only an empty parking lot stared back at me. "What do you expect me to tell this girl? What do you expect Bentley to tell her when she can't sleep because she's afraid he's coming for her?"

Silence.

"Every day for the rest of her life, she's gonna live in fear," I said. "That's on you."

"Tell her then," he said. "Shit, I'll confess to it if it's such a big deal."

If it's such a big deal. As though murder was a casual occurrence.

"You'll derail my legitimacy in the courtroom if you do," I said. "We won't be able to convict the wife who played a giant part in this. And our only shot at finding Hudson."

"Shit. What do you want me to say, Maddie?" Sam asked. "You want me to apologize? For causing you trouble, I will. I'm sorry that this is screwing up your day. But can you honestly tell me that the guy didn't deserve it?"

I stayed silent. Of course I couldn't.

Deangelo didn't deserve prison. He deserved a slow, painful death. He deserved years of exactly what he put all those women through. He deserved what the men in prison would have done to him.

But so did Hudson.

Now, I wasn't sure if he'd ever get it.

"This is doing a lot more than screwing up my day," I snapped. "This screwed up all the progress we've made since we reconnected." Silence for a few long heartbeats. "Get rid of the phone and make sure you covered every single one of your damn tracks."

I hung up.

Bentley said nothing in the passenger seat.

I stared out the window, rubbing my face to distract from the pounding in my head.

It was complicated. This case was so complicated.

More than anyone, I critiqued the justice system. To an extent, Sam was right. If he hadn't done what he did, we may have never found Bella. I didn't even want to know what he'd done to get me the information on The Crow. Which is what got us Daisy.

But that didn't make this right. Not even because Deangelo was dead, as uncomfortable as that thought made me. I didn't oppose the death penalty for people as evil as him. The fact that Sam did it or the fact that a prison turned on the electric chair didn't make a difference to me.

My issue was the fact that Pamela likely had Stockholm's. She wasn't going to turn on her husband. Even if by some slim chance she did, we knew how these men operated. They didn't share vital information with their wives because they didn't respect them, because they didn't view them as people.

When Pamela had told us we would never find Doug, that was what she meant. It wasn't a stretch to think that even she hadn't known where he went.

The only person who would have was Deangelo. These men, they respected each other, but no one else.

If Deangelo caved and told Sam where Bella was, he would've told us where Hudson was. With enough effort, with the right plea deal, he would've told us.

Now, we had nothing.

And I could only blame myself for it.

I shouldn't have told Bentley details of the case. But if I hadn't, would we have found Daisy and Bella? Or would they be lying beneath a field of wild-flowers by now?

"I'm sorry," Bentley said, voice sheepish. "I didn't think he would—"

"He killed a corrupt politician and spent almost thirty years in jail for it." I kept looking out the windshield at the entrance to the hospital. "What did you think he would do if he got his hands on someone who methodically raped and murdered dozens of young women who fit into almost the exact same demographic as his daughter, Bentley?"

Silence.

"Yeah." Running a hand through my hair, I nibbled my lip. "That's what I thought."

"I didn't think he'd be gentle with him, but neither would either of us if we had the chance, Maddie. If we were where he'd been, we'd—"

"We'd have called the cops," I snapped. "We wouldn't have let him get away with it. We would've gotten Daisy closure. We would've done this the right way."

"Would it have been the *right* way?" Bentley asked, his voice raising now. "I know we're thinking the same things. We're both attached to law enforcement, Maddie. We know how this shit goes. We know why they didn't care to look for Daisy. In a courtroom, they would do everything to discredit her. They would say she was like Pamela. That she liked it, and she wanted him. She saw it as her way out of poverty. And they wouldn't have been wrong, because she's not a perfect victim, and we know how courts treat people who aren't perfect victims.

"A good enough lawyer might've been able to get that semen thrown out.

That was the only thing tying Deangelo to the field and he would've had that. A damn good lawyer, because he comes from money, and they always win. The people with money always win, and the poor junkie whores never get justice." He spat those words with disgust. "And then what? And then Daisy would have to trade off custody with Bella every other weekend? She'd have to live every moment of her life in fear? Would that have been better, because it was following the law? The law that you always say needs to be demolished and rebuilt?"

I hated it.

I hated that he was right.

I hated that, because of the way our justice system worked, Deangelo could've gotten away with this. He was smart enough to.

The hearing played out behind my eyes.

The dungeon in the basement? He was into kink. Daisy was too. She was more than compliant, but excited, to indulge in his same fantasies. And the lock on her door? It was just a part of the fantasy.

The blood of those other girls in the basement? Knife play. Just a sexy, *Fifty Shades of Grey* style fantasy. No one was ever really hurt. Those girls left Deangelo's home in perfect condition.

When Daisy told the lawyer that wasn't true, that she heard them begging for help, they'd pull out that book she'd written. *Silkties and Seduction.* The book where she described, in detail, violent sexual escapades with Deangelo. They'd use it as proof to show that girls like her, sex workers and drug addicts, would do anything for a chance to escape that lifestyle, to level up to Deangelo's level in our society.

A good enough lawyer, with the right jury?

He could've been found not guilty.

"But I should've told you," Bentley said. "I'm sorry I didn't."

So was I.

But wasn't that hypocritical of me to say? Wasn't I agreeing with the anonymous messenger when they told me it was best I didn't know the details?

I didn't know why I was so angry now when I hadn't been then.

Largely, I was afraid of never finding Hudson. But I'd be a liar if I said that was all. My other concern was losing Sam. And the fear that I'd already had.

He was who I thought he was. Someone like me, who believed in what was right, believed the system was broken, and sometimes broke away from it to get his justice.

But I couldn't do what he had done. In a blind rage, yes, I could kill. And I had. To save my life, or the life of someone I loved.

Those situations were when under immediate threat, however.

At a moment's notice, Sam wasn't only prepared to kill. He executed a perfect murder.

At least, I damn well hoped it was perfect, because I didn't want to spend the next thirty years of my life in jail either.

The truth was, that scared me. Knowing what Sam was capable of, scared me.

"Maddie, can we just talk about this?" Bentley asked. "Please, just—"

"We're going to go back in that hospital, and we're going to act like we are in love, and happy, and grateful to finally be reunited with Daisy. You're going to get us dinner, and we're going to eat, and we're going to pretend that we are perfectly happy." I finally met his gaze. "And when we go home, when the FBI isn't looming over our shoulders, we're gonna fight about this."

Before he could respond, I threw open my door and stepped outside.

Taking in a deep breath, I prepared to put on the best show of my life.

* * *

Maddie Castle's story continues in *Beneath the Grove*. Click the link below to get started:
https://www.amazon.com/dp/B0DSQ4TQL1

Want a free copy of the Maddie Castle prequel novella? Sign up for my newsletter and download a copy today:
https://liquidmind.media/maddie-castle-newsletter-signup-1/

The Maddie Castle Series

The Handler

Tracking Justice

Hunting Grounds

Vanished Trails

Smoldering Lies

Field of Bones

Want a free copy of the Maddie Castle prequel novella? Sign up for my newsletter and download a copy today:

https://liquidmind.media/maddie-castle-newsletter-signup-1/

Also by L.T. Ryan

Find All of L.T. Ryan's Books on Amazon Today!

The Jack Noble Series

The Recruit (free)

The First Deception (Prequel 1)

Noble Beginnings

A Deadly Distance

Ripple Effect (Bear Logan)

Thin Line

Noble Intentions

When Dead in Greece

Noble Retribution

Noble Betrayal

Never Go Home

Beyond Betrayal (Clarissa Abbot)

Noble Judgment

Never Cry Mercy

Deadline

End Game

Noble Ultimatum

Noble Legend

Noble Revenge

Never Look Back (Coming Soon)

Bear Logan Series

Ripple Effect

Blowback

Take Down

Deep State

Bear & Mandy Logan Series

Close to Home

Under the Surface

The Last Stop

Over the Edge

Between the Lies

Caught in the Web (Coming Soon)

Rachel Hatch Series

Drift

Downburst

Fever Burn

Smoke Signal

Firewalk

Whitewater

Aftershock

Whirlwind

Tsunami

Fastrope

Sidewinder

Mitch Tanner Series

The Depth of Darkness

Into The Darkness

Deliver Us From Darkness

Cassie Quinn Series

Path of Bones

Whisper of Bones

Symphony of Bones

Etched in Shadow

Concealed in Shadow

Betrayed in Shadow

Born from Ashes

Return to Ashes (Coming Soon)

Blake Brier Series

Unmasked

Unleashed

Uncharted

Drawpoint

Contrail

Detachment

Clear

Quarry (Coming Soon)

Dalton Savage Series

Savage Grounds

Scorched Earth

Cold Sky

The Frost Killer

Crimson Moon (Coming Soon)

Maddie Castle Series

The Handler

Tracking Justice

Hunting Grounds

Vanished Trails

Smoldering Lies (Coming Soon)

Affliction Z Series

Affliction Z: Patient Zero

Affliction Z: Abandoned Hope

Affliction Z: Descended in Blood

Affliction Z : Fractured Part 1

Affliction Z: Fractured Part 2 (Fall 2021)

About the Authors

L.T. RYAN is a *Wall Street Journal* and *USA Today* bestselling author, renowned for crafting pulse-pounding thrillers that keep readers on the edge of their seats. Known for creating gripping, character-driven stories, Ryan is the author of the *Jack Noble* series, the *Rachel Hatch* series, and more. With a knack for blending action, intrigue, and emotional depth, Ryan's books have captivated millions of fans worldwide.

Whether it's the shadowy world of covert operatives or the relentless pursuit of justice, Ryan's stories feature unforgettable characters and high-stakes plots that resonate with fans of Lee Child, Robert Ludlum, and Michael Connelly.

When not writing, Ryan enjoys crafting new ideas with coauthors, running a thriving publishing company, and connecting with readers. Discover the next story that will keep you turning pages late into the night.

Connect with L.T. Ryan
Sign up for his newsletter to hear the latest goings on and receive some free content
➜ https://ltryan.com/jack-noble-newsletter-signup-1

Join the private readers' group
➜ https://www.facebook.com/groups/1727449564174357

Instagram ➜ @ltryanauthor
Visit the website ➜ https://ltryan.com
Send an email ➜ contact@ltryan.com

* * *

C.R. GRAY goes by a lot of names, but the most know her as Charlie, a fantasy romance author who's finally diving into the genre she's always wanted to write in - mystery and thriller. She's from a small town outside of Pittsburgh and hopes she does her city justice in the books she works on!

If she isn't writing, she's chasing after her three adorable, but incredibly stubborn, puppers - who may or may not have some of the same bad behaviors as Tempest in the Maddie Castle series. When she isn't writing, she's watching Criminal Minds or binge reading a Kathy Reichs or Kelley Armstrong novel for the millionth time. (They never get old!)

Made in the USA
Coppell, TX
02 March 2025